Howard Gurney was born in Sydney, Australia and is the author of six novels and multiple peer-reviewed medical journal articles. He works as a medical oncologist at Westmead Hospital in Sydney and is also a professor of medicine at Macquarie University, where he undertakes clinical trials for cancer patients. His first fantasy fiction novel, *Twin*, was published in 2015.

He lives in Sydney with his wife and their five children. He has also worked in Manchester, UK and travels extensively.

Other books by Howard Gurney

Path to Chaos series (fantasy)

Twin
The Thread Frays
Chaos

Dr Christopher Walker Murder Mystery series

Murder on the Ward
Death in a Chapel
Murder at The Rocks

DEATH IN A CHAPEL

A Dr Christopher Walker Murder Mystery
Book 2

Howard Gurney

CHAPTER ONE

IN THE DEAD of night, while the Gay and Lesbian Mardi Gras parade was raging in the city, three figures pushed a mortuary trolley along a service road, sweating and panting in the heat, near the docks of Western Meadows Hospital. The wheels clattered and wobbled on the uneven surface, making it difficult to steer, and they gasped with relief when they finally reached the smooth concrete ramp that led to the ground floor of the pathology building. Their garb was not suited to the temperature and their faces were obscured – two wore thick overalls and their heads were covered, while the other was dressed in surgical scrubs, cap and mask. Together they heaved the trolley up the last slope before they reached the level floor.

They manoeuvred the bulky trolley through the double doors into the dimly lit corridor but didn't lock them. They wouldn't be there long. To the right was the door to the mortuary but they pushed past it until they reached another door on the left – the locker room, according to the sign.

With difficulty, they got the trolley through the narrow doorway. The room was small and, despite pushing the trolley from one side to the other, the door couldn't be closed behind them.

'Leave it,' said the one with a blue hat, his voice muffled. 'Let's just be quick about it.'

The other wearing a green hat grunted a reply and pulled the thick plastic cover off the trolley to reveal the bin below, normally used to hide corpses when the trolley was moved through the wards. But instead of a body, the plastic tub was full of packages, each the size of a small loaf of bread, stacked neatly and wrapped in clear plastic. Despite the dim light, the contents were clearly visible – a grey-white powder.

A locker was opened and the trio worked quickly, transferring the contents until two lockers were full. The one in surgical scrubs held the last package, trying to determine whether it would fit, while Green-hat tried to make a space for it.

'Hello,' came a female voice in the doorway.

The three froze.

'I think I'm lost.' The voice belonged to a young woman in a white nurse's uniform. She had an Irish accent. She looked at Blue-hat and her eyes flicked to the hat then back to his face. 'I think I've parked in the wrong carpark. I'm trying to get to the wards. I'm a casual. Looks like half the hospital's at the Mardi Gras.' She smiled. 'Pity I missed it.' She waved her hand over her shoulder. 'Lucky the door was open otherwise I would've had to walk around the building in the dark.' Her eyes flicked to the package that Surgical-scrubs still held, then to the stuffed locker.

She backed away. 'No problem,' she said quickly. 'I'll find my own way.'

Blue-hat moved towards her.

'I didn't see anything,' she cried as she turned. But Blue-hat was upon her before she'd taken a few steps and tackled her roughly, her head slamming onto the concrete floor. Blue-hat rose slowly upright.

The three encircled her, looking down at her unmoving body. Green-hat asked, 'Is she dead?'

Surgical-scrubs bent down to check her pulse and shook his head. 'Knocked out.'

They turned her over. She had a pretty face and rosy cheeks that had rarely seen the sun. An ugly contusion was already forming on her forehead.

'Did you hear her accent? She's probably only just off the boat.'

'What are we going to do?' asked Blue-hat.

Scrubs looked up. 'We can't let her go. She's seen everything.'

'What then?'

Scrubs looked down at the girl's face, then into the locker room, then to the door along the corridor that led to the morgue. 'I have an idea.'

A short time later they had placed her on the stainless-steel autopsy table. Blue-hat deftly threaded a butterfly needle in a vein in her elbow, while Green-hat used an ornate dagger to make a slit in one of the packages. The blade was curved and pointed with a ridge down the middle and the handle appeared to be made of a hard, dark material, studded with coloured stones.

'Where'd you get that from?' asked Scrubs.

'Our friends. A gift.'

'Looks nasty,' said Blue-hat. 'Do you reckon those Arabs actually use those things on each other?'

'Don't know.' Green-hat held the knife up to glitter in the light. 'Pretty though.'

A Bunsen burner was lit, then the knife was used to scoop a large measure of powder out of the package into a small steel beaker that was held over the flame. Soon it was liquid and was drawn up into a syringe then given to Blue-hat.

'Why do I have to do it?'

'Just get on with it.'

A few minutes after the injection, the girl stopped breathing as the strange trio encircled her, watching on like grieving relatives.

'That's it then,' said Blue-hat. 'What now?'

'Get her gear off,' said Scrubs. 'All of it, jewellery and all. And the ID card.'

The three attacked the body – ripping, stripping – and within moments the corpse was naked.

'Put everything in that bag,' Scrubs instructed.

As they stuffed the items away, a piece of white paper fluttered to the ground at Green-hat's feet. It was picked up and held for the others to see. On it was a single word scrawled in pencil.

'How'd that get there?' asked Scrubs.

'It must have fallen out of my pocket in the scuffle.'

'Throw it in as well. We don't need it now.'

After everything was stowed, Scrubs said, 'Now help me carry her.'

'Where?'

Scrubs pointed to a stainless-steel wall on the other side of the room, inset with rows of small doors.

'The morgue fridge?' said Green-hat. 'Are you kidding?'

'Just until we can get rid of her,' said Scrubs. 'There's no other way.'

The two hats looked at each other then joined in, silently acquiescing.

Green-hat threw the spoon into the bag that contained the dead nurse's clothes, then picked up the package and the curved dagger.

Before the morgue drawer was slid back in, Scrubs closely examined the corpse one last time to make sure no clues had been left. 'Okay, looks clear. Now let's get out of –'

'Hello in there,' called a male voice.

'What the …' exclaimed Green-hat.

Standing at the door was an elderly man, a clergyman by his garb – purple top, white clerical collar. 'I was on my way out when I saw the light. I don't mind coming back, but if you need any prayers for the dead, I'd be happy to say them now. Might save some trouble.' He looked at the dead nurse lying in the morgue drawer, which was still pulled out. 'Poor dear. So young.' He lifted his head back to the threesome. 'How about it?'

The trio shared a look of disbelief.

Green-hat was the first to recover. 'Of course, Father. Please, be our guest.' Green-hat gestured to the corpse and the priest came into the room. Just after he passed, Green-hat lifted the curved blade and drove it into his back. The priest gave a garbled cry and fell to the ground.

'What the fuck are you doing?' Blue-hat screamed.

'He's seen everything,' shouted Green-hat. They looked down at the priest who was now gurgling and groaning. He gave a cough, blood gushed from his mouth then he stopped breathing.

'Good shot,' Scrubs said appreciatively. 'Looks like you got the aorta. Couldn't have done better myself.'

'What are we gonna do with all this blood?' squeaked Blue-hat. 'There's no way we can hide it all.'

Under the dead priest, a huge pool of blood had gathered on the tiled floor. Even as they watched, it was already flowing towards a drain in the middle of the room under the autopsy table.

'Relax,' said Scrubs. 'This room's made for this sort of thing. We can hose it all up, quick as you please.'

Green-hat seemed somewhat mollified but pointed at the body. 'What are we doing with that then, Einstein?'

'We can't put two bodies in the fridge,' said Blue-hat.

'I've got another idea,' said Scrubs. 'A good one. One that'll leave a false trail.'

'What do you mean?'

'Leave that to me. Help me get the body into the trolley.' Scrubs pointed to the murder weapon that Green-hat held. 'And give me that knife.'

'What are you going to do?'

'Throw 'em off the scent.'

'How?'

'Never you mind.' Scrubs threw the curved dagger into the trolley tub on top of the body and quickly pulled the cover over. 'You two stay here.' Scrubs pointed to the package of white powder Green-hat held. 'And lock that away.' The trolley was pushed towards the door. 'Wait here. I won't be long.'

After Scrubs had left with the trolley, Green-hat scampered off to the locker room to dispose of the package while Blue-hat began to hose the blood into the central drain. As soon as they were finished, Green-hat energetically mopped up the residual water while Blue-hat tidied the rest of the room and placed the bag holding the nurse's personal items onto the stainless-steel table in the middle of the room.

Soon they'd completed the task and they surveyed their work. Green-hat nodded. 'You know what, I think we might just get away with it.'

Blue-hat stood with hands on hips, looking pleased. 'Where do you think –'

'Hello,' came another male voice from beyond the door. 'Hello in there.' In the doorway stood a middle-aged Asian man dressed in a cleaner's outfit. He held a garbage bag in one hand. 'You work back late.' The man smiled. 'Any rubbish for me?' His eyes went to the plastic bag on the autopsy table.

The two looked at each other and Blue-hat's hands were raised in disbelief.

'No, we have nothing,' said Green-hat, twisting away discreetly. 'We'll be leaving now.'

'Okay.' The cleaner smiled. 'You lock up?'

'Sure, sure.'

The Asian man waved then turned to leave but half-turned back. 'You seen priest? He was here but now gone. Don't want to lock him in.'

He must have seen something in the two faces because his smile vanished and he dropped the bag, then turned quickly towards the door.

He began to run.

'Get him!' shouted Blue-hat.

CHAPTER TWO

THE CHANT WAS deafening.

'Action equals life. Silence equals death.'

'Action equals life. Silence equals death.'

It came from a group of about a hundred people, mostly men, wearing black T-shirts emblazoned with a huge pair of red lips with a tablet wedged between, as they walked up Oxford Street in the Mardi Gras parade, on a sultry Saturday evening in February 1991.

Christopher Walker looked on from a street corner as the first of the parade passed by, wondering whether he'd been wrong in coming out that night. This was not what he expected. Cassandra Hollow, the flatmate of one of his work colleagues, had insisted he take her to the Mardi Gras and reluctantly he'd agreed. Admittedly, he hadn't fought very hard. Cassandra was one of the most beautiful women he'd ever met and, since he was single, he'd reasoned that he'd be a complete idiot to resist.

On the other hand, Cassandra was currently going out with his former best friend, Barry Darling, a detective in the NSW Police Service, so maybe it'd not been such a brilliant idea, after all. However, Darling could hardly be described as one of his close friends at this point in their lives.

Darling refused to let up about Felicity's death, even though it was over six years ago. He kept digging, digging – wanting to know every gory detail – never letting go. If only he'd let the past be. Then, maybe, they could be friends again.

Walker glanced at Cassandra out of the corner of his eye for the umpteenth time that evening, trying his hardest not to look like a complete perv. She could only be described as drop-dead gorgeous.

She wore skin-tight sparkling shorts with a gold belt buckle, which barely covered her lower bits. And that was about it! Her top was a canary-yellow bikini, which at least covered her nipples but exposed her perfectly shaped breasts to all and sundry. On each strap she'd attached a butterfly shape and had piled her golden locks atop of her head, somehow holding the whole thing together with colourful clips and bows. Over her shoulders she'd draped a maroon silk shawl that was so sheer, Walker wondered why she bothered to wear it.

They'd met at his terrace house earlier that evening in The Rocks and had a few drinks at his local pub, the Hero of Waterloo. Cassandra had drawn a lot of admiring looks from the crowd and James, the laconic barman, had winked at him as he handed him his schooner of Reschs Pilsener. Walker couldn't help smiling. He had to admit, it felt pretty good being with her.

After a few drinks, they'd set off along Argyle Street to Circular Quay, then made their way through Hyde Park before reaching Oxford Street about an hour before the parade.

Walker turned his attention back to the parade. It was clear that the vanguard of the Mardi Gras was a protest. Many of the participants looked thin and unwell and Walker realised they almost certainly had AIDS themselves. They waved placards saying, 'AIDS drugs now Brian Howe' and 'Approve AIDS drugs now'. After a few moments, they switched their chant. 'Bri-an Howe. AIDS drugs now.'

'He's the Minister of Health, isn't he?' asked Cassandra.

'Yes,' said Walker. 'They want AZT on the PBS. Zidovudine is a drug that works against HIV but the gays reckon the government is dragging the chain on funding it. It's approved in other countries and saving lives but I think only two people have got it in Australia, so far.'

'Well, they should approve it obviously,' said Cassandra. 'What's taking them so long?'

'Cassie, you know just as well as I do how slow the federal government is in doing anything.' She was a criminal lawyer, a good one at that, and was used to dealing with bureaucracy.

A driving disco beat started up and next came a regiment of young muscular men wearing red marching-girl hats, white underpants with silver spangles and nothing much else. They marched in lines, disco-stepping in perfect unison. Cassandra screamed out, clapped her hands and wiggled her chest in time with the beat.

Then came an army of women clad in leather and chains riding motorbikes – Dykes on Bikes, according to the sign. The parade rolled by for the next hour – scantily clad men and women dancing the salsa on the back of trucks, gay sports teams, transvestites with slim hips and expensive dresses, gays from outer space, lesbians in pink nun habits escorted by white-winged angels with pitchforks, moustachioed men in Carmen Miranda watermelon dresses, gyrating muscular young men wearing nothing but skin-tight gold lame shorts, masked Scarlet Pimpernels with backless pants, and a Julie Andrews look-alike with her young *Sound of Music* cross-dressers in matching floral skirts and knickerbockers. There were Balinese dancers with overly-long fingernails, Catholics, cowboys and cat-women, gay Novocastrians, nuns and nurses.

'The men have such fantastic bodies,' gushed Cassandra, her body squirming beside him in time with the music.

Then came a table-top truck full of dancing female models in clinging lingerie, each one looking like they'd been torn from the cover of a magazine.

'Wow,' said Cassandra, stopping her dance as the float passed. 'Those women are absolutely gorgeous. Makes me want to be a dyke.' She swivelled her face to Walker's and kissed him full on the lips. 'What about you? Imagine you and I let loose on that lot. We'd have an absolute ball.' She pushed her body against him and put her arms around his neck, pulling his mouth to hers. Walker could feel her near-naked breasts pushing into his chest through his thin shirt.

'Let's go,' she gasped when she finally pulled free.

'Where?'

'To the park. I don't want to wait to get to your place.'

She grasped his hand and strode down Oxford Street, pulling him after her. They had to wait at the lights at the corner of Oxford and College and Cassandra took the opportunity to again taste the inside of his mouth.

Once in the park, she hauled him towards a copse of weeping figs and pulled him down into the undergrowth. 'Hurry,' she groaned. She tugged off her shorts and straddled him. She moved slowly for a few strokes then pumped rapidly, not breathing, her mouth open as if she was in pain. She grunted loudly then cut off her cry by covering his mouth with hers and continued to groan into his mouth for some moments before Walker felt her body slump against his.

Finally, she rolled away and pulled her shorts back on. Her bikini top had come loose but she sat for some moments oblivious, sighing contentedly. She grabbed his hand. 'That was good, Christopher.'

She pulled her top straight, stood up and held out her hand.

'Now, let's get home so we can do it again properly.'

CHAPTER THREE

WALKER WOKE UP feeling terrible. His head throbbed, his mouth was dry and foul, and his guts squirmed. He didn't know where he was. Moments before he'd been in a grass hut lying on a dirt floor, the musty smell of rotting vegetation in his nose, but now it didn't seem right. The light was coming from the wrong direction, and instead of the raucous screech of the New Guinea birdlife, he could hear the soft twitter of parrots in a tree nearby. He heard a car. That definitely was not right!

He turned his head to see sunlight streaming through open French doors that led onto a balcony, and beyond that the gentle movement of jacaranda leaves blowing in a breeze.

He was in Australia.

He was in his terrace in Lower Fort Street.

And Flea was dead.

It was his fault.

His mind wandered back to the circumstances around her death in New Guinea over six years ago. She'd drowned. He too had almost drowned. Most of his memories were hazy and there were complete gaps, but he remembered some of what happened afterwards. In that hut. In the jungle. The things they did – the people who'd saved him. A memory hung just out of reach, like a ghost in the hallway. He could sense it but not see it. Something awful. Then he remembered part of it …

The Black began to descend.

Walker sat up abruptly.

Did that really happen?

He forced the fleeting images away. He couldn't let the Black overtake him. He had to think of something else.

Angela Chee.

Angela was training under his supervision as a medical oncologist at Western Meadows Hospital. They'd had a brief liaison after her father had been murdered and Walker thought he'd found someone who might help him finally overcome the loss of his wife. But once the murder had been solved, she'd turned away from him. Even now, he felt there might still be something there. He was attracted to her, he knew that for sure, and he thought Angela had felt the same, even if for a short time.

Then there was the problem of the metoprolol. That was one of the drugs used to murder her father and she'd been caught on security camera disposing of a large number of ampoules into a hospital waste bin. She'd refused to explain. Walker's intern Gloria had ultimately been charged with the murder of Professor Chee and admitted to using metoprolol. But why had Angela been in possession of it?

And also, Angela had demanded he explain to her how Felicity had died.

Walker pushed his hands into his face and let out a long breath. He wished he hadn't drunk so much. There was something wrong with his eyes. Whenever he looked to the left, he saw double. And his groin ached as if he'd been punched down there, as if he was all swollen.

He heard a movement behind him and twisted to see what it was.

There was someone in his bed.

Then it all came back.

Cassandra Hollow!

He turned away, leaned forward and put his face into his palms.

'Bloody hell, what have I done?'

He turned back. Cassandra's naked body was uncovered in the summer heat; full breasts, flat abdomen and long shapely legs. Even in the morning sunlight, after a heavy night of drinking, she was beautiful. He realised that the ache in his groin was from their lovemaking, which had gone on for hours. She was insatiable. He hadn't known a woman could be like that.

He remembered Barry Darling joking with him years ago that he was glad they weren't gay. 'Two men with unlimited sex drive, like we've got,' Darling had joked, 'would do nothing else. Luckily women are more restrained. It gives us a chance to do other things.'

But Cassandra was not like that. She wanted to have sex as much as he did, maybe more. His eyes moved along her thighs towards her groin. He jerked around to sit on the side of the bed.

Maybe I should go to church. It might clear my head. It was Sunday morning and the Garrison Church on the corner had a service at ten. He'd just make it. Quickly making up his mind, he tugged on the rumpled trousers that sat in a pile next to the bed and quietly made his way towards the door, pulling a creased T-shirt over his head.

'Sneaking out on me?'

Walker froze in the doorway and turned slowly. 'No. No.' He took a deep breath to stop himself from spewing. 'No. Just going to make us coffee.'

Cassandra smiled at him beneath a mop of tousled hair then propped herself up on one arm. 'No, you're not. Where're you going?'

'To church.'

Cassandra pulled the corner of her mouth down thoughtfully. 'Okay. Good idea. Can I come?'

Walker hesitated, wondering what to say when the phone rang.

Angela's tense voice came down the line. 'Christopher, I'm so sorry for bothering you on a Sunday morning.' She sounded like she might cry. 'Something awful has happened again. At the hospital. A murder.'

'Angela?' Walker glanced at Cassandra, who raised her eyebrows. 'A murder!' he said. Cassandra screwed her face up as if she didn't believe it. 'Where?'

'The chapel.'

Walker frowned at Cassandra, then said to Angela, 'Have you called the police?'

'Yes.'

'Okay, do you want me to come in?'

'I can't ask you to do that on your day off.'

'You didn't ask me, I'm offering.'

'I tried calling Cassie but she's not answering. Are you sure it's not too much to ask?'

Walker's eyes flicked to Cassandra. 'No, it's no problem. I'll be there in forty minutes.' He hung up the phone. 'Cassie, do you want a lift? I'll be going past your flat.'

'What's happened?'

'Another murder.'

'And Angela is involved?'

'Sounds like she found the body.'

'You're kidding. Again? Oooh, she's going to get a reputation.'

'Need a lift home then?'

'Yes, so I can change. Then I'm coming with you.'

'Do you think that's wise? Barry will probably be there.'

'So? He doesn't own me. And Angela doesn't own you either. She had her chance and she's cooled off.' Cassandra rolled over on the bed, not bothering to cover herself. 'Besides, I'm hot stuff. How can any man withstand me?'

He let out a short laugh. 'You can say that again.' He slapped one buttock playfully. 'Come on then, hot stuff, get your gear on. Let's go.'

CHAPTER FOUR

WALKER STOPPED AT Cassandra's flat to allow her to change into jeans and a loose top before driving on to Western Meadows. As they were driving off, Walker noted she hadn't put on a bra. He thought it unwise but said nothing.

They found Angela Chee standing hunched over outside the hospital chapel, which was not far from the main entrance. Her dark hair was pulled up at the back and held in place with a red ribbon. She looked tired. Before her stood a tall uniformed police officer who was jotting in a notepad.

'Good morning, Constable Jones,' said Walker when he reached them.

The young officer grimaced. 'How did I know you'd turn up, Dr Walker, even when this has absolutely nothing to do with you.' He raised his eyebrows. 'Or does it?'

'Not at all, officer. Just coming to help Dr Chee here. I seem to remember the last time you harassed Dr Chee you arrested her.' He put on a fake smile. 'Wrongfully, I might add.'

'There was strong evidence.' Jones closed his pad. 'Evidence never explained, for that matter.'

Angela dropped her head and Walker shifted uncomfortably.

'Now, now, Constable Jones,' Cassandra intervened. 'Let's not drag up yesterday's news.'

Detective Sergeant Barry Darling appeared at the door of the chapel and gestured to them. He was wearing an open-neck purple shirt with wide lapels and tight black trousers and gave Walker the impression he'd just been called in from a disco. 'Jones, Dr Chee, would you come in here, please?'

When Walker and Cassandra started to follow, the towering Jones blocked them with a muscular arm. 'No you don't.'

Cassandra put her hands on her hips and lifted her face to the young officer's. 'Yes I do. I'm her lawyer. You can't stop me.'

Jones jabbed a thumb at Walker. 'I can stop him.'

'Jones,' called Darling, 'what are you doing? Let them through.'

Walker smiled at Jones as he passed. 'Yes, Jones,' he murmured. 'Do as you're told.'

He followed Angela and noticed he still had that problem with his vision. When he looked to one side he saw double, so he turned slightly to reduce the effect. He'd had it a few times before after he'd drunk too much alcohol and he knew it would go away eventually.

The chapel was small and dark with only a few rows of seats and an altar near the wall away from the door. In the middle aisle, before the altar, was a body laid out face down in the shape of a cross – legs straight, arms perpendicular. Jutting out of the middle of the back was a knife; the handle appeared to be made of leather or some sort of animal hide and was decorated with a number of small white marks, and two gold discs. The blade was etched with strange inscriptions.

The chapel smelled faintly of incense with no hint of blood, and the forensic staff shuffled quietly around the small room, speaking in whispers as if a religious ceremony was taking place.

'Dr Chee,' said Darling, 'can you tell me again how you found the body?'

'Well,' Angela said slowly, 'my shift had finished and I came down here.' She looked at the body. 'And he was lying there.'

'Why were you working last night?'

'I was rostered on. Every two weeks or so I do an overnight shift. All registrars have to.'

Darling scribbled something in his pad. 'Were you rostered for last night? I mean, did you swap with anyone?'

'No.'

'Tell me, why did you come to the chapel? Were you meeting someone?'

Angela looked uncomfortable. 'I came to pray. I had a bad shift. A few people died.'

Jones interjected. 'A few?'

Angela frowned at the policeman. 'This is a hospital. People die.'

Jones didn't appear convinced.

'So, you came to pray,' said Darling, also appearing not to believe her.

Cassandra put a hand on Angela's arm. 'That's what she said, detective. Are you going to keep asking the same question or are you finished?'

He huffed. 'Detective, is it? All professional, are we?' He looked at Walker. 'How come you two arrived together?'

Angela examined Walker's then Cassandra's face. 'I couldn't get hold of you this morning, Cassie. I phoned a few times. Where were you?'

Cassandra wore a poker face. 'I was up early and went out. What are you two insinuating?'

Darling scowled at Walker. 'Nothing. Just asking, that's all.'

'Well, I suggest you concentrate on the case,' said Cassandra. Then her face softened. 'Look, Barry, I went out to get some breakfast and Chris picked me up on the way through. Angela phoned him.'

Darling looked sheepish. 'Okay, okay. Sorry.' He let out a breath and his eyes flicked to her loose top. 'Anyway, back to the case.'

He turned and walked towards the corpse and Walker followed. Angela stayed where she was, her forehead wrinkled with concern.

Jocelyn Banks, the forensic pathologist, stood near the body, directing one of the scientists to collect various specimens. The aid was on his knees and dressed in a blue Tyvek suit but Dr Banks was dressed elegantly in a neat skirt, high-heels and button-up silk top, a set of pearls around her neck.

'Hello, Wendy,' Jocelyn said with a cheeky smile. She was obviously still amused by Walker's nickname for Barry Darling. 'We meet again.'

Darling looked down at the body. 'What do you think of the knife?'

'Looks foreign. Middle Eastern maybe.'

'Do you think it's a clue to the murderer?' asked Walker.

'Don't know.' Darling shrugged. 'Maybe, or it could be to throw us off.'

'One thing we do know,' said Jocelyn.

'What's that?'

'He wasn't murdered here.'

'Oh?' said Walker, looking down at the body again.

'No blood. He was obviously killed somewhere else and placed here after he'd bled out.'

'How long ago was he killed?' asked Darling.

'No more than twelve hours,' said Jocelyn. 'He was probably carried in something or wrapped up. There're no drag marks or droplets of blood anywhere. It looks like he was placed here. Obviously positioned like that,' she added, tracing a cross with a bejewelled index finger in the air over the outstretched body. 'Made to look like some sort of religious sacrifice.'

'Maybe it was,' said Darling. 'An Arabic knife in a Catholic priest in a chapel. Sounds religious to me.'

Jocelyn raised a neatly groomed eyebrow. 'Well, I'll leave that for you to decide, Wendy.' She started to move away. 'I've got everything I need. I'll give you the autopsy report as soon as possible and will phone if I find anything significant.'

'Efficient,' muttered Darling after she was out of ear shot.

'Has to be, I suppose,' said Walker. 'It's a busy coroner's morgue. They have to get through a lot of work.'

'Dr Chee,' said Darling, 'are you up to coming back to the station to give a statement?'

'A statement?' said Angela. She looked exhausted. 'I've told you everything I know. I just found him here. That's it.'

'Barry,' said Cassandra carefully, putting a hand on his arm. 'Angela's tired. She's just come off a twenty-four-hour shift. How about we leave it for another day.'

He glanced at Angela before looking back at Cassandra. Walker wondered whether he was studying her clothes for clues. 'Another day then.'

'I'll take you home,' Walker said to Angela.

'You don't have to do that,' she said, her words slow. 'I have my car.'

'It's no problem. You look done. Anyway, it's Sunday. I've plenty of time.'

'You coming?' Angela said to Cassandra.

She glanced at Darling before answering. 'No. I think I'll have breakfast with Barry.'

As they walked away, Angela muttered under her breath, 'Thought she said she'd already gone out for breakfast.'

Walker pretended not to hear and steered her towards the carpark, trying to think of something to change the subject. As they reached the car, he said, 'I didn't know you were religious. Praying?'

She didn't look happy as she eased herself into the passenger seat. 'There's a lot you don't know about me,' she said after they were both in.

He thought of her dead father and decided he could only agree. He started the engine with a grimace. It was going to be an awkward drive home.

As they drove through the back roads of the hospital, Angela pointed to a congregation gathered in the dock area behind the hospital. 'What's that?'

Walker stopped his BMW and together they peered along the dead-end road that serviced the docks. A small crowd formed a semicircle near one wall. With a sigh, he turned down the road. 'Only one way to find out.'

Walker parked near the crowd and he and Angela got out and looked over the shoulders of the nurses and ancillary staff who had gathered. On the ground was a body, an Asian man dressed in a hospital cleaner's outfit. Crouched beside the body was Jocelyn Banks, the fabric of her skirt pulled tight, her high heels neatly together. She looked up when Walker pushed forward.

'Dead,' she said flatly. 'Many hours, at least.' She looked over his shoulder at the hospital building that loomed above them and Walker followed her gaze. One of the windows on an upper level was pivoted open.

'Suicide?' said Walker.

'Appears that way,' said Jocelyn. She looked down at the body. 'Died instantly, I'd say.' She shook her head grimly. 'All very suspicious though, given the other murder. I don't like coincidences.'

Angela spoke from behind Walker. 'I know him. One of the cleaners. He was working last night. Jim, I think.'

'Jim Nguyen,' confirmed a short woman who was also dressed as a cleaner. 'Poor man. He was always so cheerful. Why would he commit suicide?'

Jocelyn stood up gracefully. 'Christopher, would you please go and inform Detective Darling? I'll stay here with the body.' She looked at Angela who stood with drooped shoulders. 'Angela, you go and rest in the car.' She addressed the crowd in a firm voice. 'Could I ask everyone to step away at least thirty metres, please. We may be standing on evidence.'

People looked down at their feet and shifted around, and eventually began to move away, leaving Walker, Angela and Jocelyn alone with the body.

Angela stared at the corpse, appearing as if she might burst into tears. 'At least I didn't find this one.' Her voice was tense. 'What is going on in this damn hospital?'

***

After the crowd had dispersed and the forensic team had taken over, Darling and Jones made their way to the top floor of the hospital building. In a single room of the neurosurgical ward they found the open window through which the cleaner had made his final egress. The charge nurse informed them the room had been empty all weekend. Beds had been closed as a cost-cutting measure, she told them bluntly, as if the bed closures were somehow their fault.

'There hasn't been a patient in that room since Christmas,' she said as she showed them in. She stared at the open window then turned away gruffly. 'I'll leave you to it.'

The room had an empty bed, stripped down to a plastic cover, along with a bedside table and an empty chair in one corner. Jones examined the window. It was of a type meant to be kept closed, with key locks on one side so it could be opened for cleaning. Now it was swung open on a central pivot so that one side of the window was in the room and the other half outside the building.

'Can't see anything on the windowsill,' said Jones.

Darling leaned in and looked closely at the green metal surface. It appeared perfectly clean, with no evidence of blood or other material. Next, he looked closely at the floor but could find no evidence of scuff marks or any other signs that a struggle had taken place.

'Seal the door until we can get forensics in here,' said Darling. 'We should at least find the victim's fingerprints.' He looked at the open window. 'It would be impossible to jump out of that window without grabbing onto the surrounding area.'

'What if he took a running jump and dived through?' suggested Jones.

'I doubt it, Jones. I don't think even *you* could manage that without grabbing an edge. The victim was about twenty years older than you.' He glanced around the room. 'No, he had to be thrown out or he jumped himself. Either way, we should find something. Get the fingerprint team up here quicksmart.'

After Jones had left, Darling stayed in the room and peered out of the window, careful not to touch anything. Down below was an access road to the docks where the cleaner's body had come to rest. On the other side of the road was the pathology building and he searched from window to window along the top floor just below his current level. He was surprised to see Jocelyn Banks seated at a desk in what he assumed was her office. She was directly across from him, although one floor below, and he could clearly see her neat desk with a small pile of papers and a computer on it. He watched her for some moments as she worked on something, making marks on a piece of paper and occasionally writing. When nothing else seemed to happen, he began to feel more like a voyeur than a policeman and was ready to move away when Jones returned with the forensic team. He turned as they entered but thought he saw a movement out of the corner of his eye and looked back. He was sure he'd caught a glimpse of her staring directly up at him from her office as he had looked away.

But now Jocelyn was sitting at her desk, head down, as before.

With an odd feeling, he vacated the room to let the team do their work.

CHAPTER FIVE

ALI HARB WAS born in Beirut in 1965 and came to Australia with his parents in 1976 when they fled the Lebanese civil war. The family settled in a three-bedroom house in Auburn in Sydney's western suburbs. Ali's father described himself as a 'self-employed businessman' despite being on unemployment benefits, who left the rearing of his five children to his wife. She was a tough matriarch but had a soft spot for her precious sons and allowed them more leeway than she would have if they'd stayed in the family-focused suburbs of Beirut.

On many occasions, Ali's mother had bemoaned the poor standards of this new country, complaining about the Australian mothers who failed to teach their children proper manners, tolerating disrespect towards elders and allowing their daughters to walk the streets like prostitutes. At least his sisters were appropriately demure when they went out in public, but he knew his mother wished they wore a hijab to school, as was proper. But his sisters had argued that 'absolutely no one wore one in this country' and in that one thing she'd capitulated.

Like his father, Ali was also self-employed, and was currently working on a particular project that he hoped would make his family a good income. He just had to keep the parole officer off his back.

On this Sunday night, he pulled his Harley-Davidson up at the McDonald's in Auburn and went inside to meet his contact who'd promised to deliver him a prize that would earn him the respect of his Brothers, which he so craved. Plus, if things went well, he'd get a tidy sum of cash to boot.

He paused outside the door and peered through the window, searching for signs of danger. The tables were mostly full of mums and dads with their kids, and teenagers dressed in the latest fashion showing off to each other. Before he pushed open the door, he grasped a silver amulet hanging around his neck and rubbed the metal between his thumb and forefinger, while whispering the protective words that were engraved there in Arabic. *'Allah! There's no god save Him, the Alive, the Eternal. Neither slumber nor sleep overtake Him ...'*

As the final words of the prayer left his lips, he became infused with strength and knew that now he'd be safe from Shaytan's intervention. His grand-mère had taught him so. It would be enough.

As soon as he entered the restaurant he saw his contact seated at a table near the far door. At first, he ignored him while he cased the room. The air smelled of cooked meat and his stomach growled. There were long lines of people at the counter and behind it; pimply teenage boys and nimble girls were serving the hungry throng. He knew from past experience that sometimes the local cops came here for a snack but tonight they were nowhere to be seen. He made his way to the counter and noticed, with some satisfaction, the effect his patch had on the customers standing in line. The helmeted skull with yellow and red wings that rode proudly on the back of his jacket allowed him to cut a path through the crowd to the front of the line.

He ordered his favourite meal – a McFeast Deluxe with large fries and a Coke – then made his way to the table to take a seat with his contact. Ali was pleased he'd chosen a spot next to the door. The Milperra Massacre at the Viking Tavern in '84 was a lesson to be learned. A Brother should always be ready for a fast exit.

'Did you get the stuff?' he asked in a low voice after he sat down.

His contact nodded. 'But we had problems.'

'Problems?' Ali stiffened. They couldn't afford failure.

'We were seen,' said the other, quickly raising a hand when Ali began to lurch to his feet, causing him to pause. 'But we took care of it.'

'What do you mean?' he murmured, his voice tight.

The man put a palm over Ali's fist, which was curled tightly on the tabletop. 'I said we took care of it.'

'How many?'

'Three. All gone.' He chopped his hand sideways definitively.

'Three!' Again, Ali had to stop himself from surging to his feet. Instead, he leaned in closer and dropped his voice to a hiss. 'How are you going to hide three dead bodies from the cops?'

'Don't worry, we managed it.' The man leaned back, trying to give the impression he was unconcerned. But Ali saw a crack of worry on his brow.

'But is the stuff safe?'

'Safe and sound. No one suspects where it is. We're ready to move it when you are. But we better do it soon before the cops start searching the place. They'll start to put two and two together before too long.'

'Tonight. We'll do it tonight.' Ali paused. Maybe it was a trap. Maybe his contact was a police stooge. He had only been introduced to him by his Brothers a few weeks ago and they were only using him because of his job at the hospital. How could he be sure he was trustworthy? 'Are you certain it's safe?' he asked slowly, his eyes burrowing into the other's, demanding truth.

'Trust me. I would have noticed something, and no one has gone near the stash. The cops have found nothing. So far. I know how to clean up after myself.'

Ali paused for a moment longer, then smiled and gave a genuine laugh. 'That I believe. With your job, I suppose if anyone could clean up three stiffs without a trace, it's you.'

The man also smiled. 'So, we're okay then.' He looked around and leaned in close. 'Okay, we'll move the stuff tonight.'

CHAPTER SIX

AS SOON AS Walker entered his office in the clinical sciences building on Monday morning his phone started ringing. It was Barry Darling. He wanted Walker to meet him.

'On the hospital oval? What for?'

'You'll see.' Darling hung up.

The oval was a grass field, five minutes' walk from the main hospital towards a creek that eventually ran into the Parramatta River. On the other side of the oval, a long way from the hospital buildings, sat the research Animal House and also the helicopter hangar that was the headquarters of the CareFlight rescue service. As he walked down the stairs to the oval, Walker heard the low level 'whoop' of a helicopter engine warming up.

In the centre of the oval, Walker could see a blue tent had been erected and a crowd of people milled about, coming and going. Several police vehicles and white vans were parked on the grass.

'Another body?' asked Walker when Darling met him just outside the tents.

'Young woman, mid-twenties. Naked. No ID.'

'Why am I no longer surprised?' said Walker, shaking his head. 'It's as if the hospital has decided to go mad. Do you think the murder is related to the others?'

'A priest apparently stabbed with an Arabic knife, a cleaner possibly made to look as if he committed suicide, and now,' Darling pointed to the tent, 'a young woman dead from a head injury that doesn't look bad enough to kill her. Naked, but no signs of sexual assault.'

'What did you want me for?'

'I want to know whether you knew what Angela Chee did after she went home on Saturday.'

'Me? Why me?'

'You took her home.'

'I just dropped her off. I haven't seen her since. But why? You can't think she killed these three people.'

'Not by herself, perhaps,' said Darling, poker-faced. 'But there's something not right about that young woman.'

'She can't help it if death follows her.'

'Follows her? So, you also think she might be involved.'

'You know perfectly well, Wendy, that I don't mean that. It's just a saying.'

'I've never heard it.'

Walker realised he'd never heard the expression either and wondered why he'd said it. 'Sorry, I can't help you.'

Jocelyn Banks walked towards them, exquisitely dressed as usual. 'She was placed here,' she said without preamble when she reached them. 'Died somewhere else. The body temperature is ambient, which means she died over twelve hours ago. But the livor mortis – that's the purple discolouration of the skin – says she has been dead for days. The position of it also indicates the body was lying flat on the back after she died, but here she was placed on her side. She must have been murdered elsewhere. There was a cricket match on the oval yesterday, which means she was moved here overnight.'

Then came the overwhelming noise of a helicopter taking off on the edge of the field, killing off any further conversation. They looked up to see a blue and white chopper with CareFlight emblazoned on the side; it hovered above the oval for a few moments, causing the tents to flutter violently.

Darling waved at it angrily and shouted something which was lost in the clatter. A moment later the chopper flew away towards the east and the noise quickly abated.

Darling looked furious. 'Their supervisor's going to get a call from me today. Who do they think they are?' He seemed to calm down and again addressed the pathologist. 'Sorry, Dr Banks, you were saying? You said she was killed somewhere else, maybe a few days ago.'

'That's correct,' said Jocelyn. 'But not everything matches. There's evidence of rigor mortis, which, in this heat, should last less than twelve hours. And there's minimal decomposition, which also points to her being dead less than a day. It's as if she was killed in the middle of winter.'

'So the signs don't make sense?' said Walker.

Banks nodded. 'Some suggest she's been dead less than twelve hours, and others indicate it's been a few days. Our forensic entomologist reckons there're virtually no insect larvae in the body. It's as if she only just died.'

'Forensic entomologist?' said Walker. 'We've actually got one of those?'

Banks gave Walker a level stare. 'Of course we do. We're not some backwater, Christopher. And she happens to be one of the best in the world.'

Walker gave an appreciative smirk.

'Cause of death?' asked Darling.

'There are signs of head trauma but they don't seem to be severe enough to kill her. No signs of rape. I'll know more when I have the toxicology and have finished the autopsy.'

Walker wondered whether he should go back to work. The murder had nothing to do with him and he had patients to see. But then he noticed Constable Jones striding across the oval from the direction of the creek. The young policeman was wearing a pair of blue overalls and gloves and was carrying what looked like a large plastic bag. 'Looks like Jones has found something,' he said, and Darling and Banks turned to watch him approach.

'I've found this, sir,' he reported, holding the bag up. 'Looks like a nurse's uniform.'

'Good work, Jones,' said Darling.

They took it to a bench and Darling, wearing gloves, carefully examined the clothes through the clear plastic. 'Yes, looks like a nurse's,' he confirmed. 'But what's this?' He held up the bag. There appeared to be a small collection of white powder in the corner. 'Looks suspicious. And this?' Stuck against the side of the plastic was a fragment of paper, which he extracted and carefully unwrapped. On it were a few words scrawled in pencil. He held it up to the sunlight and squinted at it. 'Looks like it says "Sin talk", or maybe "Sin take".' He looked at Jones. 'Some religious cult maybe?' He waved to one of the other officers. 'Let's get some photos of this then hand it over to forensics to see what they can find out.'

Walker made his way back to the clinical buildings from the oval, climbing a set of concrete stairs that took him to the access road, which ran between the ward and pathology buildings. Overhead, an airbridge connected the buildings. As he walked towards the first set of docks that would take him to the elevators, he remembered poor Sanjeev the pharmacist who had been murdered there only a few short weeks ago, skewered through the chest by a forklift driven by his crazed ex-intern.

'Is the world going mad?' Walker muttered to himself. 'Why all these murders all of a sudden?'

He was about to climb the stairs to the dock when the sunlight caught something that was lying on the road near the entrance to the morgue and he changed his path to investigate. The thing glittered again when he drew closer and he could see that it was a small piece of white metal. He stooped to pick it up and examined it.

It looked like an old silver pendant. The edges were worn and one surface was covered with squiggles that looked like

Arabic writing. On one side was a small projection of silver, carved to look like a leaf. He looked up and down the road to see who might have lost it but there was no one in either direction. From its position, Walker concluded that it'd probably been dropped by someone using the ramp into the morgue.

A delivery man maybe?

He turned it over and the other side was mostly blank except for two Western letters, roughly engraved.

'A H,' he recited. Again, he looked up and down the road and, seeing no one, slipped the amulet into his pocket. He wasn't sure what he'd do with it since there was no official lost and found department in the hospital. He briefly considered dropping it off at security but decided against it. Instead, he'd show it to one of his Arabic colleagues to get their opinion.

Walker entered the cancer ward where he met Angela Chee, looking fresh and rested despite having found yet another murder victim only two days before. He decided not to tell her about the murdered nurse. She'd find out soon enough.

'Dr Walker, this is our new intern,' said Angela, indicating a large young man with wide shoulders and a generous smile. 'Vince Greenway.'

Greenway towered over him as he thrust out a large hand and energetically shook Walker's. 'Pleased to meet you, Dr Walker. Happy to be working with you.'

Vince's grasp was firm without being overbearing and despite himself, Walker smiled back. 'Pleased to have you on board. We were worried we wouldn't get a replacement so early in the year. What were you doing before this?'

'I was at a rugby camp in England and missed the first round of job offers. I'm really pleased this one came up. I was expecting to be relegated to the outer planets.' He smiled again. 'I heard what happened for this vacancy to come up and, although I can't say I'm happy about the ... you know

… murders,' he glanced apologetically at Angela, 'I'm pleased to be here.'

'A rugby camp in England? Who do you play for?'

'Sydney Uni. But I'm trying to make it into the Wallabies. This is my big chance.'

Walker nodded slowly. 'Impressive. So, we might have a rugby start working with us. Do you need to take much time off?'

'Don't worry. Not this term at all, not with the heat. Formal practice sessions don't start until March and this term will be just about over by then.'

'Just about,' Walker said flatly, knowing full well the terms did not change until after Easter in April. Walker turned to face the corridor. 'We'd better get cracking. Any new admissions?'

'Just one,' said Vince. 'A Mr Gleason with prostate cancer. Came in with uncontrolled back pain.' He led the way into a four-bed room and went to the furthest bed.

An elderly fellow was lying prone on the bed at an angle, his face twisted in agony. Walker shook his hand. 'Mr Gleason, you look like you're in pain. Where is it?'

'It's no better since I came in last night.' He raised a thin arm. 'Turn around, I'll point on you.' Walker did as requested, and Gleason pointed to a spot halfway up his back.

'About T6,' said Vince. Angela agreed.

'Do you have pain in the legs?'

'No, just the back.'

'Have you examined the power in his legs?' he asked Vince.

'Yes, the strength is normal. Reflexes and sensation are normal also.'

'Do your legs feel normal, Mr Gleason?'

'Nothing wrong with my legs, doc. It's my back.' He lifted his legs up and down, although he winced with pain and held his back.

'Have you had problems with your waterworks?'

'Now that you mention it, they're working too well. Can't hang on to my bladder. If I've got to go, the nurses have to bring me a bottle pronto or I wet myself.'

'Jenny, do you have any ice on the ward?' asked Walker. The nurse nodded and moved away to get some. When she returned, Walker rubbed the ice on the patient's upper chest. 'Does that feel cold?'

When Gleason said it did, Walker moved to the front of his shin. 'And now?'

'Maybe not as cold,' he said uncertainly.

'Tell me if it changes.' Walker rubbed the ice up Gleason's right leg and continued up over the abdomen. When it got to his lower chest, he started. 'Blimey, that's suddenly got real cold.'

Walker did it again on the left side and got the same reaction.

'There's a band of abrupt sensation change at the patient's lower chest, normal sensation above and reduced below,' he reported.

'That's T6 dermatome,' said Angela.

'Vince,' said Walker, standing up straight, 'Mr Gleason has an early spinal cord compression at the sixth thoracic vertebrae. Phone radiology for an urgent CT myelogram.'

'Or MRI?' suggested Angela.

'That's right,' said Walker. 'We've finally got a machine. Will they do it?'

'If *you* ask them, they will.'

'Okay, I'll call the radiologist. Jenny, let's give Mr Gleason sixteen milligrams of dexamethasone IV right away. Angela, could you call Radiation Oncology – whoever's on-call – and let them know. He'll need a neurosurgical opinion also, so let them know as well, although I suspect they'll be in theatre.'

When everyone else rushed off to do as ordered, Walker turned back to the patient. 'Lucky we picked this up early, you could've lost the use of your legs. It'll be the prostate cancer in the bone of your back, growing out of it and pressing on your spinal cord. Usually, on that part of the spine, we use radiotherapy rather than surgery, especially since we got it early. We'll start the treatment today. They'll treat with X-rays every day for one or two weeks.'

'What about the pain?' said Gleason.

'We'll do something about that as well. I'll sort out your MRI scan while the others fix you up.'

CHAPTER SEVEN

AFTER MR GLEASON was wheeled off for his scan, the team regrouped to continue the ward round. There was a consult on the urology ward and Walker asked Angela to lead the way.

The next ward over was used as a shortcut to other parts of the hospital and was separated from the cancer ward by a set of double doors. A piece of paper was stuck on the door with sticky-tape and the words 'Keep closed. Wandering patient' written on it in thick red ink.

Walker stepped through, followed by Angela and Vince, but they were pulled up abruptly by an irate elderly woman wearing a dressing gown and slippers with cotton cat ears stuck to them. She peered at Walker's face closely before stepping aside and waving them on.

'Move along,' she said. 'Just checking for aliens.'

Walker nodded and moved past but Vince stopped. 'Aliens? What do you mean?'

'Come on, Vince,' said Walker. 'Don't disturb the lady.'

'But it sounds fascinating.' He turned back to the woman who was now examining the intern's face closely. 'Have you seen aliens?' he asked politely.

'Why?' she barked. 'Are you one of them? If you are then you've forgot your hat.'

Angela moved back towards them. 'Vince, you shouldn't pander to her delusions. You should know that.'

The woman turned to face Angela and gave her the same close examination. 'Well, you're not one. You're Chinese. I've never seen a Chinese alien. And you don't have a hat.'

'Why do you say that aliens wear hats?' asked Vince.

The woman spun back to him. 'Because! I saw them. I saw them chase the man. They made him fly.' She turned back to Angela and pointed. 'He was Chinese too.'

'Who?' asked Vince. 'I thought you said aliens weren't Chinese.'

'Yes.' She shook her head. 'The man who flew.'

'Come on, Vince, let's get cracking,' called Walker, moving away.

The intern began to follow but said to the lady as he left, 'I'll come back and talk to you later.'

'See that you do,' she said gruffly before turning back to guard the door.

'That's cruel, Vince,' said Angela after they'd moved along the corridor. 'You shouldn't play with that poor demented woman's mind. You'll only make her worse.'

'On the contrary,' he said, 'I did an elective term of geriatrics as a medical student. I'm interested in dementia. I know I'm not an expert but I would say that's very unusual for dementia. An acute delirium maybe, but she looked pretty well. Otherwise, a psychiatric disease. Psychosis maybe. I'll come back and examine her later when I have more time. She seemed very sure about it.'

As they walked away, a nurse called out to them from the doorway, which they had left ajar. 'Close the door next time, would you, please? We found Mrs Carlton downstairs in the docks the other night.'

'Sorry,' replied Walker, raising his hand in apology.

Mrs Carlton glared at them while they walked away, as if she totally agreed with the nurse's reprimand.

They reached the urology ward and Angela led Walker into a room with a single bed. A head with a shock of white hair poked out from the blankets, eyes closed, mouth open and unmoving. The blankets were neatly pulled up under the chin as if the body had been slipped in between the sheets as carefully as possible so as not to disturb them.

'Good morning,' said Walker. There was no movement. 'Hello,' he called more loudly. When there was still no activity, Walker glanced at Angela questioningly.

She bent down and drew closer to the patient's ear. 'Hello, Mr Anderson. Dr Walker has come to see you.'

There was still no movement and Walker moved past her and looked closely at the man's chest but could see no respiratory movement under the tightly tucked blankets. He pulled the blankets out on one side and grasped the old man's shoulder and shook it. 'Mr Anderson.'

'Should we call an arrest?' Angela said uncertainly from behind.

'I'm not sure he's dead.' Walker bent over and looked carefully for any signs of life, his face close to the motionless gent. He placed his hand on the patient's neck and felt for a pulse.

As he did so, the old man's eyes shot open. 'Yes?' he screamed in a high-pitched voice. 'What do you want?'

Walker jumped back and crashed into Angela, stepping on her toe and elbowing her in the abdomen in the process. He spun around. 'Angela! I'm so sorry.'

Angela slid to the ground, holding her abdomen, her face twisted in pain and shock. She opened her mouth but no sound came out. Walker kneeled beside her and began to rub her abdomen, firm muscles through a thin shift. 'You're just winded, Angela. Don't worry, you'll be able to breathe in a moment.'

Angela was on her back, her forehead pinched, eyes closed, threatening tears. Soon she was able to take breaths, deeper with each one. Finally, she was breathing deeply and she opened her eyes. 'That was awful. I've never been winded before.'

Walker continued to rub her stomach but now it was more like a caress. 'I'm so sorry, Angela. Let me help you back up.' She sat up and rested for a while before allowing Walker to help her to her feet. 'Let me take you back to my office where you can rest,' he said.

She shook her head. 'I'm okay now. It's all gone. I'm perfectly fine.' She took the seat near the window. 'I'll just rest here for a moment.'

The old man was now sitting up in bed, back ramrod-straight and motionless, skinny arms grasping the blanket to his chest, pale skin with wide, staring eyes. He still looked like a corpse even though he was upright. Walker looked over at Angela who now had colour returning to her face.

'Let's come back another time, Angela,' he said. 'This old bloke can wait. I don't think we can do anything for him anyway.'

His head swivelled on his skinny neck. 'I'm not deaf, you know,' he shrieked.

'Sorry, sir,' said Walker in a loud voice. 'We'll have to come back another time.'

He put a hand to his ear. 'What?'

Walker crossed to his registrar and offered her his hand. 'Come, Angela.'

As she reached her hand to his, something on the wall caught his eye and he bent over to examine it, leaving her with her arm outstretched, a look of incredulity on her face.

'Look at this! Looks like blood.'

'What?' Angela said with irritation. She stared at the spot. 'Yes, I think you're right.' Her voice was more reasonable now.

'And on the windowsill as well.'

'And I can see spots on the floor,' said Angela, pointing.

Walker craned his head to look through the closed window in all directions. 'You know what, this room is directly below the window the cleaner was supposed to have been thrown through.' He squinted at the lock. There were scratch marks around it. 'Looks like someone's opened this but were sloppy about it. In a rush maybe.'

'So they threw Jim Nguyen out of this window and then closed it, went upstairs and opened the one above instead. Why would they do that?'

'To throw the police off the track.' He examined the surround of the window. 'There might be fingerprints. I'll have to tell Wendy.'

Angela huffed. 'Do you think he'll try to blame me somehow?'

Walker turned his head abruptly. 'Did you touch the wall just now? Or the window?'

Angela looked at the window then at her hand with dismay. 'I don't know. I was concentrating on trying to breathe. I might have.'

'Well, don't touch anything now and leave the room. I'll not have Wendy badgering you again.'

As Angela left, he looked at the old man who stared back with eyes like a pair of black marbles. 'We'll have to move you as well, sir,' he called in a loud voice.

'Eh?'

An hour later, Detective Darling and Constable Jones had returned and stood in the empty room with the ward's charge nurse.

'We need to know who was in this room on the night of the cleaner's death,' said Darling.

'That's easy,' said the nurse. 'No one. The ward was only reopened this Monday after the Christmas break. The hospital closes beds when the theatres slow down. A lot of the surgeons take a break then.'

'So the ward was empty. Were the doors locked?'

'Not that I know of. In fact, no. There's no way of locking them. Anyone could wander in. All the equipment is locked away so there's nothing to steal.'

'That means anyone could've come in here after hours and opened that window,' Darling pointed, 'and no one would have been the wiser.'

'That's right, detective,' said the nurse. 'An empty ward is just that – empty. Nothing to steal.'

He crossed to the window and examined the floor and the window surrounds. A long black scuff mark led from halfway across the room to just short of the window and he could see dark marks on the wall that could have been dried blood.

'Get the team up here, Jones,' he sighed.

Ali Harb parked his Harley in the driveway of a modest house in Auburn and noted with satisfaction that the van they'd used to move the drug cache the night before was in the same place he'd left it, under the carport down the side of the house. Today he'd complete the delivery and pick up his reward for a job well done. His contact would get half the money, even though the fool had almost stuffed the whole thing up. Three stiffs! But somehow, they had managed to pull it off. As far as he could tell, the coppers appeared to have no idea of how or where the murders had occurred. Maybe the coppers were dumber than he realised!

He stared at the house but all was quiet. His eyes wandered over the front garden, which was virtually devoid of plants but scattered with a collection of garden gnomes of all sizes. Ali grimaced as his attention went back to the house. His contact would have heard him pull up on his Harley, especially the way he'd gunned the engine before he switched it off. Ali scanned the windows, carefully trying to determine whether there was someone standing behind the crooked venetian blinds, looking out at him. He started to become uneasy. His contact should have come out by now. Maybe a gun was already trained on him? Maybe he was going to get greedy? And stupid. His Brothers would be merciless if they were double-crossed but some people were just plain dumb.

Ali tried to remain calm, brave. He couldn't let the other know he was frightened. He reached up to his neck to stroke his lucky necklace for protection.

It wasn't there!

He frantically unzipped his leather jacket and dug in under his T-shirt.

Gone!

He felt a cold chill rise in his chest. His holy protection lost! It couldn't be. It was a gift from his grand-mère when he was a baby, the only thing of hers he had left.

Heedless of the previous thought of danger, he got off his bike and strode towards the door. Maybe that fool had taken it. If so, he'd punch –

He heard a car pull up on the road behind and spun towards it. The coppers?

No, it was his contact. Ali was immediately suspicious. No one was protecting the drugs. He walked to the car and waited at the window until it was wound down.

'Where have you been?' he demanded. 'Where's the stuff?' Maybe his accomplice had delivered it without him.

'Nice to see you too, Ali. Don't worry, I haven't double-crossed you, if that's what you're thinking. The stuff's all there where we left it last night.'

'Where have you been? You shouldn't have left it alone.'

'Back to the hospital. I wanted to see if the coppers had found anything.'

'And have they?'

His contact smiled. 'A dead nurse.'

Ali frowned. 'How did they know she was a nurse?'

'*Someone* threw the bag with her uniform into the creek, despite me telling them not to. The coppers found it easily.'

'It don't matter,' snapped Ali. 'There was nothing in the bag that'll give us away.'

'I certainly hope not, for your sake. I made sure *my* prints weren't on it.'

A chill rose in Ali's chest again. Then he relaxed. 'I was wearing gloves.'

'Because I told you to. You owe me, you big Lebanese dick. If it wasn't for me, the coppers would be all over you like a rash.'

Ali's hand went to his neck, a movement not lost on the other, whose lips twisted into a smile. 'I saw something else too. Up near the mortuary ramp. I went up there to make sure we hadn't left anything.'

'Had we?'

'One of us did.' The smile widened. 'A locket, by the looks of it.'

'A locket! Was it silver?'

'Maybe. Couldn't be sure from where I was standing. A doctor picked it up. I was hiding at the edge of the building. He picked it up and put it in his pocket.'

'Doctor!' snapped Ali. 'Who?'

He ran a hand over a smooth jaw and for a moment said nothing, then got out of the car and stood facing Ali. 'I would have thought you'd be more thankful. Polite even. After all, I saved you from leaving your prints. And now I know who has a very important clue. An artefact that might lead back to a certain someone. Someone who has no business being in the docks outside a mortuary.'

Ali stepped closer and grabbed his shirt and slowly twisted until the blood was cut off, causing veins to distend in the fellow's neck. He didn't care about the drugs. Didn't really even care if the cops got suspicious. All he cared about was getting back his grand-mère's gift, his protection. 'What was the name of the doctor,' he hissed through tight lips.

The fellow's face twisted with shock as it became engorged with blood, lips moving noiselessly with the lack of air. Just when Ali thought he would black out, he let go and allowed him to collapse onto his knees. Ali grabbed his hair and pushed the head back. 'Give me the name.'

The other coughed hoarsely then took in a deep breath.

The reply was a whisper. 'Christopher Walker.'

Later that afternoon, the detectives were called to the morgue by Jocelyn Banks. Two bodies lay on slabs, one Asian and the other Caucasian, but in other respects very similar – naked with their chests cut open from top to bottom to display their insides. Darling and Jones stood nearby, watching Jocelyn and her morgue attendant, an older fellow with a prominent nose and long unkempt hair. Darling had met Johnson before.

'The wound from the Arabic knife was definitely the cause of death for the priest,' said Jocelyn, matter-of-factly. 'The blade perfectly matches the wound and it dissected his aorta. Either the murderer knew what he was doing or he was lucky. He killed him with a single stab.'

'He?' said Jones.

'It takes a lot of strength to stick a knife into someone's chest through the rib cage. You should try it one day. It's harder than it looks.'

'I'll take your word for it,' said Jones.

Banks raised her eyebrows. 'Suit yourself.' She pointed to the Asian corpse. 'He, on the other hand, is not so straightforward. He died from injuries consistent with a fall from a height. But,' she raised a finger at the two police officers, 'not consistent with jumping.'

'No?' Darling said with interest.

'A jump out of a building will usually fracture the lower limbs – ankle, femur, that sort of thing, and almost always result in compression fractures of the thoracic and lumbar spine.'

'What happened to him?' asked Jones.

'Massive head injury and a broken neck.'

'I would have thought that'd be common in a suicide of this type,' said Darling.

'No. Head injuries are uncommon and certainly not a broken neck if you jump. He hit the pavement headfirst. Not many people dive to their deaths when committing suicide.'

The men examined the body closely as if they might be able to discern the injuries. Johnson stood nearby with a sheet, ready to cover the body when they'd finished their examination.

'And another thing,' continued Jocelyn, 'he has bruises around his upper arms and wrists that suggest he was roughly handled before he died.'

'A fight?'

'Looks like it.'

'Was he already dead before he hit the ground?'

'No,' Banks said slowly. 'The impact was definitely the cause of death. But the signs indicate he was pushed headfirst out of the window. And probably conscious.'

'So he'd have screamed,' said Jones.

'I would have,' Banks said.

'Jones,' said Darling, 'let's have another look at the open window. And let's ask all the patients on the surrounding wards whether they heard anything.' He turned to the pathologist. 'Is there anything else, Dr Banks? Anything you've found that might link the two deaths?'

'Not at the moment. We've sent blood off for toxicology. I'll let you know if we find anything.'

'And what is the estimated time of death?'

'The chaplain was dead at least twelve hours. So about ten pm.'

'And the cleaner?' asked Jones.

'About the same.'

'What about the nurse?' asked Darling.

'Give us a chance, Wendy,' she said with a wry smile. 'We'll do her tomorrow morning. Come in at about ten and we'll see what we've got.'

CHAPTER EIGHT

THEY MET JOCELYN Banks in the morgue the next morning as she was just finishing an autopsy on an elderly male corpse laid out on the slab. Johnson was busy sewing up the Y-shaped incision that started just above the pubic bone and finished below each shoulder. Jocelyn was wearing a white apron over a green gown and was in the process of pulling off her mask, cap and latex gloves.

'I wanted to give you the results for the nurse and thought it would be easier to explain on the corpse. It's all very interesting.' She walked to the wall and pulled out a metal drawer that held the body covered in a drape, which she pulled back. 'I find it all fascinating.'

'What exactly?' said Darling.

'The toxicology shows large amounts of heroin, enough to kill her. The white powder in the plastic bag also came back as heroin.'

'Could she have taken an overdose, then fallen over to get the head injury?' said Darling.

'That's possible. She has a needle mark in her antecubital fossa.' Jocelyn pointed to a small red mark in the crook of the elbow. 'But who would have undressed her?'

'Maybe another drug addict who didn't want to be found out,' said Jones. 'Tried to hide the evidence of an accidental overdose so they couldn't be traced.'

'Maybe,' said Darling. 'More likely she was murdered by a lethal injection of heroin after she sustained the head injury.'

Jocelyn nodded. 'The head injury first then the injection, but it was the heroin overdose that killed her.' She looked down at the nurse's face, still pretty in death despite the ugly bruise on the forehead. 'And it's fair to say that someone else undressed her, probably whoever injected her.'

'Okay,' said Darling. 'But that all seems straightforward. I thought you said you found her case fascinating.'

'Ha ha!' said Jocelyn, raising a finger theatrically. 'The fascinating problem is the time of death. We found crystal blades in her blood, which don't come on for about three days. And that fits with the livor mortis, which takes a few days to reach that level.' She pointed to purple discolouration of the skin along the flanks and the outer surface of the legs. 'But on the other hand, there were no signs of decomposition, no insect larvae, and rigour mortis was still present, all pointing to death occurring less than a day before the body was found.'

'So what does it all mean?' asked Jones.

'There can only be one explanation.' Jocelyn paused to give the policemen a chance to jump in and solve the riddle.

They both gave her blank looks. 'I give up,' said Darling.

She raised her hands as if the answer was obvious. 'She was murdered and then the body was refrigerated.'

'Refrigerated?' said Jones. 'You mean, like in a fridge.'

She threw Jones a look. 'That's generally what refrigerated means.'

'But how would they fit the body in a fridge?'

Darling frowned at his underling. 'A big fridge, Jones, not like the one you have in your kitchen.'

He grimaced. 'Could she have been killed somewhere cold and brought here?'

'The body would have had to be refrigerated until just before it was placed on the oval,' said Jocelyn. 'I suppose she could've been moved in a refrigerated truck. But that's quite an undertaking. Why would someone go to all that trouble? If I did it to throw you off, I wouldn't have bothered to refrigerate her. I would have killed her then moved her to the oval. The fact the body was refrigerated has given you a clue.'

'Murderers aren't always clever or rational,' said Darling. 'They might have killed her and panicked.'

Jocelyn shrugged. 'Well, Detective Darling, that's for you to find out. But I would suggest you look for a refrigerator that might have held the body for a few days. And someone who has access to heroin.'

Johnson had finished with the other body and placed it in the next drawer along. He stood near them and looked down at the nurse. 'Such a sweet thing,' he said sombrely, screwing up his face as if he was contemplating the mystery of her death. 'Do we know who she is?'

Darling shook his head. 'That's the other strange thing. There're no reports of anyone gone missing who matches her description. It's as if she never existed. She's a young woman, not a hobo. There must be someone who misses her.'

Johnson grunted and looked back down to study the dead nurse's face.

'Unless the only person who misses her is also the killer,' said Jones.

Walker met the team on the ward at ten in the morning. 'Any admissions?' he asked Vince.

'Just one overnight,' he said. He read from a list. 'Rani Gnanalingam.' He stumbled over the last name. 'A forty-year-old mother of three. Sri Lankan. Admitted through Emergency with a new diagnosis of metastatic cancer.'

Walker turned to Angela. 'Have you caught up with her yet?'

She nodded and opened the file she was holding. 'Two-week history of increasing back pain. Plain X-rays show a destructive lesion in T4. The chest X-ray shows a lesion in the right upper lobe. She also has finger clubbing and has lost eight kilos.'

'Seems straightforward,' said Walker. 'Smoker?'

'Claims not to be,' said Vince.

'Unusual,' said Walker. 'Shall we see her?'

Rani Gnanalingam was a thin woman in a white hospital gown who lay in the bed, her forehead bunched up and holding her right lower ribs, obviously in pain. Walker introduced himself and asked her to show him where the pain was.

'Don't worry, Rani, we'll get you some more painkillers in a moment.' He raised his eyebrows at Jenny, the team leader, who left to organise them. 'How long have you been in Australia?'

'Since 1988.' She said the words slowly, drawing the figure eight in the air. Her English seemed good, although measured.

'From Sri Lanka, I understand? What part?'

She smiled. 'Vavuniya. Do you know Sri Lanka?'

'Not really.' *Not at all.* 'Is that in the north?'

'Yes.'

Walker guessed it would be. The woman was almost certainly a Tamil refugee who had fled the civil war. 'Did you come straight to Australia?'

'No. We went first to Indonesia. For two years. Then we were allowed to come here.'

'Okay. Rani, we've got to do more tests to find why you have the pain. A CT scan of your back and chest.' The woman nodded. 'But I have to tell you, we're worried. The plain X-ray shows something destroying your backbone. It looks like it might be cancer.'

Rani nodded her head stoically, like she'd expected it. Walker had observed this sort of reaction before in people who had already seen all nature of atrocities in their own country, as if it was only expected that the horrors they'd left behind would catch up with them eventually.

He took her hand. 'But we don't know for sure. You can't diagnose cancer from an X-ray. We need to prove it by getting a piece of tissue and looking at it under a microscope.'

'Biopsy?'

'Yes.'

'Do what you need to do, doctor. But also, you must please help me as much as you can. I've three small children.'

'We will do what we can.' Walker made a point of looking around. 'Your husband?'

'Minding the children.'

'Do you have anyone else in Sydney?'

'Friends. No family.'

Jenny returned with another nurse, holding two white tablets in a small plastic cup.

'All right, Rani, here are your painkillers. We'll do what we can,' Walker repeated.

Walker left the ward and made his way to the ground floor, back to his office. As he walked the long corridor, he slipped his hand into his pocket where he felt the amulet he'd found the day before. As he twiddled it in his fingers, wondering what to do with it, a woman came out of a door along the corridor and walked away from him. He recognised her as one of the gynae-oncologists – surgeons who operated on such things as ovarian cancer. Western Meadows had one of only three speciality units in the state.

'Fayza,' he called out.

She stopped and pivoted towards him, a generous smile on her face. Her dark hair was pulled up and she wore eyeliner winged on the edges, giving her eyes a mysterious Egyptian look.

'Christopher, long time no see.'

'I was hoping you could help me.' He pulled the pendant from his pocket and held it up for her to see. 'Do you know what this is?'

She held out a graceful palm and he slipped the piece onto it. Fayza ran a finger over the silver and glanced at the Arabic words inscribed on it, then nodded.

Her voice had a pleasant, deep pitch. 'It's a protection amulet. Very common, although this is a nice example.'

'Can you read the words?'

'I can read them but I don't need to. I know the words by heart.' She looked up. 'It's the Ayat al-Kursi. The Throne

Verse from the Quran. Probably the most famous of all verses.'

Her eyes became unfocused and she recited an Arabic poem, the words graceful and seemingly full of meaning. When she'd finished she glanced back at Walker.

'It interprets loosely as "Allah, there's no god but He, the living, the everlasting. Slumber seizes Him not, neither sleep. To Him belongs all that is in the heavens and the earth. Who is there that can intercede in His presence, except by His leave? He knows what lies before them and what is after them, and they comprehend not anything of His knowledge save as He wills. His throne comprises the heavens and the earth, the preserving of them fatigues Him not, and He is the all-high, all-glorious".'

She smiled and shrugged. 'Any good Muslim would know it. Many use it as a form of protection, recite it every night before they sleep to keep evil away.' She looked down at the amulet. 'This would have been a gift, maybe to a child by a close relative. I've one myself.' She rubbed the surface with her thumb. 'It looks very old, probably a family heirloom.'

Fayza reluctantly handed it back. 'What are you going to do with it? I'm sure it will be missed by its owner.'

Walker slipped the amulet back in his pocket. 'I'll put up a notice. If someone is missing it that much, they'll contact me.'

She opened her palms. 'I'll leave it to you. If I hear anything, I will let you know.'

Walker made his way back to his office and pulled out a sheet of paper. He wrote in capital letters: FOUND – SILVER LOCKET WITH ARABIC ENGRAVING. CONTACT DR CHRIS WALKER. He threw the amulet into the top drawer of his desk then made his way to the staff room and pinned the note on the noticeboard.

CHAPTER NINE

THAT EVENING, BARRY Darling left his lodgings and crossed Glebe Point Road then walked a short way up the hill to the Toxteth Hotel. It was a community pub with a long history, mostly frequented by locals, as well as those in-the-know from the suburbs, after a drink before the city discos opened. The pub had inexpensive but good quality meals and Darling had taken to eating there most nights since he'd moved into his bedsit a few months ago. The guesthouse didn't have a kitchen, so he couldn't have cooked even if he wanted to.

He quickly ate a hamburger then moved into the sports bar to watch the English football league. The rugby league season hadn't yet started and there was nothing better on. Arsenal was leading Queens Park Rangers by two goals. As he sat drinking a schooner of New watching the television, he was approached by a dark-haired man, just past middle-age, handing out pamphlets.

'The Glebe Society Bulletin,' he announced as he gave Darling one. 'You new around here?'

'Last six months,' said Darling. 'Grew up in Millers Point but I'm looking to buy here.'

'Buy here?' said the man with a smile. 'And so you should. Why, The Rocks gangs were our competition way back, but now we're kindred spirits, so to speak. Both staving off the "new order". Trying to maintain our communities. The big end of town on one side and the cultural cringe on the other.'

Darling smiled and said nothing, hoping he'd go away. But the man was having nothing of it.

He offered his hand. 'Evan Roberts. I organise the dinners for the society members. You should join if you're thinking of living here. We need some young blood. And if you want to buy, then getting to know the other members is the best way to find out what's coming up for sale. Most of the real estate agents are members.'

'You don't say,' said Darling, becoming interested. 'How much is it to join?'

'Ten bucks.' Roberts looked over his shoulder and back again. 'Why don't you come to the dinner next Monday night? It's at the Taste of India. Do you like something a little spicy?'

'I do, actually. Indian's one of my favourites.' He glanced up at the screen as Arsenal kicked another goal. 'You know what, I might just come. How do I sign up?'

Roberts pulled out a pen. 'Give us your contact details. You can come along next Monday and pay your membership fees at the same time.'

Darling gave him his name and when he told Roberts he was a policeman, the dark-haired man looked impressed.

'Goodo! Just what we need. More coppers.' He glanced over his shoulder again. 'As a matter of fact, I was speaking to a young woman not five minutes ago about just that. Her friend's missing. They're both nurses. Sally's her name – the girl I just spoke to, that is. Not sure of the missing girl's name. Sally went away for the weekend and hasn't seen her friend since she returned. Lives just up the road, she does. Tell you what. I'll send her down to see you.' He glanced down at Darling's address, which he'd written down. 'She's only two doors up from you.'

There was a knock on Darling's door a few minutes after he returned to his lodgings and he opened the door to a thin girl in jeans and a T-shirt. She looked apprehensive, her brow furrowed and her mouth tight. Straw-blonde hair framed a freckled face.

'Very sorry to bother you. I've just heard from Evan Roberts that you're a policeman and wouldn't mind speaking to me.'

'Happy to help.' He remained standing in the doorway. 'I'm Detective Barry Darling of the Parramatta Headquarters.' He waited for her to introduce herself. Her name was Sally Biggs.

'I understand you're a nurse?'

She nodded. 'Prince Alfred. But it's about my flatmate, Alice Cleary. She's gone missing.'

'You sure? When was the last time you saw her?'

'Last Friday. I went back to Armidale to see my folks over the weekend and I haven't seen Alice since I got back on Monday.'

'What about her family? Have you asked them?'

'She's Irish and only in Australia for a few months. I don't even know what part of Ireland she's from. The south, I think. I sublet her bedroom in my flat when my last flatmate left to get married. She answered a flyer I put up at work. She's also a nurse.'

'Is the hospital missing her?'

She shook her head. 'She's doing casual shifts all over and the employment agency doesn't keep track of her. Only contacts her if there's work.'

'Where does she usually work?'

'Prince of Wales mostly. And Sydney Hospital. But she does bits and pieces all over Sydney. We both do shift work, so I just thought we were missing each other. But on Monday I realised Alice hadn't cleaned the kitchen after I'd left it in a mess. I spilled some milk on the benchtop but left it since I was running late. But it was still there when I got home today. Alice would never have left it like that. She's very neat. I reported her missing to the Glebe police but they didn't seem too worried. They said she's probably shacked up with some fellow and would probably surface next weekend.' Sally's brow furrowed further and she shook her head. 'But she not like that. She's Catholic — not serious or anything, not a prude. But you know how they are. Always guilty about sex. She wouldn't stay at a strange man's flat at the drop of a hat. Not for days on end.'

'What does she look like?'

'Dark hair, pale skin. Blue eyes. Quite pretty. Thin.'

Darling nodded grimly. It could well be the victim. 'Do you have a photo?'

'No, I don't think so. We haven't lived together for very long.'

'Will you be home tomorrow? I'll send someone around. Or ...' He paused. The more he thought about it, Alice Cleary was probably the corpse. But he had to be careful.

'Or?'

'The body of a young woman was found in the grounds of Western Meadows Hospital two days ago.'

Sally's hand went to her mouth. 'You think it's her?'

'Could be. I could drive you tomorrow morning to Western Meadows. The body is in the morgue. It would help to get an identification.'

Sally was silent for a few moments, her face pale. Then she answered slowly. 'I guess so. I want to be sure.' Her eyes began to tear up. 'I hope not though. Oh, I hope she's holed up somewhere with a bloke, screwing his brains out.' She shook her head. 'But I don't think so.' She pinched her mouth closed. 'Okay, I'll come. I'll call nursing admin when I get home to tell them I won't be in.'

Darling reached out, took her hand and patted it. 'I'll knock on your door at seven.'

CHAPTER TEN

THE NEXT MORNING, Barry Darling drove Sally Biggs in his Holden Commodore to Western Meadows Hospital. On the forty-minute journey, Sally told Darling about growing up on a farm outside of Armidale in northwest New South Wales with her parents and younger brother. She'd had an uneventful childhood, going to the local school and then nurses' college in the town. She'd been good at netball and was a fair swimmer. Her parents seemed to love their children and each other. She'd had numerous pet cats and dogs and two boyfriends, and she missed the simple country life. Darling was intrigued, realising that he'd never really spoken to anyone who had had a 'normal' life before.

'I didn't think such a perfect life really existed,' he said. 'Why did you come to Sydney?'

'Perfect?' Sally seemed surprised. She stared thoughtfully out of the window as they passed a bank of rundown shops that lined Victoria Road at Gladesville. 'I suppose so. Some would call it boring. Nothing much happens in Armidale.' She turned back to Darling. 'But given what's happened to Alice – or what we think happened – I'm not so sure I like Sydney anymore.'

The traffic ground to a halt at the lights next to Primrose's Timber Yard. 'But what about you, Barry? Tell me about your childhood.'

Darling said nothing and tapped on the steering wheel impatiently waiting for the traffic to move. Sally turned to him but seemed to sense he didn't want to talk. She turned away and studied the timber yard.

'I was an orphan,' he said, as the car pulled away.

She remained looking out of the window as if she wasn't that interested in his story, which encouraged him to continue.

'I was left on the steps of a nursing home in Millers Point. Darling House.' She turned to him but remained silent. 'That's how I got my last name.' He glanced at her. 'I was named after a building.'

'And your first name?' she asked gently.

He gave a short laugh. 'That's just stupid. The nurses having a joke.' When she said nothing, he continued. 'You know *Peter Pan*?' She nodded. 'The kids' last name was Darling and the author of the book was J.M. Barrie. Thus, my name. Barry Darling.'

She gave a genuine smile. 'But that's lovely, Barry.'

He pretended to concentrate on the passing buildings – a public swimming pool, a school, some sort of building with grand gates and a sandstone wall – but felt pleased with her reaction.

'Where did you go to school?' she asked.

'Local school,' he said. 'Then Fort Street High.'

'What made you become a policeman?'

He smiled. 'Probably getting in trouble with the cops all the time when I was a teenager. The police became very familiar to me. Then one day, I guess I woke up and stopped stealing cars and nicking things from shops and decided to make something of myself. I wasn't particularly good at school – not like Kit.' He went quiet again, his thoughts going elsewhere.

After a pause, she continued in a soothing tone. 'So, you wanted to make something of yourself?'

'I joined the Police Force. I'm glad I did. It suits me. They call it the Police *Service* now.'

They got through the lights at a major crossroad and the traffic freed up, but they were stopped again further along. Darling stared out the window at the video shops and building supply stores, reluctant to speak more about himself.

'Was Kitty your girlfriend?'

He laughed. 'Girlfriend! Not Kitty. Kit. It's a nickname. Like the Phantom.' Darling pursed his lips, wondering why he'd added that. 'His real name is Chris Walker.' He clammed up again and drove on with gritted teeth.

After a further pause, he spoke again. 'For a while when I was a kid, he was my only friend. We used to do everything together, hang around under the Harbour Bridge smoking, ride our bikes up to Glebe to pick fights with the locals. Went to school together. It was a bit sick really. We called ourselves brothers. Neither of us had brothers or sisters, so we stuck together. I'd sleep at his place a lot of nights. We drank together when we were old enough. The Hero, the Orient, the Harbour View, wherever.'

'What's he doing now?'

'That's the weird thing. He's at Western Meadows.'

'Oh? What does he do?'

'Bugger all, if you ask me. He's a doctor. Cancer. Chemotherapy, that sort of stuff. I doubt he does anything useful.' He drove some more in silence. 'Anyway, he's a total dickhead and we're not friends anymore. Trouble is, I have to keep interacting with him with these murders.' He glanced over at Sally. 'But I can't really talk any more about it while the case is still open.'

They drove the rest of the way to the hospital in silence.

They sat together in a small room off the main corridor, waiting for the mortuary attendant to come and take them through to identify the body. Sally appeared nervous, biting her fingernail and staring at her sneakers. Darling looked around at the walls, which were decorated with various health posters, some partially torn. There was one about condoms and HIV, another about domestic violence and another encouraging teenagers to quit smoking. In the corner was a large poster in French, displaying a picture of the Eiffel Tower. A laminated A4 sheet of paper said 'No smoking' in large bold type and Darling noticed burn marks in the plastic where people had stubbed out their fags. He laughed.

Sally glanced up. 'What's funny?'

Darling suppressed a smile. 'Nothing. Sorry.'

She took in a large breath and let it out. 'I'm really nervous. I hope it's not Alice but if it is, then at least I'll know. But that makes me feel guilty. As if all I'm worried about is my own discomfort, if you know what I mean.'

'I understand.' He glanced at the door. 'They shouldn't be long. I'll be there with you.'

She bounced her leg. 'I didn't really know her, after all. We were just flatting together. I don't even know who her family are.'

'Don't worry, if it comes to that we'll track them down.'

The door opened and Johnson came through. 'Ready?' he asked.

They followed him through to another room where a trolley stood with a body on top, covered in a green drape. Sally held on to Darling's arm and they stood together to the side, away from Johnson. On a nod from Darling, the morgue attendant pulled the sheet back to reveal a pale face with a blue bruise that covered one eye and the side of the forehead.

Sally stared for some time then slowly nodded her head. 'It's her. That's Alice Cleary.' She began to cry. 'The poor darling …'

CHAPTER ELEVEN

AFTER THEY LEFT the morgue, Darling accompanied Sally out to one of the hospital carparks where they met a female officer from the Parramatta Station who would take her home.

'I have more work to do here,' Darling said to Sally. 'We'll contact Alice's relatives in Ireland through the nursing agency to give them the news. Don't you worry about it.'

'Poor things,' said Sally. 'It's a terrible thing for the family but even worse when it happens in a foreign country.'

He helped her into the police car and closed the door. 'I'll see if I can check in on you tonight,' he said through the open window then watched as the car drove away.

'Sweet girl,' he said to no one in particular.

He entered another door into the hospital then realised the surroundings were unfamiliar. The hospital had been built in the seventies as a number of almost identical buildings parallel to each other with connecting wings. As far as Darling was concerned, they all looked the same.

He wandered along a service corridor devoid of traffic and also of signage. Soon he saw a man in a white coat approaching from the opposite direction, and when he got closer, he realised it was Walker.

He hailed him. 'Kit, I need to get back to the pathology building. Dr Bank's office.'

Walker didn't seem surprised he was in the wrong building. 'Happens all the time. I still get lost if I'm not concentrating on where I'm going. Whoever designed this place did it for cost, not aesthetics.' He turned back in the direction he'd just come from. 'I have to do a ward round but I'll show you a shortcut through the cafeteria.'

Walker led him back along the long corridor that Darling recognised as the one that also served the pharmacy, bringing back memories of the director of pharmacy who had helped him with Professor Chee's murder.

Walker seemed to be thinking the same thing. 'Whatever happened to Maisie Diver? Did you ever contact her?'

'No,' Darling said gruffly. 'I'm going out with Cassie at the moment.'

'Thought you said you were young and single and that the world was your oyster, there were lots of fish in the sea or something like that.'

'Yeah, well, I like to be loyal.'

After a short pause, Walker asked, 'And how's it going with Cassie then?'

'Good.'

When Darling said nothing more, Walker stuck his hands in his pockets and kept quiet.

They walked in silence as they passed the door of the pharmacy and Darling wondered about his answer. As far as he was concerned, his relationship with Cassandra Hollow *wasn't* good. He had the feeling her passion had waned and he wondered whether she was seeing someone else. He looked sideways at Walker. Why *had* Cassandra arrived with him the day of the murder in the chapel? Darling didn't believe their story that Walker had picked her up on the way through.

Then he thought about Sally and their conversation in the car that morning. He liked her and could imagine seeing her again. But perhaps he *should* give Maisie Diver a call.

They reached the cafeteria, a sprawling room the size of a small airport terminal, scattered with tables and chairs and bustling with staff having their lunch. As they entered, Angela was coming in the opposite direction.

'Ready for the clinic?' she asked Walker.

'Just showing Detective Darling the shortcut to the morgue.'

Angela said she'd walk with them and they made their way through the crush area, negotiating the crowd of people carrying trays of food and looking for a table.

'Wendy! Kit!' called a male voice from behind, and the trio turned to see a large man waving an arm exuberantly above the crowd as he pushed through to reach them.

'Oh no,' said Darling. 'It's Blinkton.'

'Oh fuck!' murmured Walker. 'That's all we need.'

'Friend of yours?' said Angela, smirking.

Blinkton wore a blue flying suit. He looked as if he'd just come from a rescue mission, still wearing an intricate harness and with a walkie-talkie hanging from his hip.

'Blinkers,' cried Walker when he reached them. 'I thought I saw you in the distance the other day. What have you been up to?'

'Bullshit,' he replied affably. 'I know what you're like, Kit. If you'd seen me, you'd have avoided me like the plague.' He shook Walker's hand then clasped Darling on the shoulder. 'Good to see you too, Wendy. I heard you actually made it through cop school. Well done.' Then he looked Angela up and down. 'And who's this you've been hiding from me, Kit?'

'This is Angela, my advanced trainee.'

'Hi Angie.' Blinkton took a step back and leered. 'Tell you what, forget these two.' He jabbed a thumb at each of his old friends. 'How about you and me go for a drink sometime. Get to know each other. Where're you from? Hong Kong? Singapore? You look Singaporean.'

'Singapore.'

'Thought so, Angie. Do you have a boyfriend?'

'All right, Blinkers, steady on. Stop trying to crack onto my registrar, if you don't mind. And her name's Angela, not Angie.'

Blinkton threw a look from Angela to Walker. 'What? Are you two seeing each other, Kit?' He raised his hands, palms out. 'I should have realised. You always liked slim girls with dark hair.'

'No, I didn't,' snapped Walker. He looked like he would say more but then clamped his lips tight.

There was an uncomfortable silence. Blinkton appeared oblivious to Walker's reaction.

'I don't mind being called Angie,' she said, breaking the awkwardness.

Blinkton turned his hands over like a magician revealing a trick. 'See, Kit. You should experiment a bit more.' He turned his attention back to the young doctor. 'Angie. I've always liked that name. Just like the Rolling Stones song.' He began to sing it, mimicking Mick Jagger, exaggerating the 'Angie'.

Walker looked irritated. But the annoying thing was, Blinkton actually had a good voice.

He closed his eyes and began to swing his body to the music, singing into a pretend microphone.

'Okay, that's enough, Blinkers,' Walker interrupted. 'You're starting to embarrass Angela.'

But she was obviously pleased. 'That's fantastic. You have such a good voice.'

'Wanna hear more?' he said, frozen in mid gyration. 'Come out for a drink with me then.' He moved the pretend microphone to her mouth for her to speak into.

She laughed. 'Maybe. But I don't even know your first name.'

He threw the pretend microphone over his shoulder. 'Craig,' he said, extending his hand. 'Craig Blinkton. Doctor-extraordinaire on the rescue helicopters. My friends call me Blinkers.'

'Please to meet you, Blinkers. How do you know these two?'

'Went to uni with Kit here. New South Wales. We used to hang around together and through him I met Wendy.' Then his head swung back to Walker. 'And Flea.' He became serious. 'Kit, I'm so sorry about Felicity. I heard she drowned in New Guinea.' He hung his head. 'If only I was around, I could've saved her.'

Darling studied Blinkton closely, trying to determine whether he was serious. He decided he was. He seemed genuinely distressed.

Walker raised his hands. 'What do you mean, Blinkers? We were in the middle of the jungles of New Guinea.'

'But that's my job. That's what we do. We save people. And we can fly to New Guinea.'

Walker shook his head. 'This is just plain stupid.'

Then Blinkton's demeanour changed abruptly. 'Wendy, do you still have your rings?'

'What?' said Darling, startled.

Blinkton raised both fists before his own face. 'You know, the skull and the swords. Jungle Patrol. I've still got mine.'

Darling shifted uneasily. 'Might have.'

Angela interjected. 'Oh, I know what you're talking about. The Phantom Club.' She smiled cheekily. 'Yes, Barry has his rings. And he has a suit. He wears it for his girlfriend.'

Walker looked sideways at Darling who squirmed. But Blinkton shook his fists with enthusiasm. 'Rings and a suit. I knew it, Wendy! I knew you wouldn't desert the cause.'

'Were you in the Phantom Club as well?' Angela asked.

'We all were. We were among the original wave. When John Henderson started the club back in '81, Kit and I were in first-year medicine and Wendy was in police school. We grabbed it with both arms.' Blinkton hugged his arms to his chest. 'We even went up to Brisbane to one of the meetings.' He smiled fondly. 'Remember, boys? At John's place? A great day joining with others of the brotherhood.' He paused and tipped his head towards Angela. 'And sisterhood as well.'

Walker took a step away. 'I really don't think Angela is interested in all this.' He beckoned her. 'Perhaps we should get started on the ward round.'

'Oh, no,' said Angela. 'I find this all fascinating. Blinkers, do you have a Phantom suit as well?'

'No. But I'm really pleased that Wendy has one.' He addressed Darling, who was now scowling. 'Where'd you get yours from? Perhaps I should get one too.'

'Can't remember,' said Darling.

'No worries,' said Blinkton. 'I reckon Frew will help me out.'

'Frew?' said Angela.

'The publishers of the comic. They're based here in Sydney.' He turned back to Walker and Darling. 'Remember, guys? The club newsletter on the back page of the comics? Whatever happened to that?'

When neither of them answered, he looked at his wristwatch. 'Great talking to you, boys but I've to get back. I'm on call. Fantastic to catch up.' He raised his arms to encompass both Walker and Darling. 'And great to see you two together again. That sort of friendship can't die, no matter what.'

'We're not friends,' Darling said quickly. 'This is a relationship borne out of necessity. It's certainly not a friendship.'

There was an uncomfortable silence as Blinkton threw questioning glances at Walker and Darling. Then he took Angela's hand in his. 'Well, at least it was a great pleasure to meet you, Angie.' He lifted her hand to his lips and kissed it. 'And remember my invitation for a drink. I'm serious.' With that, he turned and strode away.

The trio stood together, staring at his back as he retreated.

'Interesting character,' said Angela. She glanced at Walker. 'I quite like him. He's got a great voice.'

'Always was a bit strange,' said Walker. 'But at least he was a lot of fun.'

'And a brother-in-arms, by the sounds of things.' Angela wore a wry smile. 'You must have been a formidable trio in your day.'

'I completely lost touch with him,' Darling said curtly. 'I heard he got into a bit of trouble and was admitted to hospital.'

'Hmm,' said Walker. 'He started in Emergency Medicine and then just dropped off the radar. I heard he had a nervous breakdown. His family are quite rich and had him in a private clinic somewhere. Then when I started here at the Meadows, I heard he was in helicopter rescue. Haven't had a chance to catch up with him though.'

'At least it looks like he got over his depression or whatever it was,' said Darling. 'Bit strange how he wears his flying gear to the cafeteria though.'

'Oh well,' said Angela, stifling a grin. 'It must be a relief to know that other people also like to dress up, Detective Darling.'

Darling tried to look annoyed but, despite himself, gave a short laugh. 'I thought you two had something to do? I suggest you get on with it.'

CHAPTER TWELVE

WALKER AND ANGELA finally got to the ward to find Vince Greenway waiting for them. 'How are we going with Mrs Gnanalingam?' asked Walker. 'Did we manage to get a biopsy of anything?'

'The lesion in the lung is too small and the radiologists are worried about biopsying the bone in T4,' Angela said. 'They say it's too close to the spinal cord.'

'Are the radiation oncologists lined up to start radiotherapy to prevent a spinal cord compression?'

'Yes, but they want biopsy proof of cancer before they start.'

'Damn, how annoying. She has a destructive lesion, clubbing, has lost almost ten kilograms and has something in her lung. What more do they want?'

Angela flipped open the chart. 'We're trying for sputum cytology but she can't cough anything up. Should we do a bronchoscopy?'

'Maybe,' said Walker, frustrated. 'Let's go down to radiology and look at the films. Maybe we can find something else to biopsy.'

The CT scans were stored in an area behind the main desk in the radiology department with different slots for each ward. Vince had gone ahead and already found the patient's films.

'Thank God for small mercies,' said Walker. 'At least they haven't lost the films.'

Vince started to put the films up on the viewing box but the first few were the wrong way around and Walker took over. 'If you don't mind,' he said, trying to sound kind. 'It's faster this way.'

The CT of the chest showed a white area in the right upper lobe that looked like a tumour, and there were a few enlarged lymph nodes in the centre of the chest. Walker turned his attention to the CT scan of the spine, which showed an obvious dark area in the fourth thoracic vertebra. He studied it closely to see whether there was any evidence of the tumour in the surrounding soft tissue that would be easier to biopsy. Then he noticed the abnormal area also involved the disk between that vertebra and the next bone down.

'Has this been formally reported?' he asked sharply.

'Not yet,' said Vince. 'I've only shown it to them to see whether they can biopsy it. They're behind in their reporting.'

Walker blew out a breath and faced his two underlings. 'Shows you the importance of actually looking at your own X-rays.'

'What do you mean?' asked Angela. 'I did look at them.'

Walker tapped on the dark area between the vertebrae. 'Cancer doesn't do that.'

'What?'

'See there.' He pointed to the dark area at the bottom of one of the vertebrae and traced the mass with his finger, showing it extended into the area below it. 'Cancer doesn't grow out of bone into a vertebral disc.'

'Oh, oh,' said Angela. 'Sorry, I didn't see that.'

Walker spoke to the intern. 'Try to get some sputum, but don't send it for cytology looking for cancer. Send it to microbiology.'

Vince looked confused. 'Microbiology?'

Angela frowned at the CT films. 'Are you sure?'

'She's from Sri Lanka and spent time in Indonesia, maybe in a refugee camp. Ask her.'

'Should we get a Mantoux test?'

'Waste of time,' said Walker. 'Positive or negative, it won't help. The evidence is there. We need proof.'

'What are you two talking about?' said Vince, looking from one to the other. 'A Mantoux test?' He looked back at the scan. 'TB?'

'Potts disease,' said Walker. 'Tuberculosis of the spine. Look it up.'

Later, after the ward round had finished, Walker and Angela took the back stairs to the outpatient clinic. For the first few flights they walked side-by-side in silence, Walker conscious of the slap of her sandals on the concrete stairs. The air in the stairwell was hot and humid and he made a joke that he'd have preferred to be at the beach.

Angela let out a lavish sigh. 'Yes, please. Anything to get this dress off and feel the cool air on my body.'

When they got to the bottom, Walker held the door open for her and she smiled at him and gave a giggle as she passed. For some reason, he felt like they were on a date.

He decided he'd risk it. 'Talking about the beach, what are you doing this Saturday?'

'Nothing,' she said. 'Do you want to take me to one?'

'I'd love to. If you want to, that is.'

'Sure. Which one?'

'I usually go to Tamarama.'

She gave him a brazen smile. 'That's topless, isn't it?'

'You don't have to,' Walker said quickly. 'I go for the bodysurfing. No surfboards and sometimes the waves are great.'

Angela smiled. 'I'm okay with that. Shall I come to your place Saturday morning? We can go from there.'

CHAPTER THIRTEEN

WALKER INCHED ALONG Victoria Road on his way home, windows down, sweating in the heat, with MC Hammer blaring out of his radio about not touching something.

He tapped his fingers on the steering wheel and jiggled in his seat in time with the music. When he was halfway across Glebe Island Bridge, the traffic came to a dead stop and the radio switched to 'Unchained Melody' by The Righteous Brothers. Walker swore under his breath, both for the traffic and for the song, which he disliked. Ahead, a gridlock of cars was struggling to cross the city. There was talk in the news about a cross-city tunnel and he wished they'd stop debating and just get on with it. The traffic was just as bad for those leaving the city, making the bridge a carpark in both directions. He looked over the line of vehicles on the opposite side to see the skeleton of the new Glebe Island Bridge. Construction had only just started and it would take a few more years to complete.

Behind him, a large motorbike growled; the air was full of exhaust fumes and Walker contemplated rolling up the windows. He looked in the rear-view mirror and saw the noise was coming from what looked like a Harley-Davidson ridden by a bikie dressed in a leather jacket, despite the heat. He wished the fellow would thread his way through the traffic like they normally did and get out of his hearing range. He looked out to his left at the stretch of water called White Bay and noticed a medium-size container ship moored at the Glebe Island docks. The name of the boat was displayed in white peeling paint near the bow – *Sintak-5*. Rust showed through parts of the hull and railing, and on the dockside of the ship, two partially rusted cranes sat unused.

'What a rust-bucket,' he muttered to himself before turning his attention back to the traffic ahead. It was still not moving. Probably something to do with roadworks for the new bridge, he surmised. He blew out an exasperated hiss. Maybe he should move. He thought about a small house in Epping or even Parramatta. They were both close to work. And also close to Angela. He'd heard that Barry Darling was living in Glebe. Maybe he should move there. At least he wouldn't have to contend with this. The traffic still hadn't moved and his thoughts roved to his former friend. *What a dickhead you are, Wendy!*

But immediately he felt a pang of guilt. Guilt about Felicity. Darling had probably loved Felicity and couldn't forgive him for letting her die. And now Walker was sleeping with his girlfriend. He sighed. *I'm a total loser.* He shook his head despondently. 'What am I doing?' Then he realised the double vision he'd got after sleeping with Cassandra had finally disappeared, just like he thought it would.

The cars in front finally started to move and he glumly shoved the car into gear. As he drove off, he glanced over at the rusty ship again, moored at the dock. There was something about it that was off-putting. As he drove forward, he let the image of the boat linger, glad to think of something other than Darling, Cassandra or Felicity.

'What is it about that boat?' he muttered to himself. Had he seen it before? He didn't think so. Something about the name then? *Sintak-5.*

Then he had it! It was the name written on the piece of paper found with the nurse. Darling had thought it was 'Sin talk' or 'Sin take', but now seeing the ship and visualising the piece of paper, he was sure of it. The scrawled writing was a ship's name!

But why a ship? What could that have to do with a dead nurse found thirty kilometres inland? He began to have doubts. *No! I'm sure.* He vowed to call Darling as soon as he got home.

***

Walker met Darling at the Captain Cook Hotel after seven that evening. They'd rarely drank at that pub when they were younger, tending to go to the Hero of Waterloo or the Mercantile down at The Rocks, but the Cook had now become a sort of neutral territory for them both, a familiar place to meet but one that did not dredge up old memories.

Walker ordered the beers and they sat at one of the tables down the back that had a view of Darling Harbour through timber-framed windows. As they eased themselves into their seats, an overweight fellow wearing a shabby suit came through the front door of the pub, surveyed the crowd from the doorway, then spotted them.

'Oh crikey!' Walker said in a low voice. 'Just what we need. A union bagman to talk our ears off.'

'We'll have to remember that in future,' said Darling. 'This is Bruce Rowntree's watering hole.'

Rowntree was balding, with the red face and sweaty skin of an avid drinker, and he came towards them wearing a knowing smirk, then pulled up a chair. 'The dynamic duo. What brings you two together? I thought you hated each other.'

'Fuck off, Bruce,' said Darling, failing to look up as he took a sip of his beer.

'I seem to remember it had something to do with your wife, Kit,' Rowntree continued unperturbed. 'Wendy here, not forgiving you for letting her die, or something like that. Or was there more to it?' He looked from one irritated face to the other. 'Or did Wendy here sleep with her, maybe?'

Walker curled his hand into a fist and ground his teeth.

Darling grabbed the fat man's tie and jerked it hard. 'You're a fuckin' turd, do you know that, Bruce?' He jerked the tie again causing Rowntree's head to shake and his sleazy smile to disappear. 'Now apologise to Christopher.'

Rowntree's smirk slowly returned and his podgy eyes darted from Walker to Darling. 'Looks like you two love each other after all. Standing up for each other. I knew this schoolboy enmity was all a show.'

Darling pushed Rowntree in the chest again but let the tie go. Bruce left the tie in disarray and flicked his head at Walker. 'I do apologise though. And I am sorry about your wife. I liked Felicity. She had character. And she kept you two real. What I said was a bit harsh. But I can't stand you two pretending to hate each other's guts when you're the best friends you'll ever have.' He jerked a thumb at their half-empty glasses. 'I'll get you a beer. My shout?'

As Walker watched Rowntree amble away, he noticed a large fellow dressed like a bikie sitting at the bar. He looked Middle Eastern and the design of his jacket reminded him of the bikie who'd been behind him on Glebe Island Bridge. As soon as he saw him, the bikie turned back to the bar. On the back of the jacket was the profile of a skull wearing a winged helmet.

Now Rowntree was out of earshot, Walker took the chance to tell Darling about the ship at Glebe Island.

'The *Sintak-5*,' Darling said uncertainly. 'It's a bit of a stretch.'

'I'm sure of it.'

'But what would a container ship have to do with a dead nurse at Western Meadows? How did her body get there?'

'You heard Jocelyn Banks. The body was refrigerated. Maybe she was killed there and taken out to the hospital to throw you off the trail?'

'A bit elaborate,' said Darling. 'And what would a nurse be doing rummaging around the docks?'

Walker shrugged. 'I don't know, but I think you should look at it.'

'Maybe.'

'This about that boat at Glebe Island?' asked Rowntree, who was standing over them clasping three schooners of beer.

Walker looked up at him in surprise.

'What do you know about it?' asked Darling.

'Not sure what your interest is but I'm worried that it's being unloaded by non-union workers.' Rowntree took a seat. 'I want to have a look at it.'

'I thought the prime minister was sorting out the dock disputes,' said Walker. 'I seem to remember something on the news recently.'

'Hawke's trying to get the Waterside Workers to accept an agreement. A pay rise in exchange for new job classifications.'

'A pay rise. That sounds good to me.'

'Yeah, but it's weakening our position long term. The stevedore companies want more casual positions and more redundancies. I think Patrick Corporation will screw us in the end. It'll be okay while Labor is in, but as soon as those deadshit Liberals are back in power, they'll put the boot in. We want to put a stop to non-union workers infecting our docks. I want to have a look at that ship. It's a dead sitter for non-union work.'

Darling rubbed his chin. 'Kit thinks the ship might be tied up with a murder. It might be illegal goods they're unloading.'

'Doesn't matter whether the goods are illegal or not,' said Rowntree, pointing a belligerent finger. 'Whatever you unload, dirty or clean, it has to be done by members of the WWF. If there're any scabs involved, I wanna know about it.'

'I thought scabs were strike-breakers, Bruce. There's no strike.'

'They're fuckin' scabs whether there's a strike or not. You gotta be a card-carrying union member to work the docks. If you're not then you're a scab and deserve what you get.'

'Well, we want to look at it as well,' said Walker, drawing a frown from Darling.

'Let's do it together then,' said Rowntree.

'But there's a problem,' said Walker. 'I checked the shipping news. It's leaving tomorrow morning. We have to do it tonight.'

'Tonight!' said Darling 'I can't get a warrant that quickly. It's impossible.'

'I don't need any warrants,' said Rowntree. 'I'm a union representative. I can do an inspection any time I like.'

'I don't know,' Darling said dubiously.

'Wendy,' said Walker, 'this might be our only chance. Once the ship's gone, that'll be it. It's tonight or never.'

Darling looked from Walker to Rowntree then took a gulp of his beer and leaned back in his chair. 'All right then. Tonight. But we've got to do it in secret. I don't want to lose my job over this. I'm trying to buy a house.'

'A house,' said Rowntree putting on a sweet voice. 'How domestic. And here I was thinking you cared two hoots about justice.'

Darling looked sheepish and was silent for a few moments. Then he leaned forward and put his forearms on the table. 'All right, we'll do it tonight. But we've got to do it my way.'

CHAPTER FOURTEEN

JUST BEFORE NINE o'clock that night, Walker and Darling waited in Blackwattle Park at the bottom of Leichhardt Street in Glebe. The water lapped quietly against the sandstone wall on the edge of the bay and a light breeze rustled the leaves of the peppercorn trees above. The pair stood together, both turned towards the path that led down from the street above. A streetlamp lit the path at the top but where they stood it was dark.

'Do you think he'll come?' asked Walker.

'Who knows,' said Darling. 'Bruce Rowntree looks after himself, *numero uno*. I wouldn't be surprised if he's forgotten. He's probably propped up against the bar at the Captain Cook, burning some poor sod's ear off about the importance of the union movement.'

There was a noise to their left and a shadow appeared on the path that led around the water's edge.

'Shh!' hissed Darling and he jerked Walker further back into the shadows.

A figure came closer, a man on a pushbike. They could hear him puffing and each inhalation caused the orange end of a cigarette to flare. The figure stopped before them in the light – Rowntree, dressed as usual in a shabby suit with one trouser-leg tucked into a sock and a fag hanging out of the corner of his mouth. He coughed after he stopped but somehow the cigarette stayed put. 'Thought you two'd get cold feet. I'm surprised to see you here, quite frankly.'

'Good evening to you too, Bruce,' said Darling. He made a point of examining Rowntree's bike, a rusted old dragster that somehow had retained the pink handlebar streamers. 'Nice set of wheels, Bruce. Did you nick it off your little sister?'

Rowntree groaned as he dismounted and let the bike fall to the ground. 'Yes, I did, as a matter of fact. She owes me.'

Walker looked down at the bike. 'You going to just leave it there?'

'Who's going to steal it?' He looked across the bay towards the Glebe Island Bridge. Just beyond was the shadowy hulk of a docked ship. 'That it?' He took a deep drag on his cigarette. 'Let's get going then.'

Darling led the way to a small rowboat that bobbed in the water at the end of a jetty. One by one they got in, Rowntree last, wobbling and splashing, threatening to overturn them all.

'Watch what you're doing, Bruce, you fat arse,' Darling hissed.

Rowntree sat down hard, dropping his fag into the water in the process. 'It's not me, it's you two. You've got the distribution all wrong. Don't you know how to arrange yourselves in a fuckin' rowboat?'

'If you lost a few pounds you'd do better,' replied Darling. 'And since when have you been an expert sailor?'

Rowntree pulled down the sleeves of his suit jacket, which had risen up in the kerfuffle. 'I'm the one who works on the docks, remember.'

Darling let out a short laugh. 'Docks, not boats. Hauling your wobbly arse around a wharf telling union members what to do isn't sailing.'

Rowntree frowned, pulled a crumpled packet of Winfield out of his jacket pocket and lit one. 'Just start rowing, will ya.'

'And I wouldn't call it work either,' muttered Darling, as he placed the oars into the locks.

'I'll row,' said Walker, manoeuvring himself into place. But his first few strokes were ill-timed and unbalanced, and the boat took off in an arc. The right oar flipped out of the water, sending up a spray into Rowntree, who had arranged himself at the stern.

'Watch what you're doing,' yelled Rowntree. 'You've drenched me fuckin' fag, you dickhead. Where'd you learn to row, at one of those poofy private schools?'

'Sorry, Bruce,' said Walker. After a few more strokes he got the hang of it and soon they were making steady progress towards the bridge. When they'd moved away from the shore, he said, 'You know I went to Fort Street, Bruce. Same as Wendy.'

Rowntree said nothing as he pulled out another cigarette, lit it and drew back deeply. He blew out a lungful of smoke and pointed over Walker's shoulder with the cigarette. 'You need to pull to port, Kit, or you'll end up at the timber yard.'

Darling rolled his eyes. Walker pulled harder on his right-hand oar, making the boat swing to the left. When he glanced over his shoulder, he was silently pleased that he'd picked the correct side. He was never really sure about port and starboard.

'Fifty-fifty guess,' grumbled Rowntree, his normally ruddy face partially hidden in the muted light afforded by the city skyline.

When they were halfway across, Walker noticed Rowntree look down at Darling's hand, which rested on the gunwale.

'You're wearing your ring,' he said. Walker could just make out a change in Rowntree's face, as if he was smiling. 'Going to catch a few criminals, Bazza? Brand 'em with the mark of the Phantom?' Walker saw the red cigarette tip point towards him. 'You and the Ghost-Who-Walks here?' Rowntree gave a throaty chuckle.

'Fuck off, Bruce,' said Darling as he looked away.

After that, they moved in silence across Blackwattle Bay. The Glebe Island Bridge was a low structure that connected Balmain to the city and had a pivot span that could be opened to allow nautical traffic to pass. At this time of night, the span was closed and a few cars could be seen crossing the bridge. Before it, a new bridge was under construction, a massive structure that when finished, would be thirty metres above the water level. Construction had just begun and the silhouette of the foundation spans could be seen jutting out from the headland on each side, like crippled hands reaching out. The construction site was silent and dark, with cranes silhouetted against the starry sky like an abstract painting. Walker rowed past the western side, dipping his oars carefully to avoid any noise, as if the foreboding structure above them was an enemy fort guarding a strategic military asset. Even Rowntree seemed unsettled; he examined the red tip of his cigarette then stubbed it out on the gunwale.

They moved under the low span of the existing bridge as an occasional vehicle rattled overhead. When they reached the other side, Walker stopped rowing and twisted around to view the large vessel moored just ahead at the Glebe Island dock. The city lights from across the bay showed a dark, rusting hull and a deck half-full of containers. It was not particularly large, and on the port side, the tops of two cargo cranes could be seen. Near the top of the hull was the name *Sintak-5* in white. Thick mooring ropes secured the boat to a low concrete dock that appeared devoid of activity. In the distance, towering over the dock area, was a line of large concrete silos used to store cement, by the look of the logo.

'What should we do?' asked Walker.

'Listen,' said Rowntree, raising a hand.

After a moment, Walker could just make out a series of deep thumps, as if work was underway at the other end of the ship. Closer to them, the dock was dark but he could see the ship's bridge was illuminated from the dockside, confirming that unloading was occurring.

Rowntree pointed to the dock near the stern of the ship and in the dim light Walker could just make out a ladder. 'Tie up there. We'll all go and have a look.'

'Are you sure that's a good idea?' asked Walker. He frowned at the dark hull looming above them. 'Maybe we should come back in the day.'

'It'll be gone then,' said Darling. 'You said the shipping report said it's leaving tomorrow for Melbourne. It's now or never.'

'Chickening out, are you, Kit?' said Rowntree.

'No,' Walker snapped. 'Just being careful.' To prove he wasn't a coward, he turned the rowboat towards the ladder. With a few more strokes they were up against it and Darling secured the boat with a line around the metal rail.

Rowntree hauled himself up first, followed by Darling and Walker, and they stood side by side at the top. At the other end of the boat, a crane was unloading containers. Two men could be seen up on the boat and two more on the dock, but otherwise the wharf appeared deserted.

'Working back late,' said Rowntree. 'They'd better be paying overtime. And they,' he jerked his thumb at the dockworkers, 'better be union members.' He strode towards them.

'What are we supposed to do?' Walker asked nervously. 'At least he's got a reason for being here.'

'Play it by ear,' said Darling as he followed Rowntree.

CHAPTER FIFTEEN

DARLING AND WALKER held back and lingered near a gangway, which led to a low, open door in the side of the hull. They watched Rowntree walk towards the dockers, who were struggling with something towards the stern of the boat. The crane hook was caught on an edge of a pallet and one worker was kneeling on the ground while the other was bent over beside him. They both jerked around when Rowntree spoke.

'Hello, fellas. Where's your boss?'

Almost immediately, a squat fellow dressed in shorts and orange safety vest came out of the shadows. 'Hey! You're in the wrong place, mate. Get a move on.'

Rowntree swung around to face him, pulled his fag from his mouth and pointed with it. 'You in charge?'

'What's it to you?'

Rowntree pulled a laminated card out of his top pocket and held it up. 'Union inspection. WWF.'

Seeing that all attention was now on Rowntree, Darling hissed to Walker, 'Stay here and keep a lookout. I'm having a look around.' Before Walker could reply, Darling scurried up the gangway and disappeared inside the hull.

The cargo hold was empty and dim in the reflected light of the dock. Most of the containers were stacked towards the rear of the boat where the unloading was underway, and at the other end of the hold were a number of pallets that held machinery of some kind, covered in clear plastic. Darling made his way towards them, not sure what he was looking for.

He sensed movement in the darkness between the machinery and froze. After a moment, a man stepped out of the shadows, dressed in an orange boilersuit.

'Yes, please?' He looked to be Middle Eastern, or maybe Indian – Darling couldn't be sure in the darkness.

'Hello,' said Darling. Now he wasn't sure what to do, what to expect. He realised how weak his plan had been. Was he expecting to find drugs or other contraband sitting in the open? 'Do you mind if I look around?' he asked.

The man remained silent then retreated into the darkness.

'What are you doing here?' came another voice from behind and Darling spun around. Standing in the doorway near the containers was a large bearded man, his face partially in darkness. The voice was thickly accented but Darling couldn't place where he was from.

'I'm a police officer. Do you mind if I look around?'

There was a pause and in the dimness Darling could see the man's head swivel, as if to check whether he was alone. 'What do you want?' Then after another pause. 'Do you have a warrant?' Darling thought the accent was Arabic.

'Are you the captain?'

'Yes. You should have come to me before you came on the ship. Do you realise you're trespassing?'

'Sorry. I'm investigating a murder. I thought I saw someone run in here.' He realised how weak his excuse sounded.

'Murder! There has been no murder here. Was there a murder nearby?' Again, the head swivelled, searching. 'Are you alone?'

There was something in the man's tone that made Darling feel uneasy. 'No, there're others.'

'I think you should go. There's nothing for you here.'

'Okay. Sorry to disturb you. If you see anyone, please let the police know.'

The man said nothing but remained still, watching from the shadows.

Darling made his way to the door that led to the gangway from where he could see Walker staring at something that was happening further along the dock. But just as he stepped through, a hand grabbed the sleeve of his coat, stopping him. In the darkness, Darling could just make out a face and a strip of orange. It was the other man who had hidden near the machinery. Darling was about to speak but the man put his finger to his lips and shook his head. His hand moved down Darling's arm then encircled his fingers, and Darling felt something pushed into his palm. As soon as he grasped it, the man backed away into the darkness.

Back along the dock, Rowntree was having a loud discussion with the supervisor, and the dockers had returned to their unloading. As soon as Rowntree saw Darling descend the gangway, he held up his arms to bring an end to the conversation. 'All right, all right, I can see everything's in order. Sorry for the trouble. I will bid you fellas a goodnight.'

When Rowntree reached them, he asked in a low voice, 'Find anything?'

Darling shook his head then looked down at the piece of paper in the palm of his hand. On it, a few words had been scrawled in thick marker – *Meet Bald Rock 2 nite.*

He looked up. 'Feel like a beer?'

It was after eleven when they reached an old sandstone pub situated in a backstreet, a short walk up the hill from the docks. Inside, a blues guitarist was playing 'Crossroads' and the poster on the door read 'Noel Davies, Bald Rock Hotel, Balmain. 8–11.30 pm'. Walker shouted them each a Tooheys and they stood at the bar listening to the musician. Eleven-thirty came and the sailor had not turned up and the musician was playing his final tune. The barman called last drinks.

'Looks like he's chickened out,' Rowntree said.

'Or was trying to throw us off the scent,' said Darling. He looked at his wristwatch. 'We'll wait for a few more minutes. Want another?'

Darling bought middies and they drank them as they watched the locals stumble out the door on their way home. Finally, the barman asked them to be on their way, so they downed the rest of their beers and made their way outside as the publican closed the door behind them.

The street was quiet and dimly lit, lined by small factories on one side and a few houses on the other, all in darkness. There was no one to be seen.

'That's that then,' Rowntree announced. 'Not sure I like the idea of rowing a boat across the bay at this time of night. I might look for a taxi.'

'Typical,' said Darling. 'Leave all the dirty work to us, as usual.'

'Steady on, Bazza,' said Rowntree. 'Can't you phone one of your cop buddies to pick you up? Is your rowboat so precious?'

'I borrowed it,' said Darling.

'Not my problem.' Rowntree burped loudly and moved in the direction of Victoria Road, the major route to the city. 'I'll see you blokes later.'

'I hope you get mugged, you lazy bastard,' Darling called after him. Rowntree raised two fingers without looking back. 'What about your sister's bike?' he yelled, but Rowntree completely ignored him. Darling turned back to Walker. 'What about you, Kit? You going to piss off as well?'

'Come on, Wendy,' he said, turning in the opposite direction that led back down to the docks. 'I've got to work tomorrow.' He set off up the street without waiting to see whether Darling followed.

At the end of a factory, the street curved sharply down the hill towards the water. As Walker turned the corner, he saw two men struggling on the opposite side, next to a graffitied wall. One was dressed in orange.

'Hey,' he yelled, then glanced back to see Darling break into a trot. When he looked back again, the man in orange was on the ground and the other fellow was running away towards the water.

They ran to the fallen man and Walker crouched beside him while Darling ran on in pursuit. Then Walker noticed a huge pool of blood and a large knife protruding from the man's neck. He wasn't breathing. A quick check of his pulse confirmed he was dead. From the amount of blood, he figured that the knife had severed the carotid artery. Blood soaked the clothes and was now streaming down the gutter towards the bay. There was no more blood flowing from the wound.

Walker stood up, not sure what to do. The man was beyond help. Maybe he should help with the chase. Just when he decided he should follow Darling, he saw him jogging back up the street towards him.

'Lost him,' he gasped when he reached Walker. 'He ran like a rocket. Pulled away from me then disappeared up a side street. He could be anywhere.' He looked down at the body. 'What about him?'

'Lost him too.'

'You sure? Shouldn't we try something?'

Walker shook his head. 'He's lost his total blood volume. There's nothing to resuscitate.'

'Shit.' Darling gazed along the street and then at the body. 'I'm going to have to call the local team in.' He didn't look very happy. 'I'm going to get in a lot of trouble for this.'

'Why? You can't help it that the bloke was a champion sprinter.'

'Not that. I wasn't supposed to be investigating that ship. And now look what's happened. One thing though.' He reached into his pocket and pulled out something. 'He dropped this.'

Walker peered at it in the dim light. 'What is it, a condom?'

Darling unfurled the latex fully.

'A surgical glove,' said Walker. He moved to examine it more closely. 'You only see that brand in hospitals.'

Darling nodded. 'And I bet you a million dollars it's from Western Meadows.'

CHAPTER SIXTEEN

IT WAS NINE in the morning, and the sunlight shining over the calm water of the harbour detailed the exhaustion on Darling's face as he watched the *Sintak-5* steam out towards the arch of the Harbour Bridge. He squinted in the dazzling light, hands on hips, as the ship rounded Peacock Point on the edge of Balmain before the bow was lost to view.

'A big fat zip,' said Darling. He'd called the local police in for the murder and had quickly convinced them to organise a warrant to search the *Sintak-5*. A horde of police had searched the ship from top to bottom, but apart from a few bootleg CDs of Faith No More, Bon Jovi and Aerosmith, their search had been fruitless. There was certainly no evidence of heroin or other contraband, even using the sniffer dogs. The captain had stood on the dock while they searched, silent and brooding, but had politely thanked the police when they'd finally finished. If anything, Darling thought the captain was too cool, offering no complaint of the police intrusion onto his apparently faultless ship, which had delayed his planned departure to Melbourne by over two hours. The captain confirmed the murdered man had been one of his crew, a Bangladeshi they'd picked up in the newly opened Laem Chabang port in Thailand only ten days earlier. The man was a good worker who'd kept to himself, so the captain didn't really know much about him. He claimed he had no idea why the man was off the boat the previous evening and also no clue why anyone would want to kill him.

'What now?' asked Walker, who was sitting on a stack of pallets near the water's edge.

Darling turned to him with a scowl. 'Certainly not following one of your harebrained clues, that's what. I must have been mad to listen to you.'

'Come on, Wendy, a man was murdered last night. A man who was supposed to be meeting you in secret. You can't tell me that's not suspicious.'

'That means nothing,' snapped Darling. 'He could've been looking for an easy entry into Australia. You know, some boo-hoo story about oppression or persecution or some such nonsense. I bet he was no more than an asylum seeker.'

'Is that all?' Walker scoffed. 'Just an asylum seeker.'

Darling swore under his breath. 'I'm going home for a shower. You can do what you want.' He began to walk towards the gate of the docks.

'Doesn't explain why he was murdered though,' Walker called out his name. Darling ignored him.

Forty minutes later, hot and sweating, Darling arrived home, having made his way on foot around the water's edge before slogging up Glebe Point Road to his lodge. He took a quick shower and put on a clean set of clothes then headed to one of the local cafes. He sat at a table on the street and ordered a cappuccino and a plate of bacon and eggs. Finally satiated, he leaned back in his chair and looked at his watch. Ten thirty!

'Hi, Barry.'

He looked up to see Sally Biggs, dressed in her nurse's uniform. 'I'm on my way home from night duty.'

He pushed a seat out for her and ordered two cappuccinos.

'Any news on Alice's murder?' She looked exhausted, with dark smudges under her eyes, and Darling suspected it was from more than just the night duty. Sally noticed him looking at her and she straightened her hair self-consciously then pulled her hands across her face as if she were trying to smooth the creases in her skin. 'I'm not sleeping so I've volunteered for nights. I'd rather be working while it's dark. Safer to sleep during the day, although it's been so hot, I rarely get any.' She gave him a damsel-in-distress look.

Darling wondered whether he should offer her to stay with him, then realised it was a bad idea. She was attractive, and if it was found out he was having a relationship with the friend of a murder victim, it wouldn't look good. He could wave any chance of a promotion goodbye. Besides, there was Cassandra. He wasn't sure whether she was a keeper and he wasn't even certain whether she was limiting herself to him alone. But then again, he couldn't be sure. Maybe he should try monogamy for a while. He decided not to take the bait.

Looking up at the sky, he changed the subject. 'Looks like it's going to be another scorcher. Do you have a fan?'

Sally looked disappointed then shrugged. 'I'd rather have air conditioning.'

'Air conditioning,' huffed Darling. 'This is Glebe, not Darling Point.'

'If I owned my own house, I'd get air conditioning no matter what the cost. I hate the hot weather. Sydney's too humid. Back home in Armidale we get dry heat.'

'Are you thinking of buying a house here?'

Sally made a face. 'On my salary? And with interest rates like they are?'

'I'm looking,' said Darling, glad to be talking about a safe subject.

'In Glebe? To buy? Why here? You'd do much better out in the suburbs where there's room to breathe. No one wants to live in the inner city. Too close and grubby.'

'I love it,' said Darling, leaning back in his chair and looking up and down Glebe Point Road. 'I predict that people will start moving back in.'

Sally guffawed in disbelief. Then she surveyed the houses on the other side of the street. 'How much do you need?'

'I reckon over two hundred thousand to buy something half-decent. House prices have stabilised after the craziness of a few years ago but there's talk of another boom. I want to strike while the iron's hot. The Police Credit Union will lend me the dosh but I need at least ten percent for a deposit. I've saved twenty thousand but want another five as a buffer.'

Sally whistled, impressed. 'Twenty thousand! Well done. What are you after?'

'A two-bed terrace. Nothing too big.'

She nodded. 'I reckon you should be okay.' Then she gave a fake, sweet smile. 'Two bedder, hey? Do you need a tenant to help you pay the mortgage?'

Darling raised his eyebrows, impressed with the suggestion. 'Maybe I will. Good idea.'

They drank their coffee then she asked, 'Anything on Alice? I'm really serious about not sleeping at night with the thought of a killer around.'

Darling paused before speaking. 'I can't say much, but I can tell you that the killer is not from around here. We think she was killed at Western Meadows Hospital.'

Sally let out a breath. 'That's a relief. But are you any closer to finding him?'

Darling patted her hand then stood up. 'Try to get some sleep, Sally. Have a cool shower then hit the sack. You look exhausted.'

'Thanks,' she said wryly. 'Is that why you've rejected my obvious charms? Because I look a mess?'

He smiled. 'Get some sleep. If you like, we can have a beer and a steak tonight at the Toxteth.'

CHAPTER SEVENTEEN

CHRISTOPHER WALKER AWOKE late on the Wednesday morning, having tossed and turned all night. He'd fallen asleep thinking about the stabbed man in orange but in the early hours had forced himself to wake up from a nightmare. He then sat in Felicity's armchair reading a book until sleep finally took him. But the dream had returned and repeated itself throughout the night until he finally awoke exhausted after 9 am.

In the dream, he'd been watching Jocelyn Banks doing an autopsy on the man whose flesh was now orange rather than the suit. Over and over, she'd shown Walker how to peel the flesh, starting at the vertex of the scalp and working around the head in strips as if it was a piece of fruit, carefully slice away the skin to leave a thin layer of white tissue over the bone. He watched appreciatively as she deftly negotiated the ears, eyes and nose, so the skin came away in a continuous strip that curled up neatly on the table beside the head.

Then Jocelyn had asked Walker to start on the corpse's legs while she worked on the arms, showing him how to slice away large slabs of flesh, being careful not to cut into the muscle. Walker tried but he wasn't very good at it and kept swearing in frustration as he produced an untidy mess of skin fragments at the foot of the table. Jocelyn kept encouraging, telling him that he'd improve with practice.

He woke many times to break the dream but every time he drifted off again, he was back at the same place, assiduously slicing, trying to match Jocelyn's skill.

Finally, they'd finished and Jocelyn swung a cleaver in her hand, smiling with excitement.

'Now for the good bit,' she said, licking her lips. She lifted the cleaver. 'I hope you're hungry, Kit.'

He'd jolted awake, breathing hard, his head groggy, with a cold sweat on his chest and brow, then stumbled into the shower and stood under the cold water trying to clear his head to rid himself of the images.

He thought of Angela. He really liked her and she'd agreed to go to the beach with him.

Then another memory forced its way into his head.

Felicity on the day she'd died.

He felt the Black rising again from within his chest.

But this time he forced himself to remember.

They were walking up a shallow, fast-flowing creek following their guide, an elderly local who knew the area and also the languages of the various tribes. There'd been a heavy storm that morning in the north. They were hurrying but Walker knew it was not because of the storm. The guide and Felicity kept looking back over their shoulders for the danger that would come from that direction, not where they were headed to. Something had happened. To somebody else who they'd met on their travels. A man. A geologist. Walker looked back but all he could see was the shallow creek and dense vegetation. Their guide was in the lead and Felicity was next, and Walker watched as she splashed confidently over rocks that jutted above the surface, not caring that her feet got wet. She looked back and gave him a smile, one of encouragement; a sign to will him to be brave, to keep him going. And then he saw it. Over her shoulder. A wall of water sweeping down the waterway towards them.

He stood in the cold shower and pushed his knuckles into this forehead to force the memory away. No! Whatever happened back then could not be the cause of the foreboding he felt!

He thought of something else – Cassandra, naked in his bed after the Mardi Gras, rutting in the park like animals.

Yes, that was it! That was the cause of the guilt that now filled his chest and guts and threatened to devour him. He'd slept with Cassandra and she was going out with Barry Darling.

He let the cold water flow over his face, trying to wash away the shame. He took a deep breath and made a decision. He'd tell Wendy. It was the only way to assuage the blackness that filled him, forcing the nightmares, stealing his sleep.

Today he'd go to Darling and confess what he'd done. He was glad he'd made the decision. Quickly, before he could change his mind, he dressed and made his way to the car.

As he drove away, his thoughts turned again to Felicity.

Walker found Darling in the meeting room of the police station in Parramatta. Jones stood before a corkboard attached to one wall and Darling was on the phone. He slammed it down just as Walker entered.

'Head office in College Street is sending out a pair from the homicide squad.' Darling made a face as if he'd just stepped into something disgusting in his best Italian shoes. 'The detective inspector says we'll need the help since there are three murders. But I don't know why we need them. We solved the last murder in quick time. I don't need some phoney hot-shot sticking his nose into our business. We're perfectly capable.'

'When are they coming?' asked Walker.

'This morning.' Darling turned to the large corkboard. 'So, we better get on with it.' He looked over his shoulder. 'What do you want anyway, Kit?' he snapped.

Walker realised that now was not the time to confess his crimes. 'Just seeing how you're getting on.'

Darling gave him a queer look, then addressed Jones. 'Okay, let's try to summarise what we've got.'

They looked up at the board, which was mostly bare except for several squares of paper fixed along the top with pins. Three names and designations were listed: Otto Reilly –

Catholic priest; Alice Cleary – Nurse; Jim Nguyen – Cleaner. Under each name was another piece of paper with the details of their deaths. Above the names was a single piece of paper with Western Meadows written on it. Three pieces of string, secured by thumbtacks, joined each of the victims to the hospital.

'Firstly,' said Darling, 'there's the priest killed with a Middle Eastern knife, his body laid out in the shape of a cross in the hospital chapel. We don't know where he was killed but it was not in the chapel.' He spoke quickly, as if they'd gone through the same evidence a number of times.

'That sounds like someone trying to frame the murder as some sort of religious killing,' said Jones. 'Trying to throw us off.'

'Next we have an Irish nurse who, according to the employment agency, was supposed to be working a casual shift in the geriatric ward. It was her first time working at Western Meadows. She was killed by a heroin overdose, administered by an unknown person or persons. Forensic evidence points to her body being refrigerated after death and, taking that into account, she could've been murdered at the same time as the priest.'

The three stared at the board as the words sank in.

'Then we've Jim Nguyen,' Darling continued, 'a Vietnamese cleaner who appears to have been thrown out of the fourth-floor window to his death, made to look like a suicide. That also happened at the same time as the other two.'

'So that's three deaths where efforts were made to hide the place and nature of their deaths,' said Jones thoughtfully.

Darling nodded. 'Well done, Jones. Yes, already that's a clue. Why were they going to such great pains to hide where the murders were done? Then we also have the Bangladeshi sailor from the *Sintak-5* who was stabbed to death by a male person, as yet unidentified. The ship was searched and there's absolutely no evidence of illegal activity or substances. The boat wasn't even in Sydney when the murders occurred. It was still en route from Bangkok.'

'Where was it?' asked Walker.

'Off the coast of northern New South Wales, near Newcastle. It didn't arrive into Sydney until the day after the murders.'

'What links them?' asked Walker. 'An Irish nurse, a Catholic priest, a Vietnamese cleaner and a Bangladeshi sailor. I doubt they even knew each other, especially the nurse. It was her first time at the hospital. You can hardly claim it was some sort of conspiracy of a gang or the like.'

'Good point, Kit,' said Darling. 'None of the killings seem planned. They look as if they were made up as they went along, including the sailor.'

'As if the killers were caught doing something they didn't want anyone to know about,' added Walker.

'Agreed,' said Darling. 'What then? What about the heroin? Traces were found in the plastic bag that held the nurse's uniform, which was thrown into the creek behind the hospital.'

'So, this could be about drug smuggling,' said Jones. 'Heroin out of Southeast Asia. We know that's mostly trafficked by the motorcycle gangs.'

'And the Arabic knife,' said Walker. 'Do you think that's a link to the Middle Eastern criminal gangs?'

'Maybe. What have we found out about it, Jones?'

He flicked to a page in his notepad. 'It's called a *jambiya*.' Jones pronounced the word slowly. 'Definitely from the Middle East.' He looked up. 'But not from the places where the drug gangs are from. The knives are usually bought by tourists in the bazaars of Yemen.'

'Where's Yemen?' said Darling with a questioning look.

'South of Saudi Arabia,' said Walker. 'Where do the drug gangs hail from?'

'Lebanon mostly,' Jones answered. 'They seem to be linking with the bikie gangs in Merrylands and Auburn.'

Darling pinned a photo of the blade on the corkboard under the priest's name and they stared at it, mesmerised.

'It's a cheap version by the look of that wooden handle, probably a tourist trinket.' Jones looked down at his pad again. 'The hilts of the expensive ones are made of ivory or rhinoceros horn and are worth a small fortune. But the blade is real. Apparently, it's a formidable weapon in a fight.'

'Looks it too,' said Walker. 'I don't think I'd like that jabbed between my ribs.'

'Or into your belly, ripping up through your intestines and liver.' Jones smiled and yanked his arm upwards as he acted out the movement. 'Very effective.'

Darling grimaced. 'Do they usually just come like that? I can't imagine it would be safe carrying it around without some sort of wrapping.'

'Usually it's in a curved scabbard made of wood,' said Jones.

'Of which we've no trace.'

'But if we find the scabbard, we might find our murderer,' said Walker.

'Or murderers. I can't imagine one man could've carried out all three murders by himself,' said Darling.

Again, they stared at the mounting evidence before them, trying to piece the complex picture together. As they watched, Jones added the word 'heroin' under the nurse's name and then linked it and the photo of the knife with string and thumbtack. He turned questioningly to Darling who gave a firm nod. Jones seemed pleased.

Then Darling stirred. 'Let's go back to the nurse and assume she was murdered somewhere at the hospital. Why was her body refrigerated? And where was the fridge?'

'Delivery truck?' suggested Jones.

Darling shook his head. 'Why a truck?'

'What if it was used to deliver the heroin?' said Walker. 'You know, disguised as a shipment of meat or something?'

'I doubt it. Too elaborate. They're more likely to put drugs in cans of baked beans or in furniture, not something that needs refrigeration. Are there any fridges in the hospital?'

As he spoke, Jones added a further piece of paper under the nurse's name with 'refrigerated' written on it.

'Lots of freezers are used for storing research samples, all over,' said Walker. 'It's a teaching hospital and there's a lot of research done. But mostly they're freezers, not fridges. And none are big enough to fit a body.'

'There's one place I can think of,' Darling said slowly. He clicked his fingers. 'The morgue?'

Walker's mouth opened and he tapped his forehead. 'Of course. The morgue. Who would think to look for a missing person in a morgue fridge? Yes, the more I think about it, it would have to be the morgue fridge.'

'Who has access to the morgue on a Saturday night?' Darling continued. 'In particular, the night of the Mardi Gras. We also need to find where the heroin went. And we're also looking for a wooden scabbard that would hold a curved dagger. Jones, get a detail to search the locker rooms, toilets and other rooms around the morgue. Anywhere the drugs could've been stored.'

'I'm onto it, boss,' said Jones, moving towards the door. 'I'll nip up to the hospital and ask Dr Banks.'

Before he could leave, two figures entered the room, stopping Jones in his tracks.

In the doorway was a man almost as large as Jones, but older, with thick-rimmed glasses and ears that stuck out like a set of open car doors. Peering around from behind him was a younger woman, blonde with a slim build.

'Detective Sergeant Darling?' said the man. 'I'm Senior Detective Sergeant Royce Wills.' He tipped his head. 'And this is Detective Constable Thelma Bianca. I think you're expecting us.'

Jones looked from the pair and back to Darling, wearing an unwelcoming frown.

Detective Wills swung a doleful face at Jones. 'And who are you when you're home, sunshine?'

Jones's stature became straighter. 'Constable David Jones, sir. I'm helping with the case.'

Wills looked back at Darling. 'That might explain your progress. Or lack thereof.' He raised his chin towards Walker. 'And you?'

'Dr Chris Walker. I'm a cancer specialist from Western Meadows.'

'Cancer specialist?' Wills examined the board with its collection of photos and connecting string lines and faced Darling again. 'Detective Darling, can you please explain why you have a potential suspect here with the results of your investigation on full display for all to see?'

'Suspect?' said Walker.

'Quite possibly,' Wills said calmly. 'At this stage, everyone is a suspect.' He pointed to Walker. 'And I've seen your name on the run sheets. You were involved with the case involving Professor Chee, if I'm not mistaken.'

'Well, I work at the hospital where the murder occurred, if that's what you mean.'

'Murders,' corrected Wills. 'A veritable abundance of murders.' He addressed Darling. 'Did you know that the Parramatta district now has the highest concentration of murders on record for New South Wales and probably Australia? And they're all centred on Western Meadows Hospital.' He turned back to Walker. 'Why is that?'

Walker grimaced. 'Well, I'm sure we're all safe now that you're here, Detective Wills.'

'*Senior* Detective Sergeant Wills.'

Walker ignored him and addressed Darling. 'Will that be all, Detective Sergeant Darling? I'm needed back at the hospital.' He smiled at Wills. 'You know, saving lives and all that.'

Wills returned an empty smile. 'By all means, doctor. I'm sure we will be meeting again.'

As Walker left, Wills maintained his plastic smile and turned to the board, and the female constable moved in beside him. 'Now, Detective Darling, please try to explain what you've got here and we'll see whether we can make some sense out of it all.'

CHAPTER EIGHTEEN

WITHIN AN HOUR of meeting Royce Wills, Darling felt like he'd been relegated to grunt work, being sent to do the sorts of things that he usually got Jones to do. Using the information that Darling had given him, Wills had come to the same conclusion that the murders may have occurred at Western Meadows morgue and had ordered Darling to investigate.

He and Jones found Jocelyn Banks in her office on the second floor of the pathology building. It was a neat, utilitarian room with a clean desk and a healthy fern sitting on a filing cabinet near the window. She looked up when they entered, appearing to have been writing a report in a neat hand on a form. Darling raised his eyes to her window. One floor up and directly opposite was the room from where the cleaner had been thrown.

'Dr Banks,' Darling began after she'd greeted them, 'we've reason to believe the nurse's body may have been stored in your own morgue fridge.'

Jocelyn looked surprised. 'Here?' She frowned thoughtfully then slowly nodded her head. 'Yes, I see that makes sense. I don't know of any other fridges large enough to hold a body in the hospital. And, as I said before, a refrigerated truck just sounds too fanciful. Too complicated.' She leaned back in her chair. 'Well, that certainly narrows down the suspects.'

'The body would have been stored after hours, otherwise people would have seen,' said Darling. 'And the nurse was rostered on for night duty. Who has access after hours?'

'Me,' said Jocelyn. 'And the morgue attendants. That's about it. This is a forensic morgue so access is limited. Not even the hospital administrators have access.'

'The morgue attendants then. Who are they?'

'Well, we have two – Clive Johnson and Quentin Boon. Johnson is on duty today. He'll be in the lunch room this time of day.'

Darling raised a hand. 'Jones.'

He nodded and moved away.

'And who was on duty on the evening of the Mardi Gras?'

'That was a Saturday night, so no one was on duty. One of them would have been on call. I'd have to look that up.'

'And Quentin Boon. Where would he be?'

'He's rostered to start at four this afternoon. We're in catch-up mode. There's a backlog of autopsies and the murders here haven't helped. The whole team is doing overtime.'

Darling nodded. 'We'll catch up with Boon after four then.' He rubbed his jaw. 'Dr Banks, we also think the murders might have occurred here.'

'You mean in the morgue?'

'Or near here. We haven't been able to find the murder site. The priest was stabbed to death. That's very bloody and hard to hide. But there are no traces in the hospital or dock area.'

'So?'

'So, do you think the murders could've happened in the autopsy room?'

Jocelyn rubbed her forehead. 'Very clever. Yes, that could be the case. This place is built for dissecting bodies and dealing with fluids efficiently. The autopsy room would be the perfect place for a stabbing murder. You could wash away all the blood. Even if we found traces, it would be impossible to match it with the deceased's. All we can do is blood typing, but we have so many go through here, any match would be inconclusive.'

'Is there no other way?'

She shook her head. 'There's a method for matching DNA being developed in the UK by Professor Jeffreys at the University of Leicester. It might be useful one day but it's too unreliable at the moment. And we can't do it anyway.'

'What about fingerprints?'

'Maybe,' Jocelyn said doubtfully. 'Everything is scrubbed clean between cases. You'd have to be lucky.'

'We'll try anyway. We need to get a lead from somewhere.'

She raised a finger. 'Answer me this – why would the nurse be refrigerated but the other two bodies left out in full view?'

'Heat of the moment? We suspect these murders weren't planned. The murderer, or probably murderers, were almost certainly panicking.'

'Can't have panicked too much. They've done a pretty good job of throwing you off the track so far.'

'Don't remind me. I have a head-office jerk on my back trying to break my balls.'

'Sounds uncomfortable.' She smiled. 'And probably anatomically impossible.'

Darling stood. 'I'd better catch up with Jones. This is the first lead we've had.'

Darling found the young constable in the lunch room talking to Clive Johnson. He nodded to Jones and sat down beside them as Jones spoke.

'Sir, Clive Johnson was just telling me that he was up in Newcastle on the weekend of the murder.'

'That's right,' said Johnson. 'I was visiting my brother all weekend. We were fishing.'

'Fishing? Where?'

'Off the coast. Doug's got a twenty-eight-foot Bertram. We were out all day on the Saturday and didn't get back till late.'

'What'd you catch?'

'We were after bluefin tuna but all we got was whiting.' He grinned. 'Still, it was a good day.'

'How far off the coast did you go?'

'You've got to go a long way for bluefin. Over fifty K. The boat can take it. It's fully rigged.'

'Just the two of you?'

'Yeah. We've been doing it for years. The weather was good.' He grinned again. 'We know what we're doing.'

Darling made a few notes in his pad. 'Could you please give Constable Jones your brother's contact details? We'll need to speak to him, and anyone else who saw you up in Newcastle on the day.'

He frowned. 'What's this about? The murders? You think I've got something to do with them?'

'We're checking everyone, Mr Johnson. All routine. No need to worry.'

Johnson didn't look happy. 'If you must. I'll give you his number. But I've gotta warn you, Doug don't trust no coppers. He'll give you a hard time.'

'Why is that? Has he been in trouble?'

'Spent six months in Maitland for dealing drugs a few years ago. Now every time something happens up his way, the coppers come buzzing around like blue-arsed flies, asking questions.'

'Drugs? What type?'

'Smack. Weed. Mostly smack.'

'Heroin?' said Jones.

'That's what I just said, didn't I? But he doesn't do it anymore. He's clean. Like I said, don't expect a friendly welcome from him. Don't be surprised if he tells you to stick it up your arse.'

Darling stood and Jones rose with him. 'We'd appreciate you not contacting your brother, Mr Johnson. We'd like to talk to him without any prompting.'

He smiled, showing a row of grey teeth. 'No worries. Always like to please the law.'

As they moved away, Darling murmured to Jones, 'I'll bet you next week's pay that he'll be onto this brother within the hour. You'd better call him as soon as you can.'

As Jones strode away, Darling called out, 'And we need to catch up with Quentin Boon at four. I'll meet you in the morgue.'

'Dr Banks,' said Darling when he caught up with her in her office again, 'we interviewed Clive Johnson and he claims he was fishing with his brother in Newcastle.'

'I'd believe him,' said Jocelyn. 'He's a bit of a rough diamond, our Clive. But I've always found him to be an honest worker. I can't imagine him murdering anyone.'

'He's used to cutting up bodies. Does it every day. I've seen him chopping into bodies with gay abandon. Perhaps he's become desensitised. Finds it easy to kill?'

'There's a big difference between cutting into a corpse and a living, breathing person, Detective Darling, believe me. Take me, for instance. I know my way around human anatomy better than anybody, but I would make a hopeless surgeon. It's a totally different approach, a different level of care.'

'I'm talking about Johnson potentially stabbing a priest, not carefully dissecting him. And you said so yourself – the single stab wound in the aorta. Was that a lucky shot or was it done by someone who knew what he was doing? Done it before. On corpses.'

Jocelyn nodded thoughtfully. 'I see what you mean. But I still can't believe Clive would wilfully murder another person.'

'We'll catch up with the other morgue attendant this afternoon.' He looked at his pad. 'Quentin Boon.' He raised his eyes. 'Did you look up who was on call the night of the Mardi Gras?'

'Oh yes, sorry, I said I'd do that.' She moved to a filing cabinet, opened the top drawer, flicked through a few folders then pulled out one and ran her finger down the page. When she glanced up, she gave a look like she was about to snitch on her best friend. 'It was Clive Johnson. Quentin Boon was on during the day and Clive was on call after six.'

Darling nodded and scribbled into his pad with some satisfaction. 'Now we're getting somewhere.' He snapped his pad shut. 'All we need to do is comb the autopsy room and the rest of the morgue. I have a team doing that as we speak. Care to join me?'

Jocelyn accompanied Darling to the autopsy room, which was now scattered with forensic officers in white coats, working with brushes and powder, collecting fingerprints. One fellow was on his knees before the drain in the centre of the floor and was carefully scraping black muck into a paper envelope with a paddle-pop stick.

'I'm not sure how all this is going to help, Detective Darling,' drawled Jocelyn, leaning on the doorjamb with her arms folded. 'We carried out autopsies on all the murder victims here, so you're bound to find their blood samples. And if Clive Johnson is a suspect then – given that he works here every day – finding his fingerprints will mean nothing.'

'But what if we find the prints of someone who shouldn't be here?'

Jocelyn raised her eyebrows. 'Good point.' She uncrossed her arms and pushed herself upright. 'I might leave you to it then. Looks like you'll be here for a while.'

'Sir,' came a voice from the corridor and they both turned to find Jones smiling widely, holding a brush and a paper envelope. 'We found white powder.' He gestured with his head towards a door behind him. 'In the locker room.'

'Ah ha!' cried Darling, glancing at Jocelyn triumphantly. He rubbed his hands. 'Whose locker?'

Jones paused for effect and his smile widened even further. 'Clive Johnson.'

'Did you get hold of Johnson's brother?' Darling asked later that afternoon after the forensic team had left.

'Yes, sir. He confirmed the story.' Jones glanced at his pad. 'They set off from Jensen's Point Marina on Lake Macquarie at about six in the morning and travelled off the coast for about thirty nautical miles, caught some whiting and finally got back into port at about eight pm.'

'What was his demeanour? Did he give you a hard time?'

'Not at all. Seemed very helpful. The story sounded pretty neat though.'

Darling let out a laugh. 'Johnson got to him obviously. We'll have to check the others on the list he gave us, but I suspect you'll have to drive up to Newcastle yourself and talk to someone at the marina.'

They walked through the morgue doors. The slabs were devoid of bodies and a thin young man wrapped in a green theatre gown was setting up a tray for the next autopsy, pulling the equipment from a green bucket and laying it out on a stainless-steel table covered with a blue paper mat. On a cursory look, it might have been mistaken for a carpenter's tray – a mallet, a saw and a large set of shears. But the scalpels, hooked scissors and metal probes hinted at another purpose.

The man glanced up at them and froze in the act of placing what looked like a wide butcher's knife on the tray. He kept hold of it as he smiled. 'Can I help you?'

He appeared to be in his late twenties with a sallow face and a head of dyed orange hair, dark at the ends. He looked unhealthily thin. There was a stud in his nose and his right earlobe was pierced with a gold earring.

'Quentin Boon?' said Darling. 'I'm Detective Darling and this is Constable Jones from the Parramatta station. We'd like to ask you some questions, if you have the time.'

Quentin turned to face them. The arm with the cleaver hung at his side. 'Of course. How can I help? Is it about the murders?'

'Why do you say that?' asked Jones.

Quentin smiled at Jones. 'What else is there for you to be investigating? Three murders? You wouldn't have to be Einstein.'

'Where were you on Saturday night, two weeks ago?'

His forehead creased in thought then his face brightened. 'Why, at the Mardi Gras, of course! I was in the parade. I went as an angel.'

'An angel?' Jones said dumbly.

'Yes!' Quentin gushed with excitement. 'I looked absolutely fabulous. Big white wings, a tutu and a beautiful sparkling wand. Oh!' His arms swept out delicately to each side as if they were angel wings, then raised them to rest softly on the back of his head. 'And a gorgeous gold and silver halo.' He let out a sigh. 'It was such a glorious night.' He smiled brightly again at Jones. 'Were you there?'

He took half a step backward before he caught himself. 'No,' he grunted, his voice unnaturally coarse. 'I was on duty with the rest of the boys.' He coughed nervously. 'Men. They were men. Policemen.'

'Really,' said Quentin, raising his eyebrows suggestively. 'I'd love to meet them.'

Darling threw Jones an admonishing look then addressed Quentin. 'So, you were at the Mardi Gras. Do you have any witnesses?'

'Why of course. Lots of people.' He raised a finger as if he'd had a sudden thought. 'Dr Walker. He was there. I waved to him from the parade. He was standing on the corner and I'm sure he saw me. He was with this drop-dead gorgeous woman. Blonde. Long legs. Great tits. She was hanging all over him.'

'Blonde,' said Darling. 'You sure? Not an Asian girl?'

'Oh no, detective. Definitely not Asian. An Aussie girl. And she looked hot-to-trot. I'm pretty sure Dr Walker had a great time that evening. Why don't you ask him?'

Darling grimaced and made a note in his pad. 'Yes,' he said gruffly, 'I think I will.' He began to move away then stopped and turned. 'Jones, get a list of names of those who can corroborate Mr Boon's story.'

'Names?' Jones said stupidly. He turned to the young morgue attendant who now wore a coy smile. Jones looked terrified.

As Darling walked away, he heard Quentin's voice take on an intimate tone. 'Now, Constable Jones, why don't I start with my details – address, phone number and anything else you want. And if you like, perhaps I could have yours …'

CHAPTER NINETEEN

AFTER LEAVING THE morgue, the two police officers made their way to the hospital security office and asked to speak to the manager. They were directed to a tall chap of Indian extraction with dark curly hair and a young face, although Darling suspected he was at least fifty years old.

'We need information about who has access to the morgue after hours,' said Darling. 'Do you keep a record of who is issued with keys?'

The chap seemed keen to help. 'Is this about the murders? No worries, sir. I'll see what information I can give you.'

He bent to open a safe under the bench and pulled out a spiral-bound book with 'KEYS' written in thick red ink on the cover. He flicked through a few pages. 'We've a system, you see.' He smiled proudly. 'I'll have that information for you in a jiffy.'

The fellow continued to flick from page to page, going back and forth, but slowly his keen smile turned to a frown.

'Is there a problem?' asked Jones.

'No problem,' the manager said quickly. Then he straightened and cleared his throat as if he was about to make an important announcement. 'There have been three keys issued. One to Clive Johnson and one to Quentin Boon. They are both mortuary attendants.' He snapped the book closed and smiled with satisfaction.

'And the third?'

'To the director, of course. The third key would have been issued to the Director of Forensic Pathology, Dr Jocelyn Banks.' His full lips opened into a wide smile that revealed flawless white teeth. 'And a beautiful lady she is. A credit to our institution.'

'Are you sure no other keys have been issued? Perhaps to staff who have since left and forgot to return them?'

The fellow raised an admonishing finger. 'Never! There's a rule. No keys, no pay cheque. Those wishing to leave this institution must return all keys issued to them and we must sign off their chit as proof of the transaction or they will fail to get their final pay. We're very insistent and particular on the matter.'

'Could the keys be copied?' asked Jones.

He frowned. 'No. They are special keys. Locksmiths know it's illegal to copy them.'

'But it's technically possible?' Jones persisted.

The man shook his head once and again waved a finger. 'It is not done.'

'But if a locksmith had the correct equipment, *could* they copy the key?' said Jones.

'As I've faithfully and earnestly declared, it is highly illegal.'

'But can *you* get copies made if you need one?' asked Darling.

'Me? Of course.' He smiled. 'We must be able to make copies.'

'And who does that?'

'We've a locksmith we send them to.'

Darling threw Jones a look and sighed. 'Jones, kindly get the name of the locksmith then meet me in the morgue. I think it's time we had another talk to Clive Johnson.' He turned back to the security officer. 'Who was the last mortuary assistant to leave the job?'

The man reopened the book and ran his finger down the page. 'There were two in the last five years. Frank Naim and Ahmed Mohammed,' he said without raising his head. 'But it's definitely recorded that the keys were returned. Both over two years ago.'

'Two years?' said Darling. He turned to his junior officer. 'Check them out anyway, Jones.'

Darling and Jones found Clive Johnson in the autopsy room, cleaning up after a procedure. The stainless-steel table was bare and washed clean, and he was hosing the last evidence of the autopsy down a central drain, spraying the policemen's shoes when they came closer. Jones gave a yell and Johnson jerked back as if he'd only just seen them, then turned off the hose, a questioning look on his face. He leaned back against the autopsy table and frowned when Darling and Jones came close to him on either side.

'Mr Johnson,' Darling began, 'we'd like to ask you a few more questions about the night of the Mardi Gras.'

'You mean the night of the murders,' said Johnson, matter-of-factly.

Darling nodded. 'Can you go through the timeline of your movements on that day?'

Johnson glanced nervously at Jones, who held his pen poised over his notebook. 'I've already been through this. And you've spoken to my brother.'

'We'd like to go over it again,' Jones insisted.

Johnson rubbed his chin thoughtfully. 'Well, like I said, I went up the coast early that morning and me and my brother took his boat out fishing.'

Jones read from his notes. 'You said you left in his twenty-eight-foot Bertram from Jensen's Point Marina, Lake Macquarie, at roughly six thirty in the morning.' He glanced up. 'Is that correct?'

'About that time, yes,' Johnson said, clearly uncomfortable. 'Why are you asking again?'

'And that you went about fifty kilometres off the coast,' Jones continued. He snapped his pad closed. 'That's a long way. Did you encounter any other vessels on the open sea?'

'What do you mean by encounter? We saw some other fishing boats and a few container ships, if that's what you mean.'

'Did you go close to any of those vessels, particularly a container ship?'

'Not close. We keep out of their way.'

'Did you come into physical contact with any other vessel at any time? Did you negotiate any sort of rendezvous?'

'Rendezvous? What do you mean by that? We were out fishing, not having a flamin' cocktail party.'

'Let's leave that then.' Jones examined his notes again then looked up sharply. 'What time did you get back in?'

'Let's see,' said Johnson. He bent his head and rubbed his chin in contemplation, although Darling could tell he was nervous. 'I think it was about eight in the evening.'

'That's a long day,' said Darling.

'We enjoy our fishing.'

'We understand you were on call for the mortuary after six pm that day,' continued Darling doggedly. "How can you be in Newcastle when you're on call?'

Johnson hesitated. 'Well, usually we *are* back by four or five. It's unusual to be called in. And, after all, I'm on call for a morgue, not an emergency room.' He smiled showing stained teeth. 'My clients are usually going nowhere in a hurry. There's never any rush. Plenty of time to get back, if need be.'

'Mr Johnson,' said Jones, 'I interviewed the owner of Jensens Point Marina and he says you came in earlier.' He glanced down at his pad. 'More like four in the afternoon.'

'Joe Strider! He wouldn't know his arse from his brains. He's pissed most of the time. I doubt he'd even be there at four, let alone eight. More likely he'd be up the pub by three getting even more pissed.'

'Why eight pm?' Darling persisted. 'Why so late? It would be coming on night-time.'

'Like I said, we like our fishing. And there was a mighty ebb tide that afternoon. It was slow work coming in. Took an extra hour at least. There was a full moon so it was a king tide too. It was tricky coming back in through Lake Entrance.' He seemed to remember something. 'And we had to help a man and his boy. Their runabout engine had conked out and they were being dragged out to sea. We offered to tow them, which slowed us down even more.' He let out a short laugh. 'Ungrateful bastard he was, too. As soon as we reached the marina, he cranked his boat back onto his trailer and pissed off without even a thank you. That's gratitude for you!'

'Did you get a name?'

'No,' said Johnson.

'Can you remember the name of the boat or registration number?'

Johnson frowned. '*Dream Catcher* or *Dream Weaver*, something like that. Something about a dream. And the number was something like "OY1N". I remember thinking it sounded like an Irishman saying "Ian".'

Darling nodded to Jones, who snapped his notebook closed. 'Thank you, Mr Johnson,' said Darling. 'We will be checking these details.'

'Why?' asked the morgue attendant. 'Do you think I had something to do with murder while I was in Newcastle?'

'We'll see,' said Darling as they left.

CHAPTER TWENTY

JONES FOUND FRANK Naim in a panel-beating shop, just off Parramatta Road in Granville, an industrial suburb not far from Western Meadows. Naim had left a forwarding work address with hospital security and Jones was pleasantly surprised that he was so easy to track down. Naim was a thin young man of moderate height with neat hair and clean blue overalls who was crouched beside a convertible, working on the rear bumper. He didn't appear fazed by a uniformed policeman entering his premises and seemed happy to talk.

'Yes, I worked at the Meadows,' he said in answer to Jones's question. 'In the morgue. I left about two years ago.'

'Cutting up bodies not your cup of tea?' asked Jones, with a smile.

Naim smiled in return. 'It was a bit ghoulish but I didn't mind.' He waved a spanner around the workshop. 'This is not as interesting but it's better pay.' He put the spanner in a pocket. 'But what's this about?'

'Routine enquiry. I need to know whether you still have a key to the morgue.'

'Key?' Naim looked puzzled. 'Why would I have a key? I wouldn't have got my final pay if I hadn't returned it. You should check with hospital security.'

Jones scribbled something in his notebook. 'As I said, just a routine enquiry.' He looked up. 'How did you get on with your work colleagues?'

Naim seemed to become tense. 'Fine. Why?'

'Clive Johnson?'

'Yes, Clive.' Naim noticeably relaxed. 'Nice bloke. Never caused me any trouble. Another fellow replaced me. Don't know his name.'

'And Dr Banks?'

Naim hesitated before speaking. 'Why, what has she been up to?'

Jones was struck by the tone of Naim's reply – more curious than defensive. 'Why would you think Dr Banks would be up to something?'

Naim raised his hands. 'I'm not saying anything about anyone. I'm out of all that now.'

'Out of what?'

Naim paused again and studied Jones's face carefully. 'What's this all about?'

'I'm not at liberty to say,' said Jones. 'But if you know anything about suspicious or illegal behaviour you should tell me.'

Naim waved his hands. 'I have no proof about anything illegal.'

'Proof?'

'Look, I told you. I don't know anything. I didn't like working there, so I left. That's all I can say.'

Jones examined Naim carefully. He had a feeling he knew something but it was clear he would get no more out of him today. 'One other thing. Where were you on the evening of the Mardi Gras?'

'That's easy. I was at the Parramatta Speedway. I work in the pits with the sprint cars.'

'Do you have witnesses?'

'Are you kidding?' Naim grinned. 'Got your pen? I'll give you a list.'

Ahmed Mohammed was harder to find. The forwarding address he'd given the hospital was a house that had been demolished for the F4 motorway extension in 1989. To make matters worse, the name was common and there was a half a dozen of them listed on the clunky police database that had been recently introduced. None of those names matched the date of birth on the hospital records but Jones knew that meant nothing.

He was able to exclude two when he found that they were currently in jail. Another had an address listed in Queensland and he managed to find one more at a registered address in Auburn. When Jones knocked on his door, it was opened by an elderly gent in a wheelchair.

'Ahmed Mohammed?' asked Jones, his hopes receding.

'Yes.'

The fellow looked ancient. 'The Ahmed Mohammed involved in Medicare fraud in 1985?'

The old man was annoyed. 'Yes, but what's this all about? Can't you cops leave me alone? Can't you see I've suffered enough?'

Jones half-turned and let the screen door close. 'Sorry to bother you, sir. I was looking for someone who used to work at Western Meadows Hospital. My mistake.' Jones made his way back along the front path.

'What do you want?'

The new voice that came from the house was different, younger. Jones turned back, his hand still on the front gate. Inside the door was the shadow of a man standing behind the screen door.

'Are you Ahmed Mohammed?'

The shadow indicated the wheelchair-bound man. 'This is my father who I'm named after. I heard what you said. Why do you want to speak to me?'

'You used to work in the morgue?'

'Yes.'

Jones returned to the front door. Inside was a swarthy-looking fellow with a dark beard and a shaved head. He had tattoos on his neck and arms.

'We're making routine enquiries,' said Jones.

'Is this about the murders?' he asked coolly.

'You know about it?'

'It's in the papers.'

Jones tried to study the fellow, although his face was partially hidden by the shadows. He could make out his eyes – intense, calm. He didn't look afraid. 'I won't be able to help you,' said Ahmed. 'I left the hospital three years ago.'

'We're speaking to everyone who worked in the morgue in the last five years.' The fellow said nothing. 'Did you get on well with everyone?'

'Good enough. Weird place. Weird job. Bound to make people a bit weird.'

'You or them?'

He paused. 'Them.'

'What do you mean by weird?'

'Just that. They deal with death. They chop up dead bodies. Bound to make you see life differently. It's not healthy.'

'Is that why you left? Too weird?'

Ahmed hesitated, as if considering his words. 'Got a better job.'

'Where?'

'Bouncer at the Royal Oak.'

'Is that where you were the night of the Mardi Gras?'

Again, the fellow appeared to think before speaking. 'Yeah. Started a shift at ten. Didn't finish until after three.'

'Do you mind if I check with your boss?'

'Do what you like. It's a free country.' He stared at Jones. 'Anything else I can help you with, officer?'

'No,' said Jones. 'No, that will be all. For now.'

CHAPTER TWENTY-ONE

SENIOR DETECTIVE SERGEANT Royce Wills called a meeting the next day in the Parramatta station to discuss progress. Darling, Jones and Constable Bianca were in attendance. He faced them in the meeting room, half-sitting on the table towards them, his head bowed and eyes closed as they each reported what they'd found, like he was memorising every detail.

Finally, he raised a hand to call a halt to the reports and cleared his throat in preparation for his judgement. 'So we have Clive Johnson and his brother off the coast of Newcastle at the same time that the *Sintak-5* was steaming down the coast towards Sydney,' said Wills.

'I've checked Steve Johnson's record,' said Jones. 'He was in Maitland jail in 1982 for dealing in heroin. Six months. He's been clean since then but the locals have been keeping an eye on him. There's been a few investigations where he was taken in for questioning, but nothing stuck.'

'What about Clive? Any record?'

'A few speeding offences. Nothing else.'

'Does his story stack up?'

'Some of it,' said Jones. 'He was definitely witnessed leaving the Jensen's Point Marina on the Saturday morning in his brother's boat. The marina owner claims they returned at four in the afternoon. But Johnson's alibi does not stack up. He claims he helped rescue a fisherman and his son in a stranded runabout, caught in the outgoing tide. According to the registration number he gave us, the boat is owned by a,'

Jones read from his notes, 'Mr James Kerridge of Charlestown. The boat was called *Dream Runner*. But Mr Kerridge says he wasn't even in the country on that day, let alone on Lake Macquarie. He was on an oil rig in Bass Strait. And he doesn't have a son. Lives by himself.'

'Good work, Jones,' said Wills.

'Thank you, sir.' He threw a guilty look at Darling.

'What about the other morgue attendant?' asked Wills. He glanced up at the names on the corkboard. 'Quentin Boon? Does his story stack up?'

''Yes, sir,' said Jones. 'Several witnesses attest to him being part of the parade in the city. I ID'd him myself on a video tape of it. Just like he said.' Jones raised his arms above his head. 'Angel wings.'

'Doesn't mean he's not tied up in it, if this is a heroin racket,' insisted Darling.

Wills raised a finger. 'True, but not murder, and that's our focus right now.'

'Yes, sir,' mumbled Darling, trying not to sound sullen.

Wills looked at the corkboard again. 'Keys,' he read, then swivelled to Darling. 'Are they all accounted for?'

Jones answered instead. 'Yes, sir. I checked back over the last few years and all keys had been returned by previous employees. There are three keys – one each for Johnson, Boon and Dr Banks. I also checked on the two morgue attendants who left in the last few years. Frank Naim checks out. The other one, Ahmed Mohammed, is a bit shifty. I'm in the process of checking his alibi but he definitely returned his key.'

'Do it,' ordered Wills. 'Leave no stone unturned.'

Jones continued uncertainly. 'There is another thing, sir.' He looked at Darling then back to Wills. 'I haven't been able to discuss this with Detective Darling but both Mohammed and Naim gave me a feeling that something is not quite right in the morgue.'

'What do you mean?'

'They refused to say anything specific but one hinted about possible illegal activity and the other said that the work environment was ...' Jones paused.

'Was what?' demanded Wills.

'Weird, sir.'

'Weird.' Wills gave a satisfied nod. 'Right. Good,' he said. 'I think that fits nicely.' He raised his arms as if was making a proclamation. 'I'm satisfied we have everything we need.' He closed his eyes and leaned back on the table, both palms resting on the surface. 'This is what I think happened. The Johnson brothers met the *Sintak-5* off the coast of Newcastle in the Bertram and picked up a shipment of heroin. The Bertram is big enough to easily carry a drug load. They bring it back to Lake Macquarie and then one or both of them drive it down here on the night of the Mardi Gras.' Wills flicked a finger at Bianca. 'We have to check what sort of vehicles they have. It needs to be big enough to carry the booty.'

'Steve Johnson has a Nissan Patrol,' volunteered Jones. 'A 4.2-litre diesel.'

Wills nodded as if he'd expected it and closed his eyes again. 'For some reason, they bring it here and store it in the lockers before they distribute it. Probably consider the hospital a safe haven.' He paused, eyes still closed as if he were praying. Then he continued, his voice slow and thoughtful. 'Then that night they were disturbed, first by the nurse. She could've been lost and was walking through the wrong part of the hospital.'

'Poor girl,' said Bianca, shaking her head. 'Wrong place, wrong time.'

Wills opened one eye and glared at her as if she'd interrupted his train of thought. She dropped her head sheepishly and pretended to study her notes.

Wills continued. 'Then the other two came upon them, the priest and the cleaner. They stabbed the priest in the morgue. There would have been blood everywhere but they were able to clean it up. Then they threw the cleaner out of the window.'

'Why stab the priest and not the cleaner?' asked Jones. 'Why not stab them both?'

Wills nodded his head solemnly, as if Jones had made a good point. He closed his eyes reflectively, as if to emphasise the great computation that was taking place in his forensic brain. His eyes snapped open. 'The priest's body and the knife were already on their way to the chapel. They had no weapon to use so they had to improvise.'

Darling said, 'It's a bit complicated, isn't it? Throwing him out of a window. They took a great risk being seen.'

'They were obviously improvising,' said Wills. 'They knew they couldn't hide the bodies so they had to make sure all the evidence led us anywhere else but the morgue.'

'There's something that worries me,' said Darling.

Wills pursed his lips and raised his eyebrows indulgently. 'And that is?'

'Something the old lady said. She said she saw aliens chasing an Asian man.'

'Well, they were probably dressed in theatre gear. She mistook them as aliens. Or the more likely explanation is that she's a demented old lady and imagined the whole thing. I think it has no relevance to this case.'

'But if they were wearing theatre gear,' Darling persisted, 'why didn't she say they were doctors or nurses or something like that? Why aliens? There must have been something about their appearance that looked unusual. You know, out of this world.'

'Really, Detective Darling,' said Wills, 'is that the sort of nonsense you accept as evidence? The prattling of a demented old woman? Where is the logic in that? You did a good job with the Chee murder, Darling, but now I'm beginning to think it was a fluke.'

Darling was stern. 'With all due respect, sir, I think it's logical –'

'That will be all, detective,' interrupted Wills. 'What I need now is for you to focus. We've two suspects, Clive and Steven Johnson. We've a motive, heroin smuggling, we've the method, and Clive Johnson definitely has the means. All evidence points to at least two of the murders taking place in the hospital morgue and that one of the bodies was stored there. We've traces of heroin in the bag that contained the murdered nurse's discarded uniform and we've traces of the same drug in Clive Johnson's locker. Both Clive and Steven Johnson admit to being off the coast of Newcastle at the same time as the *Sintak-5*, which was en route from Thailand, a country known to be major source of illegal heroin supply. A sailor on the *Sintak-5* who had arranged to meet with you was murdered before he could speak to you. If this is not an open and shut case, I don't know what is.'

Darling stood stock-still, his face blank. For some moments, he didn't answer. Finally he dropped his head. 'Yes, sir. I have to agree with you. It *is* a watertight case. I'll get right onto it.' He motioned to his offsider. 'Jones. Draw up the arrest warrants.'

CHAPTER TWENTY-TWO

THE HOMICIDE SQUAD arrived at Johnson's weatherboard house in Toongabbie, a modest suburb near Western Meadows Hospital, at six on Friday morning. Senior Detective Sergeant Royce Wills led five officers wearing bulletproof jackets, ably aided by members of the Special Weapons and Operations Section. A police helicopter hovered overhead.

It was a fresh morning, cooler than the previous week's stifling heat, and the sun was already up, illuminating the cloudless eggshell sky above them. Darling and Jones had been excluded from the operation for 'operational reasons', and they looked on from a short way up the street, standing on the neatly trimmed grass verge of one of the neighbouring homes, morning dew still on the ground.

The SWOS team knocked in the front door to allow the armed officers to surge through the house and a short time later a handcuffed Clive Johnson was led out through the door, dressed in shorts and a T-shirt and looking as if he'd been rudely awakened. The operation had been timed to occur at the same time as an identical one in Newcastle, which would apprehend Johnson's brother, Stephen.

Clive Johnson was guided into the back seat of a police car, looking dazed and confused. Within moments he was whisked away, leaving the team to go through the house for evidence at their leisure.

'Looked like a pretty neat operation,' said Jones.

Darling made a rude noise with his lips. 'Johnson certainly doesn't give the impression that he's a master criminal. The whole thing smells of overkill to me.' He jerked a thumb into the air. 'A helicopter, for fuck's sake. What were they expecting?'

'Detective Wills is meticulous, if nothing else,' said a female voice behind and they spun around to see Thelma Bianca, neatly dressed in uniform with her blonde hair tucked under her cap, her young face fresh and unadorned by makeup. 'Never leaves anything to chance. It's why he has such a high arrest rate.'

'I would have thought that conviction rate would be more important,' said Darling, although he immediately regretted it. It sounded petty.

'How come you're not in on it?' asked Jones.

Bianca twisted up her nose. 'Wills said he wanted experienced men on the job. Men he could trust.' She spoke plainly but Darling could sense her frustration.

He turned back to the house, which now had blue and white checked tape draped across the front fence and door. 'Looks like all the action's over.' He turned back to the junior officers. 'Shall we go for coffee?'

Thirty minutes later they'd arranged themselves around a small table on the footpath outside an Italian restaurant on George Street in Parramatta. Darling had ordered them all cappuccinos.

Both junior officers had taken off their headwear and were staring out at the morning traffic, appearing uncomfortable. Initially, Darling thought it was him that made them uneasy, but when he noticed Jones and Bianca surreptitiously glancing at the other, he deduced the real reason. Darling smiled to himself, and for some reason, the irritating gnaw in his stomach caused by Wills blatantly stealing all the kudos seemed to lessen.

'So, Thelma, are you married?' he asked pointedly. Jones's head snapped towards him but Darling ignored the scowl.

She took a long sip of her cappuccino before she answered. 'No, and before you ask, I don't have anyone special.'

'What a coincidence,' Darling said mischievously. 'The same goes for Jones.' He smiled at Jones but his scowl only deepened and Darling was sure his ears had turned red. He addressed Bianca again. 'Where do you live?'

'Leichhardt.'

'Inner city. Great. Jones here lives at …' Darling's brow knitted. 'Where *do* you live, Jones? I've forgotten.'

'You've never asked, sir,' he grumbled, then addressed Thelma. 'I live in Hunters Hill.'

'Lah-de-dah,' said Darling, throwing a wide grin at Bianca, inviting her to join in. 'North Shore, eh? So did you go to one of those fancy private schools? Joeys? Kings? Scots?'

'Saint Ignatius,' Jones said in a low voice.

'Riverview?' Thelma gushed. 'I went to Loreto.'

'Really?' said Jones, becoming more animated. 'That's at Kirribilli,' he said to Darling.

'I know where Loreto is,' Darling said sullenly. 'I grew up in The Rocks across the harbour.'

But the two young officers now ignored him completely as they leaned towards each other and launched into a long conversation about friends they might have in common, teachers they'd had, school excursions and the like. In a short time, they discovered they'd finished school the same year.

Darling slumped back in his chair, all the fun having gone now the couple were getting on so well. He glanced glumly up and down the street, which was slowly filling with pedestrians as one by one the shops opened. His thoughts drifted back to the arrest. All the evidence pointed to Clive Johnson being involved – the drug remnants in his locker, the fact that he was on call the night of the murder, his means of access to the *Sintak-5*, which almost certainly had transported the heroin from Thailand to Sydney. But it just didn't feel right. And to cap it all off, that wanker Wills was taking all the credit for the work he'd put in. *Well, me and Jones.* He looked over at the young officer who was now smiling and talking eloquently with Thelma. What was it with these private school kids? It was like a club. A club he'd never been a member of. He'd gone to Fort Street High, admittedly selective, but still a state-funded school. Same as Chris Walker. They were never in the same league as these private school kids. Even now, years out of school, they still got the best jobs. He scowled to himself. *I bet my left testicle that Wills was a snotty-nosed private school prick.*

'What?' said Jones. The pair were giving him a quizzical look.

'What?' said Darling, acting dumb, but realising he must have spoken aloud.

'Did you say something about your testicle?' Jones and Bianca were both wearing childish grins.

Darling pulled out his wallet. 'All right, you two. Time to get to work. I'll pay.' Now he felt like a grumpy uncle chaperoning two teenagers.

The young officers went back to their chitchat but Thelma broke away again as Darling was pulling out a twenty dollar note. 'Detective Darling, do you realise that we both went to the same high-school dance?' She was beaming with wonder. 'We were in the same room. We might have actually been dancing next to each other.' Her smile focussed on Jones, who returned it with the same childish awe.

Darling ignored them as he pushed his chair back and went to the counter to pay, his stinking mood having now returned.

CHAPTER TWENTY-THREE

WHEN ANGELA PULLED up her Honda Accord in front of Walker's terrace in Lower Fort Street just after eight that Saturday morning, the temperature was already in the high twenties. Walker appeared at the door wearing an old pair of Crystal Cylinder board shorts and a T-shirt.

'It's going to be a scorcher.' He smiled. 'I'm glad you came early. We'll have a chance to find parking.'

Angela wore a loose white cotton dress that revealed a floral bikini beneath it. She had a large straw beach bag on her shoulder and a floppy sunhat on her head. She gave him a shy kiss on the cheek, which he attempted to return but mistimed and ended up kissing her on the ear instead. They both laughed.

'Okay, that's the awkwardness over and done with,' she said, still smiling. 'Shall we go?'

There was already traffic as they drove through Bondi Junction and Walker was glad when most cars turned off down Bondi Road. Walker took the next major road left and snaked his way down the hill towards the coast. Instead of trying to make it all the way to the beach, which he knew would already be full of cars bustling for a spot, he made his way to his secret spot on a back road over Tamarama gully. From there it was a short walk down stairs and through a park to the beach.

They picked a spot on the left side of the wide sandy crescent towards the rocks and threw their towels down on the already hot sand. It was a glorious day and the surf was good, but not so large as to close the beach.

'Do you bodysurf?' he asked. He was itching to get into the water.

'No, but you're welcome to. I'll get a bit of sun.'

He pulled off his T-shirt, kicked his thongs onto the sand then raced down to the water. The waves were perfect for bodysurfing and he spent the next forty-five minutes swimming out through the waves and catching them in. He was good at it and could often get on the waves faster and go longer than the other swimmers. There was another fellow a few years older than him nearby, who also knew what he was doing and they spent some time in companionable pleasure catching the waves, never speaking but often smiling to each other at the end of a particularly good run.

Walker caught a large wave and for some moments was in the barrel before it broke. He rode it all the way to the shore then stood up and looked in Angela's direction, hoping she'd seen him. But to his consternation, she wasn't looking at him at all. Her attention was captured by a man kneeling beside her, engaging her in conversation. She was on her stomach, but even from the water's edge he could tell she was topless. She was smiling.

Walker made his way, dripping and puffing up the beach towards her. As he neared, the fellow glanced up at him and Angela turned her head and upper body to see him, which had the effect of showing off her naked chest to the man. He was sure the fellow glanced down at her before Angela lay back down. She grabbed a top from her bag and pulled it on, then sat up.

The fellow stood up and smiled. He was larger than Walker and had a rugged look. Then Walker realised who he was.

'Vince?' he said.

'Dr Walker.'

He immediately felt a lot better. The fellow may be bigger and better-looking, but Walker was his boss. 'What are you doing here?'

'Same as you, I expect. Trying to dodge the heat. I saw Angela lying here and I couldn't believe it. Do you live around here?'

'No. I live in the city.'

'*In* the city. Who lives *in* the city? What do you live in, an office building?' He laughed as if he'd made a clever joke.

'The Rocks, actually.'

'Oh.' The young doctor made a face then screwed up his forehead thoughtfully. 'Aren't they all housing commission places?'

'Not all,' Walker said coolly. 'And you? Where do you live?'

'Coogee. Near New South Wales Uni.'

'I thought you went to Sydney Uni?'

'I did. I still play rugby for them.'

'How are your Wallaby aspirations going?'

'This is the big year. Sink or swim. I either make it into the national team or I knuckle down and become a real doctor.'

'Well, good luck with it.' Walker smiled and said nothing more, hoping Vince would get the hint.

'Well, I'll leave you to it.' Vince waved to Angela then walked away towards the rocks at the side of the beach, and Walker was relieved to see him join a pretty blonde girl who looked his type. Beautiful, he thought smugly, but no match for Angela.

'How was your swim?' she asked.

'Refreshing. You should've come in.'

'I'm happy here. I love the feeling of the sun on my skin.'

'You can go back to it if you like. Sorry to interrupt.'

Angela smiled cheekily. 'You just want to see me with my top off.'

Walker was about to disagree but he caught himself. After a pause, he said, 'Of course I do. You're beautiful. I *do* want to see you topless.'

Angela said nothing and continued to smile. After a moment she pulled her top slowly over her head and threw it onto the sand. She raised her eyebrows. 'Well?'

Walker gave an exaggerated nod of approval. 'Mmm. Acceptable.'

'You've seen me naked before, you know.'

'Yes, but not in full sunlight.' He made a point of examining her from top to bottom. 'I wish I had your skin.'

Angela rolled her eyes. 'Now you're going too far,' she said, but Walker could tell she was pleased.

They lay on their bellies on the towels next to each other and Walker welcomed the feeling of the sun drying him. He put his head on his arms and turned towards Angela and she did the same. She closed her eyes, a contented smile on her lips.

Walker relaxed his mind and allowed himself to daydream. Shortly after, he became aware of a group of friends talking nearby.

'How did you go last night?' a woman asked.

'You wouldn't believe what happened to me,' said a man.

'I saw you leaving the pub with Janet. You've always had a thing for her. Did you two do it?'

'Well,' said the young man slowly, 'I'd had a bit to drink.'

'So you couldn't get it up,' another girl snickered.

'No, that wasn't the problem.'

'What then?'

'We were halfway home when she went for me.'

'While you were driving?'

'Yeah. She had my pants down and … well, you know.'

'Wow!'

'I thought we should stop and I pulled up in that park near Bronte – you know the place.'

'Yeah. And?'

'Well, we found a nice spot in the bushes. But when I finally got her knickers off, I realised I was busting for a piss.'

'Err, don't tell me! You didn't, did you?'

'That's disgusting,' said the other girl.

'No, of course not. I walked off to take a leak in the bushes but there was some sort of bog there. My leg disappeared up to the knee in this disgusting pond of crap.'

'Yuck!'

'I managed to pull myself out … but it really stunk. When I finally got back to her, she started gagging.' One of the girls laughed. 'No, I mean it!' he continued in a disbelieving voice. 'She actually vomited.'

The other girl also laughed. 'You idiot.'

'How to spoil the mood,' said the first girl.

'Then she wanted me to drive her home but when we reached the car, she said I still stunk. She got a taxi. I don't think she'll want to see me again.'

The two girls laughed hysterically.

Walker opened his eyes and saw that Angela, too, was having a quiet chuckle. Her head was close to his and she was looking into his eyes. 'Do you want to go for a swim?'

They hurried together over the hot sand and were glad to get their feet in the water, where they waded out until it was just above their knees.

'Oh, the water's cold,' said Angela.

'It's warm when you get used to it,' said Walker, although he had to stifle a grimace when the thrashing water hit his abdomen. Then, just to show how it was done, he dived through the next wave and swam a few strokes out until the water was up to his neck.

He turned. Angela was holding her arms out, her fingers splayed like a Balinese dancer as whitewater crashed against her thighs.

'Coming in?' he called.

She squealed like a little girl as she jumped through the next wave, clasping her arms together over her bikini top to stop it coming off. Then, to his surprise, she dived through the next wave and quickly swam out to him.

'Show me how to bodysurf,' she demanded when she reached him, beaming, seemingly exhilarated by the cold water.

'Sure, but we have to go out further.'

They swam out and Walker stopped with a handful of other swimmers just where the waves were breaking.

'You have to pick the wave,' he said. 'Like this next one.' The wave was larger than the last and he estimated it would break just after the spot where they were treading water. He let it go past. 'Just before it comes, you've got to swim and kick like hell to get up the speed. When you feel the wave moving you forward, put your arm out in front and the other hard down by your side. You need to stay in the wave. Don't let it spit you too far forward.'

The next wave came and Walker did as he'd instructed and bodysurfed towards the shore, then did a forward tumble to get off the wave just before it turned to mush. Underwater, he spiralled back out to sea and broke the surface doing freestyle back out to Angela. 'Now you try.'

She missed the next wave but caught the one after, and Walker was impressed that she did just as he'd said and made it close to the shore. She swam back out, grinning with childlike delight.

'I did it! The only problem is my top came off.' She didn't seem particularly concerned, having put everything back in its rightful place.

'Wear a rash shirt next time.'

They spent the next thirty minutes bodysurfing. Finally they left the water together, dripping, and trudged back to their towels, which they collected and kept moving to the grassed area beyond the sand. Angela sat at one of the tables near the cafe, shaded by an umbrella, while Walker got a couple of coffees. They sat together looking out at the surf as they dried off.

Walker glanced at Angela, taking in her slim figure, olive skin and long, glistening dark hair. She'd donned a short top but still wore her bikini bottoms. Her toenails were painted red.

How had they drifted apart? Her father's death had undoubtedly complicated matters. And there was still the issue of her throwing away a bag of drugs. Had she intended to kill her father but backed out at the last minute? Or had she been involved in the murder? No, he couldn't believe that. All he knew was he wanted to get to know her better.

'What are you doing tonight?' He'd tried to be nonchalant but she looked away, uneasy. It certainly wasn't the reaction he'd wanted.

She gazed towards the rocky headland, avoiding his eyes. 'Oh, I'm going out to the pub.'

'Who with?' He realised how he sounded then tried to cover his abrupt words. 'I mean ...' He smiled sheepishly. 'Are you going out with Cassie?'

Now she looked at him with a frown. 'No,' she said tightly. 'Why Cassie?'

'Nothing. I don't know. I was just asking.'

'If you must know, I'm having a drink with Craig Blinkton.'

Walker was stunned. 'Blinkers! You're actually going out with him?'

'Why not?' she snapped. 'He asked me. You were there.'

'Yes, but I thought you were only being polite. Blinkers!' he repeated. 'But he's not your type.'

Angela let out a terse laugh. 'Not my type? So you know all about me, do you? What is my type then?'

Me, he wanted to say, but instead, 'Well, not a buffoon like Craig Blinkton. He's a helicopter doctor, of all things!'

'I find that very interesting, thank you very much. Much more interesting than stuck-up surgeons and high-and-mighty physicians, if you must know.'

They'd raised their voices and a few people seated at neighbouring tables were looking at them. Walker leaned in closer and dropped his voice. 'I'm not high and mighty.'

'Who said I was talking about you?'

He leaned back in exasperation and stared wordlessly towards the breaking waves on the shore. Then he stood up stiffly. 'Well, we'd better get back then. You'll want to get ready for tonight.'

Angela stood quickly, grabbed her things and without waiting, began to retrace their route back to the car. Walker followed a few paces behind but caught up to her when she stopped for cars at the road. In the park opposite the beach they walked uneasily, side by side, neither looking at the other.

Finally he said, 'Angela, I'm sorry about the way I reacted.' He spoke softly and kept his eyes forward. He wanted to tell her the truth. 'I was going to ask you out to dinner – to the Thai restaurant in Epping – and I was disappointed that you couldn't join me.'

She walked silently until they reached the steps that would take them up to the car. Then she said, 'Well, I'm sorry I reacted as I did as well. It would have been nice to go to dinner with you.' She stopped on one of the concrete steps. He could feel the heat rising through the soles of his sandals. 'Perhaps we can do it another time.' She dropped her eyes. 'I'm … I'm sorry now that I'm going out with Craig. If I'd only known …'

'Sure.' Walker looked away. 'Another time. Bad timing, that's all.'

He felt her fingers on his chin, guiding his head towards hers. Then he felt her lips on his. He stood still, eyes closed, savouring the moment, not wanting to ruin it. Finally, he couldn't help himself and he cradled her head in his hands and kissed her more passionately. She returned with equal vigour for a moment before breaking away.

'I need to get back,' she gasped.

She turned quickly and left him standing on the stairs.

CHAPTER TWENTY-FOUR

IT WAS EARLY afternoon by the time they reached Walker's terrace, and Angela immediately left, saying she had a few things to do. It had been an uncomfortable trip home with neither of them speaking, both lost in their own thoughts. Walker stood at the gate as she drove away. A few things to do? Get ready for her big date with Blinkton, in other words.

There was no breeze and the air was stifling, so he walked through his front door, aiming to grab a beer from the fridge. But straightaway he knew something was wrong. In the front room, the cushions had been pulled off the lounge and the loose change in the jar he kept on the mantelpiece was scattered on the fire hearth. However, the television was not stolen. The kitchen was equally a mess and he noticed the back window was wide open. He went upstairs and all the drawers in the bedroom were pulled open and clothes strewn across the floor. In the other small room he used as an office, the desk drawers had been pulled out and turned over onto the floor. A bowl of loose change was still full of coins and small notes. As far as he could tell, nothing had been stolen.

Walker shrugged. It didn't make sense. He'd been broken into many times, usually by druggies, and the first thing to go would be the TV, video and any money. He walked out onto the veranda and looked up and down the street, seeing no one except a boy kicking a soccer ball.

The phone on his bedside table rang and initially he ignored it, then reluctantly went inside to answer it. He picked up the handset with a sinking feeling, hoping it was not Cassandra. It was Darling. He said he needed to meet Walker that evening. Something he wanted to talk about. He was taking Cassandra out that night and hoped Walker could meet him at the Epping pub beforehand.

'I've just been broken into,' said Walker. 'Got in through the back window.'

'Anything stolen?'

'No, that's the strange thing. Nothing.'

'You probably disturbed them. They were probably going out the back window as you were coming in the front.'

'Maybe,' said Walker. But it didn't seem right. They hadn't even taken the money. He decided he didn't want to talk to Darling about it. He was a copper but wouldn't be bothered with a break-in where nothing was stolen. Walker decided he wouldn't even bother the local cops. 'Probably just kids,' he said.

'Probably,' Darling agreed. 'God knows *we* did it enough.'

Walker grunted a noncommittal reply. He didn't want to talk about the 'old days' with Darling. 'Okay, I'll meet you at the pub.'

Later, as Walker drove along Victoria Road, he wondered what it could be that Wendy wanted from him. Something about the murders perhaps? Probably not. Maybe something about Felicity. If it was, he decided he'd finally have it out with him. It was no business of Darling's. Walker didn't care whether he'd secretly loved her or not. Flea was *his* wife. He owed Darling nothing.

He turned off Victoria Road at West Ryde and, as he wound along the road that ran along the railway, he became convinced it was Felicity that Wendy wanted to talk about. He began to feel aggressive, shoving the gears up and down roughly as he took the corners. Tonight, Wendy would finally get what was coming to him.

But as he parked his BMW, Walker had a sudden revelation that it might not be about Felicity at all. He turned off the engine and sat staring blankly out of the front window at the other cars in the carpark. He realised Wendy might want to talk about Cassandra. All the anger abruptly disappeared. Now he felt an overriding sense of guilt. And something more. Remorse.

He trudged slowly up the back steps of the Epping pub and as soon as he got to the top, he saw Darling at a tall table close to the bar. He was wearing tight white jeans and a striped Lacoste polo top, making Walker feel underdressed in his checked shirt and stone-washed jeans. By the time he reached him, Darling had got them both a beer.

Walker was thankful that he began to talk about the murder case. 'Clive Johnson and his brother are in custody. We've a pretty good case against them.' Darling told him how they thought they'd met the *Sintak-5* off the coast of New South Wales in Steve Johnson's boat, taken the drugs back to Newcastle and then by car to Western Meadows to hide them before delivery. The murders happened at the hospital because their movements were accidently observed by the poor victims. 'All three in the wrong place at the wrong time,' he concluded.

'Sounds like an open and shut case,' Walker said grimly. He didn't say it, but he was just thankful that Angela had nothing to do with it. He couldn't see how she could have, but she did have a habit of coming across dead bodies in suspicious circumstances.

'Seems like it,' Darling agreed morosely.

'You don't sound very happy about it. I thought Wills would have been pleased with you.'

'Senior Detective Sergeant Royce Wills, if you please,' he corrected in a mocking tone. 'He's trying to take the credit, of course. But that's not what's bugging me.' He frowned. 'I just don't believe that Clive Johnson would be mixed up in all of this. He doesn't seem the type.'

'Who else then? The other morgue attendant apparently had a great alibi.'

Now Darling looked uneasy. He stared into his beer glass but didn't drink. 'Quentin Boon? Yes, he did have an alibi. A good one. He was in the Mardi Gras parade. We have a video.'

'Oh?' said Walker. He shifted in his seat, took a swig of his beer and looked around the bar.

'Yes. Says he saw you there.'

'Me?' He frowned as if he was trying to recall. 'He might have done. I was there, all right.' He drained his glass then pointed to Darling's half-empty schooner. 'Want another?'

Darling ignored the request. 'Says you were there with a girl. Good-looking. Sexy.'

'Oh?' Walker pulled his mouth down, as if he was giving the idea considerable thought. 'There were plenty of women there.' He gave a short laugh. 'You know what it's like. The gays attract good-looking women like bees to a honeypot, for some reason.'

Darling faced him squarely. 'Swears she was a blonde. Last time I looked, Angela has dark hair.'

Walker leaned back and slowly shook his head. 'Wasn't Angela. As a matter of fact, Cassandra asked me to take her.' He picked up his glass to take another swig but put it back down when he saw it was empty. 'We were both free so I said yes. Didn't she mention it to you? You were busy, as I recall. Angela was working. But you'd remember that.'

'He said she was all over you like a rash.'

'What! Cassie? Wendy, that's ridiculous.' Walker stood and picked up his glass, ready to go to the bar. He tried to sound nonchalant. 'He obviously got that wrong. Must have been thinking of someone else.' He gestured with his empty glass. 'Why don't you ask Cassie?'

'I will,' Darling said gruffly.

Just then, Cassandra came through the door wearing a sheer grey dress that looked more like an undergarment. As usual, heads turned as she threaded her way through the crowded bar.

'I was just asking Kit here,' said Darling without preamble when she reached their table, 'whether you were together at the Mardi Gras.'

She gave a wide smile and kissed Darling on the cheek. 'Oh?' she said coolly, glancing at Walker. 'And what did he say?'

'I'd be more interested in what you've got to say,' answered Darling, equally cool.

She didn't bother to look at Walker again. 'Why yes, we were there together. I asked him to take me. I didn't want to go alone and both you and Angela were working. Didn't I mention it to you?'

'No, you didn't.'

'Didn't I? Oh well.' She looked around the room, as if the conversation was of no consequence. 'You did get mixed up in those murders straight afterwards, I suppose.' Her attention returned to the two men. 'Are either of you going to buy me a drink?'

Walker stood. 'I was just going for another.' He was glad to get away. 'Chardonnay?'

As he stood at the bar, he peeked back at them. They seemed deep in conversation and Darling looked serious but not angry. Walker wished he knew what she was saying. He realised he was a hopeless liar but he had a feeling that Cassandra was an old hand at it. She was resting her delicate fingers on Darling's shoulder and had her thigh pressed against his as they spoke. Walker turned back to get the barman's attention, wishing he'd never slept with her.

When he got back, they were talking about the band they were going to see later that night – a Midnight Oil tribute band at the Tracks nightclub downstairs. Walker breathed a silent sigh of relief. Disaster averted, for the moment at least! Now would have been a good time to disappear, but he'd already got himself another beer, as well as one for Darling and a wine for Cassandra. Now he'd have to stay until he'd finished. He gulped a large mouthful but it tasted bitter on his tongue.

'What's Angela up to?' Cassandra asked. 'How come you're not out with her?'

'She's on a date,' he said, happy to tell them. Maybe they'd feel sorry for him.

'A date?' said Darling. 'Who with?'

'Blinkers, can you believe it?'

Instead of being suitably astounded, Darling merely smirked. 'That's right. He did ask her out that time in the hospital cafeteria.'

'I thought she was only being polite,' Walker grumbled.

'She seemed to like him.'

Walker refused to answer, knowing Darling was just trying to be nasty. He felt a jab of anger and almost blurted out what Darling's own girlfriend got up to, but he stopped himself. Instead, he looked down at his watch. 'Time to go.'

But before he could move away, someone joined them from behind. 'Wendy! Kit! Great to see you.'

Craig Blinkton stood at the table, smiling like a Cheshire cat with Angela beside him, her eyes dropped glumly. They were holding hands and Walker looked meaningfully at Angela's enclosed in Blinkton's big fist, then up at her face. She lifted her eyes to him then pulled her lips into a tight line. 'What are you doing here?' she asked in a low voice.

Blinkton's smile grew even wider. 'Lovely for us to all be here together. Just like old times.' He made a show of looking around. 'Where's your date, Kit?' Then his attention fell onto Cassandra. 'And who are you, beautiful?'

'Cassandra Hollows.' She smiled widely and held out her hand for him to shake but he leaned forward formally and kissed the back of it.

'Craig Blinkton, at your service.' Walker rolled his eyes when Blinkton snapped his heels together, raising his body to attention. 'I'm an emergency doctor on the helicopters. I save lives.'

Darling mouthed a silent obscenity and shook his head.

'You all coming to the see the band?' Blinkton continued. 'It should be great fun.'

'I'm off,' Walker said loudly before anyone could say another word. He gave a vague wave towards the group then shouted stiffly above the noise, 'See you all another time.' He gave Angela another look, then turned on his heel and pushed his way out through the crowd.

CHAPTER TWENTY-FIVE

THE TASTE OF India was a small restaurant on the corner of Bridge Road and Glebe Point Road, and that Monday night, Sally Biggs and Darling pushed open the door into a wall of curry, sweaty heat and voices raised in conversation. The spices stung his eyes and nose, and Darling heard Sally's rasping cough behind him. He was already sweating when they'd arrived because they were late and had walked at a fast pace down the hill to the restaurant. But the heat and humidity in the air gave him the sensation that he was directly inhaling an old man's armpit, one who dined exclusively on cumin and turmeric. His first thought was that they should leave and find a quiet bar up the street.

Sally was suitably attired in a singlet, shorts and sandals but, trying to impress, Darling had worn jeans and a long-sleeved shirt. Now he wished he hadn't. He could feel the sweat already pooling in his groin.

Evan Roberts was towards the back of the restaurant at a table with about a dozen others, and he caught sight of them immediately and beckoned them over. Too late to back out! Darling had subconsciously taken Sally's hand when they'd entered and he now led her as they threaded their way through the throng. Halfway to the table, he realised what he'd done and looked down at his hand then at Sally sheepishly. She just smiled. To his surprise, it felt right.

He'd invited Sally on the spur of the moment when he'd seen her on the Sunday afternoon, the day after he had been out with Cassandra. All through the evening at the pub and nightclub, Cassandra had been distant with him, flirting outrageously with Craig Blinkton. He hadn't spent the night with her.

Roberts had reserved them a place opposite each other at the end of the table and he and Sally sat down on flimsy fold-up chairs, the type often used in community halls.

'We've already ordered,' said a white-haired woman with a thin face and cultured voice to his side. 'Are either of you vegetarian?'

'No,' said Darling, raising his hands. 'I eat anything.'

'I'm vegetarian,' said Sally.

'You are?' Darling asked incredulously.

The woman smirked. 'You know each other?' She laughed. 'No problem. We ordered vego just in case. Lentils and another dish with red kidney beans.'

'Yum,' said Sally.

'I'm Charlotte Smithson, the Glebe Society secretary. Welcome aboard.'

Darling had brought a two-litre cask of Yalumba Chardonnay and poured Sally and himself a glass. He offered some to Charlotte but she declined, pouring herself a measure from a bottle in an ice bucket behind her. As far as Darling could tell, it was some sort of foreign thing, maybe French by the name. He raised his eyebrows at Sally who made a face in return. They seemed to share the same thought. Imported bottled wine! Maybe they were out of their league.

They were introduced to Charlotte's husband, a philosophy professor at Sydney Uni, and another Asian-looking couple by the name of Ruben and Iris Lee. Ruben was next to Sally and therefore diagonally opposite Darling. They were on the end of the table and with the noise of the restaurant, Darling realised it would be difficult to engage the rest of the group in any meaningful conversation. Soon after, Ruben became engrossed in a conversation with the professor, and Iris started to talk to Charlotte about society business, so Darling resigned himself to the fact that he and Sally would have to provide their own entertainment. Again, he wished they were somewhere else. A subdued bar would be perfect, maybe with soft jazz playing in the background so they could talk.

'How's the house hunting going?' asked Sally. 'Any leads?'

'Not yet. Been too busy with work.' He glanced along the table and everyone else seemed to be ignoring them. 'How about you? Dreaming of Armidale?'

'Maybe,' she said, a bit too seriously for Darling's liking. 'This thing with Alice has thrown me. I'm not sure I like living in Sydney. I'm thinking of going back.'

'Armidale!' Darling felt like he'd been hit with a hammer. He was dismayed that she might leave, but at the same time bewildered that he should care so much. He'd only just met her. He didn't know what to say. 'But –'

'I hear you're a police officer,' interrupted Ruben from Sally's side. His spoke slowly and with a slight stutter.

Darling turned his attention to him. 'Yes, at Parramatta.' He felt as if he was a robot, his thoughts still on Sally's revelation.

'Very important job,' said Ruben. His voice was cultured Asian-English, as if he was born in Asia somewhere but had gone to a public school in England or private school in Australia. Australia probably, thought Darling, still in a haze. The man had an Australian accent.

Ruben was talking again. 'Where I come from, the police have a very hard time. We don't know how good we have it here in Australia. Australians are so law-abiding, despite all their so-called larrikinism.'

'Where are you from?'

'Papua New Guinea. From Wewak. Do you know where that is?' He continued when it was clear that Darling did not. 'North coast, up towards the Indonesian border. It's fairly safe there. But in other areas, like the highlands, it's becoming pretty hairy.'

His wife, Iris, had overheard and joined in. Darling had a feeling it was one of their favourite topics. 'The *raskols*,' she said. 'They're getting worse and worse every year since independence. And Port Moresby!' She rolled her eyes. 'You may as well beg to be killed! Living in compounds. Needing personal guards. What sort of life is that?'

'You're from PNG?' was all Darling could say.

'Well, originally,' Ruben explained. 'My family has a business in Wewak. But I went to school here in Sydney. We go back every year.'

'Do you know the highlands?' Darling asked, suddenly interested. 'Southwest of Mount Hagen?'

'A little. It's very dangerous there. But the cultural shows are something to be seen. Mount Hagen, Goroka. They're quite an experience.'

'I had a friend,' said Darling. 'A woman. She died in the highlands. South of Mount Michael. Do you know it?'

Ruben shook his head. 'I've been through there but don't know it very well. How did she die? Hold-up on the road?'

'Drowned.'

'Drowned!'

'You seem surprised.'

'Not many foreigners drown in New Guinea. That sounds very strange. How did it happen?'

Darling felt as if a heavy mantle had fallen onto his shoulders. Even a native of the country found it hard to believe Felicity had drowned. It was just as he'd suspected. Walker's story was a lie.

'She was married to a friend of mine. He was with her. They were travelling upriver to the Misapi Mission and got caught in a downpour.'

Iris seemed shocked. 'Did they have a guide? They should've had a local guide. A local wouldn't have got caught in a flash flood. They happen all the time there.'

'Yes, they had a guide, according to my friend.' Darling examined their faces carefully. They seemed honestly appalled.

'Well, I'm very sorry,' said Ruben. 'Was it long ago?'

'Six years.'

'Her husband must have been devastated,' said Iris. 'Did he manage to get her body back to Australia for burial? The red tape in PNG is unbelievable, if you don't know your way around.' She held up her hand and rubbed her fingers and thumb together. 'You know what I mean.'

'No,' Darling said bluntly. 'They never recovered the body. Washed away. My friend was apparently almost drowned and spent a month in a grass hut in the middle of nowhere. By the time the authorities got to him, there was no trace of her remains. One of the locals also drowned and the rest had no idea what had happened. The husband also had no idea. Or so he says.' He took a gulp of his wine and cradled the glass between his palms, brooding.

Ruben raised his eyebrows. 'You don't believe him? Do you think there was foul play?'

Darling's mind raced as he thought through what had been said. He vaguely became aware that Sally had reached her hand across the tabletop towards him. Finally, he focussed on it and jolted back to the present, grabbing her hand and looking sheepishly at those around him. 'Foul play? No. The police said they investigated thoroughly.'

Ruben gave a dismissive laugh. 'Thorough? I doubt that very much. If there was no bribe exchanged then I know how thorough it would have been.'

Darling was agitated. 'Do you think it's worth me going there? To get the truth?'

Ruben shrugged. 'Maybe. I don't know about such things. But if you know someone there it will help.'

'I do,' he said quickly. 'A policeman at Mount Hagen. The one who tracked down the husband.'

Ruben and his wife exchanged glances. 'Well, then you have a chance,' said Ruben.

'You can't be serious,' said Sally, still holding his hand. 'You can't go to New Guinea.' She turned with disbelief to the others then back to Darling. 'It's been six years. And what about Alice's murder?'

'That's been solved,' he said. 'I've got nothing else that's urgent at the moment.'

The waiters arrived, placing plates of food along the table and the spicy aroma became more pungent. The party began to tuck in, Darling and Sally forgotten.

Sally leaned closer and dropped her voice. 'Barry, are you serious? That's such a long way to go.' She bit her bottom lip. 'And we've only just started seeing each other.'

He grabbed her other hand and held them both in his. 'I think I might have to. It's something I really feel I need to do. I don't think I'll ever rest until I know what happened.'

'Why?' Sally insisted. 'You're not her husband. What is she to you?'

'We grew up together. We were close.' He let out a long breath. 'I just can't get over her death. And I don't trust her husband, Kit. I don't trust his story. Call it policeman's instinct. There's something not right about the whole thing.' His thoughts drifted elsewhere again. 'I just don't trust him,' he repeated tightly.

She squeezed his hands. Finally, his eyes drifted back to hers.

'Do you want me to take you home, Barry?' she asked softly.

CHAPTER TWENTY-SIX

THE NEXT DAY, Darling phoned the Mount Hagen police station and asked to speak to Sergeant Martin Kora of the Royal Papua New Guinea Constabulary.

'The last time we spoke, you talked about the Jungle Patrol,' said Darling when Kora came to the phone. 'And you said that you stand against evil.' He paused to allow the words to sink in. 'I'd like you to know that I too stand against evil. *Stamus Contra Malo.*'

There was a moment of silence on the other end. Then softly, 'Do you wear a ring?'

'Two rings.'

They exchanged a few more secret words, then Martin Kora let out a short laugh. 'It is gratifying to know that the Patrol extends to other shores.'

'For me also.'

'How can I help you, brother?'

'It is said "The Phantom has a thousand eyes and a thousand ears".'

'That is true.'

'So, I need you to be my eyes and ears.'

'Gladly. For what purpose?'

'There's something about the death of Dr Walker's wife that has never sat right with me. I would like to find out as much as I can.'

'I will help you if I can.'

'That's good,' said Darling. 'As they say, "No man can refuse the voice of the Phantom."'

'That is also true, Detective Darling.' There was a pause. 'Since you've brought up the issue of Dr Walker's wife, there's one thing I must ask you.'

'Please, call me Barry.'

'Okay, Barry. It's the doctor's name. Christopher Walker. The Ghost Who Walks. I've asked myself many times – can it just be a coincidence?'

'I think so. I grew up with him. He knew nothing of the Phantom when he was younger. It was me who pointed out the importance of his name.' Darling paused, thinking of the past. 'There was a time when he was one of us. He took the oath, owned the rings. But I think he has moved on. He no longer sees the importance.'

'Not like us.'

'Well, Martin, you and I are at the coalface. We see the evil of mankind.'

Kora grunted on the other end of the phone. 'I can smell it. The jungle reeks of it. And not just the locals – the *raskols* – although they are bad enough.'

'No?'

'No. The greed of mankind has seeped into our world. No longer are we the innocent people existing off the land, earning our keep with our hands, kneeling in the soil. The evil of the world has come to us in the guise of international corporations. Mining companies. And it's not only gold and copper, the honest riches of the old world, which they seek. Now they've discovered the currency of the modern world. Oil.'

'Yes, I've heard. Chevron, I think. But isn't it good for the local economy?'

'Good to line the pockets of the greedy. Very little trickles down to those who have cared for the land for generations. They've found oil and gas to the west and south of Mount Hagen. Next year they will build a great pipeline from Iagifu in the highlands down to the coast so they can pump away what has slept in our ground for millions of years. They will bleed the soul out of our country.'

'Well, as it is said, "The Phantom will never refuse a challenge." You must remain steadfast and do what you can.'

'It is also said, "It is better to die on your feet than to live on your knees."'

'I wish I could help.'

'It is for us who live here to carry the burden. But if you ever would like to visit, you will be most welcome.'

'I might just do that. I have annual leave coming up. I'd like to see a new frontier where the Jungle Patrol stands fast against evil.'

'I think you will be surprised how easy it is to get here. We're only a one-hour flight from Port Moresby.'

'I would like to see where Dr Walker was found.'

'That would be harder. That is a long trip by rough road and by boat. Are you sure you want to?'

'I feel I need to. I need to find out the truth about Felicity Walker or I will never rest.'

There was a pause on the other end of the phone. Darling looked out his window at the paved streets and tame sculptured gardens of Parramatta and suddenly, more than ever, he wanted to go.

Then Sergeant Kora spoke again. 'I will do it, brother. Let me know when you can come.'

CHAPTER TWENTY-SEVEN

BARRY DARLING WAS exhausted when the Toyota Hilux finally pulled up outside of the Plumes and Arrow Inn near Mount Hagen airport at midday on a Thursday in late February. He'd spent the last two days travelling from Sydney to Brisbane, and then by Air Niugini Airbus to Port Moresby. Due to the late arrival, he'd had to stay overnight in a motel near the airport and was given the 'good' room next to the generator. But he'd had a terrible night's sleep due to the rumble of the motor, as well as the constant rabble of drunk people arguing, screaming and fighting all night. He was very relieved the next morning when the ageing twin-prop Fokker Friendship finally took off for the one-hour flight to an airstrip ten kilometres from Mount Hagen.

Sergeant Martin Kora met him on the tarmac in over thirty-five-degree heat, the excited policeman immediately giving him the secret handshake, which Darling was pleased to return despite his exhaustion. Kora was a stocky local with short-cropped hair and a large smile, dressed in short-sleeved shirt, blue cargo pants and black boots to mid-calf. He quickly escorted Darling out of the stifling heat into the terminal building.

'Be careful of the sun,' he said in excellent English, smiling broadly. 'You expats cook up nicely in no time at all.'

Darling's thoughts immediately went to the cannibalism, which had previously occurred in these parts, and he had to stop himself from replying with a wisecrack. It was too soon to test his host's sense of humour.

Darling was silently glad that the hotel was so close to the airport. He badly needed a shower and a beer, in that order, and wasn't in the mood for a prolonged conversation. To his relief, Kora explained that the inn was run by an expat Australian. Darling didn't think he could stand another night in an establishment like the last one in Port Moresby. However, he began to have second thoughts when Kora led him into the hotel lounge. There they found a man – clearly white – dressed as a local native, complete with a grass skirt, wooden shield, bow and arrows, and brightly painted face, entertaining a group of Japanese businessmen who were happily snapping away on their cameras.

'Who's that?' asked Darling.

'Why that's Peter Spencer, the owner.' In answer to Darling's obvious look of dismay, Kora added quickly, 'It's not fake, you know. Mr Spencer is an initiated member of the Jiga tribe.' When Darling still appeared dubious, he pointed at the wiry white man. 'See.'

At that point, Spencer produced a short piece of bone and proceeded to push it through a hole in his nose, much to the delight of the Japanese, who laughed uproariously as they took more photos. 'You can't do that if you've not been initiated.'

Kora seemed to sense that Darling was near the end of his tether, and he quickly led him away towards his room. 'How about you have a shower and I'll meet you back here at four for a beer.' He smiled as he reached the door of Darling's room. 'My shout. I'll introduce you to one or two of the local drops.'

'Sounds like just what I need,' sighed Darling and they parted after a firm handshake.

Just after four o'clock, a washed and rested Darling made his way to the lounge and was pleased that Spencer and the Japanese businessmen had disappeared. A few moments later, Kora arrived, still dressed in uniform, and ordered them both a drink.

'My plan is to let you have a day's rest here before we set off to where I found Christopher Walker. Perhaps you would like to visit the police station tomorrow?'

'Sure. Are there any sights to see?'

Kora grimaced. 'Not really. The street markets, I suppose. But I wouldn't recommend walking around by yourself. The local *raskols* like to get up to no good, especially if they know you're new around here.' He thought for a moment. 'There's the Mount Hagen Pioneer Club, which is next to the markets and pretty good on Friday nights. I expect the local expats will want to meet you.' He raised a finger. 'But we can't stay late. I would like to leave early on Saturday before sun-up, to get a good start. The roads are not so good.'

The next morning, Kora picked him up and drove into town along rutted bitumen, past dusty ramshackle buildings painted in bright yellows, reds and blues, and plastered with grand signs displaying their wares – Maggi, Cold Power, two-minute noodles, Klina laundry soap. The police station was a low building that looked like a fortress, besser blocks with drawn shutters and surrounded by a tall metal picket fence. Kora parked around the back. Inside, he was introduced to a young officer by the name of Dave Berum, moustachioed and muscular, wearing wraparound sunglasses, even though they were in the office.

After introductions and small talk, Darling asked them not to mind him and to get about their work. He watched them for thirty minutes or so and soon realised that police work was probably the same the world over. Endless paperwork, idle phone calls, visitors complaining about one thing or the other, and only occasionally punctuated by a real issue that needed to be sorted.

On the wall behind Kora's desk was a poster of a black man dressed in what Darling initially thought was a red Phantom suit, the figure adopting a powerful pose on a beach with palm trees behind. But then he realised it was an advertisement to encourage the use of condoms to prevent the spread of AIDS. Across the top, large white text declared 'Condoman says', and then a cartoon speech bubble of the man saying, 'Don't be shame, be game.' In his hand, the Phantom lookalike held a box of condoms and at the bottom of the poster were the bold words 'Protect yourself'. Darling wondered whether Kora had the poster displayed because he agreed with the sentiments or because it reminded him of the true Phantom. He didn't think he should ask in front of the other staff.

He excused himself, and after another warning from Kora about the local *raskols*, he made his way to the town markets, a covered area just off the main road that sold local produce and cheap clothes. Rows of tables were covered with displays of colourful fruit and vegetables, some of which he could recognise and others he could only guess at. Except for a collection of youths who glared at him as he passed on the road, he was not bothered. When he returned to the station, Kora drove him back to his hotel and promised to pick him up that evening for dinner at the Pioneer Club.

From the outside, the club looked as ramshackle as the buildings that surrounded it. Inside it was timber and Laminex and a small bar sold ice-cold beers at a cheap price. Darling bought them each an SP lager and Kora led the way to a group of whites who were sitting on cane lounges in an open room.

He was introduced to Dawn, one of the local whites who managed a coffee plantation to the north of Mount Hagen. It soon became clear she knew a lot about what went on in the area. She rattled off numerous community organisations she'd been involved with, such as the local Red Cross, Farmers & Settlers Association, Golf Club, Pioneer Club, the Pony Club, and others Darling didn't recognise.

'Good news about Saddam Hussein,' Dawn said conversationally. When Darling raised his eyebrows in question, she continued, 'I guess you're out of the loop. He's announced the withdrawal of Iraqi troops from Kuwait.'

'That's nice,' said Darling. 'About time we got some good news out of the Middle East.'

'But the Iraqi soldiers are setting fire to Kuwaiti oil fields as they retreat.'

Darling grimaced. 'Great. There goes the petrol prices. Wonder what will happen to Saddam.'

'Probably nothing,' said Kora. 'The Americans will offer him protection, for sure. It's always the same with powerful men. They get off scot-free.'

Dawn became keenly interested as to why an Australian policeman would be in Mount Hagen. She said that most of the group were betting he was part of the Australian Federal Police on a training program and she was surprised when Kora announced he was investigating the death of an Australian woman from six years ago.

'Yes, I seem to remember that,' said Dawn. 'Terrible thing.' She shook her head. 'And a bit surprising. Most deaths around here are due to murders, both locals and whites. Rape is also common. But a drowning is unusual, especially when they had a local guide. He also died, from memory.'

Darling found the conversation disquieting, only increasing his compulsion to see the site where Felicity had died. 'Did you meet the husband,' asked Darling, 'Christopher Walker?'

'I did. A few times,' she said slowly, as if recalling. 'The last time was in Mount Hagen hospital after the drowning. He looked like he'd only just survived himself. And no memory of the event apparently.'

'Apparently?' said Darling, trying to calm his intensity. He had to stop himself from pressuring the woman.

'I remember speaking to him,' she said. She screwed up her forehead as she searched her memories. 'I had the feeling he was keeping something back.' Her eyes flicked to Darling's. 'You know how you get a feeling? As if he could remember more than he was letting on.' She sighed. 'But it was all thoroughly investigated.' She frowned again. 'The strange thing is that they never found the bodies.'

They were joined by a thin wiry man by the name of Jim, Dawn's husband, who broke the train of the conversation by handing his wife a shandy before energetically shaking Darling's hand. 'Well, you came on a good night,' he said. 'There're a few of the original pioneers here, or at least their relatives.'

'Oh?' said Darling, glancing around at the people who were each caught up in their own conversations.

'That over there,' said Dawn, pointing to a thickset middle-aged man with a full head of hair, 'is Daniel Leahy. He's the nephew of Mick and Danny Leahy who were the first white men to explore the highlands. Daniel's a good bloke. Runs a successful trading company with his cousin and has given a lot back to the community. Part of the Salvation Army. It's rumoured that he might get a knighthood next year.'

'You don't say,' said Darling.

'His uncle Mick was a character though,' said Jim, smiling. He pointed to a portrait on the far wall. 'That's him. Dead now. The Leahys were real adventurers. They saw and did it all. Gold mining, tribal wars. They helped save a few whites attacked by the locals. Lost a few too. Got in trouble with some international league about being overzealous in his personal protection. Mick himself claims he'd shot over one hundred of the local natives in self-defence. He fought Gough Whitlam to stop PNG independence but then supported it afterwards. Strange, since Margaret Whitlam was bridesmaid at his own wedding. But it was for discovering gold that he's most remembered.'

'Is there much?'

'Mostly all mined out now,' said Dawn. 'Oil is the new currency. They've found huge fields to the west of here at Iagifu and Hedinia.'

'There's a rumour they've been searching to the east as well,' added her husband. 'The Australian Bureau of Mineral Resources were really hot on it a few years ago. I helped them a few times. They had a geologist, Alf Runsack, searching through the area south of Okapa. Come to think of it, he knew your Walker fellow. They sometimes travelled together. The doc and his wife were helping with the TB service and they would sometimes travel from village to village with Alf.'

'Really,' Darling said with excitement. 'Is he still here?'

Jim went silent then gave his wife a look, who frowned at him in return. 'Well, strange thing,' he said slowly, rubbing his cheek. 'Alf also disappeared around the same time.'

'What!? Did he drown too?'

'No. By all reports, they'd split up a few days before. Alf had gone further north while the doc and his wife returned to Misapi Mission. But none of 'em made it.'

'What happened to him?'

'Not certain,' said Jim. 'The Goroka police looked into it but found nothing. I understand that's why the Mount Hagen police got involved. The Goroka mob were searching for Alf so they had no one to investigated the Walkers. But it doesn't take much imagination to work out what happened to Alf. The tribes here are a rambunctious lot. One day they're your best friend, the next they figure you're a sorcerer and come after you with a machete. No one dies around here of natural causes. If a chief dies from old age, the rest of the tribe start looking around for the sorcerer who cast the spell. If Alf was anywhere near the village at the time, that would have been enough for them to blame him and conk him over the head with a club or shoot him full of arrows. And way down south, it would never be found out.'

That night, on the way home in the car, Darling mulled over the stories he'd heard that evening. It was clear that New Guinea was a fascinating place but fraught with danger, and he wondered again at the stupidity and neglect that Chris Walker had shown in bringing his wife here.

Soon, he'd finally see where Felicity had died with his own eyes. Somehow, he had to get to the bottom of her death.

CHAPTER TWENTY-EIGHT

THE MOUNTAINS TO the east were shrouded in mist when Kora, Dave Berum and Darling set out the next morning in the Toyota, with Darling in the front passenger seat. Before they left, they got a full tank of diesel, which Darling gladly paid for. Initially the road was good, but soon it became potted and Kora had to weave to keep the tyres safe.

'With the oil companies coming into the west, we can expect the roads to improve,' Kora said after they'd hit a particularly deep pothole. As it was, the going was slow and by lunchtime they'd only reached Kuniawa, a collection of shacks on the highway that looked like a smaller version of Mount Hagen.

Darling noticed a police station. 'Why were you sent to search for Chris Walker and not the coppers here?' he asked.

'Small station,' said Berum. 'If too many coppers leave town, all hell breaks loose. And the Goroka crew were involved with another murder,' confirming what Dawn had said the night before.

They stopped for a lunch of flour balls and coffee and were soon on their way again, turning off the highway onto a dirt road, which rapidly turned to mud after the first river crossing. They rumbled along through open land alternated with thick jungle, following the ridgelines and valleys in a southeasterly direction.

The sun had become obscured by tall mountains to the west when Darling began to feel unsettled. They'd been driving along worn tracks and twice he and Berum had had to get out of the vehicle to guide it through thick mud halfway up the wheels. On each occasion, the young policeman had pulled out his gun and nervously scanned the trees and gullies all around, as if expecting an attack. Kora wore a permanent frown and more than once glanced at his wristwatch nervously, his jaw set tight. The western sky rapidly darkened as they drove down a steep incline, bouncing recklessly over rocks and ditches; Darling noticed Berum constantly turning his head to check the jungle around them.

Finally, Kora pulled up on the edge of a fast-moving watercourse. 'The Tau River,' he said. 'After this, we'll be safe.' He sounded relieved but his forehead was still bunched up.

'Safe,' said Darling. 'From what?'

'The local tribe,' said Berum. 'They would attack us if they saw me.'

'Why?'

'Retribution,' he said, and began to study the surrounding bushes again, failing to elucidate. He finally took off his sunglasses as night fell.

Darling examined the river in the gloom; it looked to be about thirty metres wide. He couldn't tell how deep it was and couldn't see a track on the other side. 'Is it safe to cross?'

'It was last time,' said Kora. 'The water is a bit higher.' He looked over his shoulder at the track behind. 'But we can't stay here.' He pushed the truck into gear and drove into the stream, but instead of going straight across, he pointed the truck upstream.

'Where are you going?' Darling exclaimed, but Kora just gritted his teeth harder.

The night had come on quickly and Darling could now barely see the water level before them, and the bank on the other side was a continuous shadow of low trees. Then he saw a gap and felt the vehicle swing towards it. For a moment, the front of the four-wheel drive lurched downwards and the back lifted up as it floated in the current, and Darling grabbed the passenger handle at the top of the windscreen. The truck stopped for some moments, the back wheels spinning in free water, and Darling wondered whether he should open the window and swim for the shore. But then the front wheel found purchase and the truck crawled forward, and finally up onto the other bank. Kora drove a few more metres then came to a halt and pulled on the handbrake.

'Made it,' said Berum, slapping Kora on the shoulder. He smiled broadly, his frown dissolving.

'Is it always that difficult?' Darling asked.

'I've only done it once before,' said Kora. 'When I came searching for your friend.'

'Are we safe now?' he said, staring into the shadows that surrounded them.

'Of course,' said Berum. 'This is my land. My tribe.'

'And on the other side of the river?'

'Our enemy's.'

Darling grimaced. 'Nice to know. Do we need to come back this way?'

'No,' said Kora, still smiling, 'but it's faster. Otherwise we have to go through Goroka. Not as much fun.'

Kora flipped on the lights and took off again, climbing up a steep track that, thankfully, was not too muddy. Soon they reached the top and Darling thought he could see huts on the side of the road in the dim moonlight. They crossed a narrow bridge and Kora finally pulled the vehicle up on the road between a collection of huts.

'Lufa.' Berum beamed. 'My home. We will be welcome here.'

CHAPTER TWENTY-NINE

WALKER WAS NOT looking forward to clinic that afternoon and uncharacteristically procrastinated in his office, tidying his desk and throwing out bits and pieces he didn't need. He opened the top drawer and saw the silver locket and idly examined it for a few moments before slipping it into his pocket. No one had contacted him about the notices he'd put up in various staffrooms around the hospital, so he decided he should probably hand it into security.

Sighing loudly, he dawdled towards the Cancer Centre. Angela would be doing the clinic with him and he wasn't sure he wanted to see her. The last time they'd been together was at Epping pub. He didn't want to think about what that oaf Blinkton had got up to with her. Walker still couldn't understand what she saw in him.

The other thing that worried him was that he had heard that Barry Darling had gone to New Guinea, of all places. He had put up with Wendy's acrimony about Felicity's death for years now. He knew that Wendy had loved his wife, so he had tolerated his actions, initially by ignoring him and then eventually by cutting off all contact. But since they had been forced together with these recent murders, it had started all over again.

So what was Wendy up to now? It had to be about Felicity! What was he digging for? If only he could remember what had happened in that hut …

When he arrived at the clinic, one of the nurses looked up and threw him a lewd smirk. 'Angela has already started, Chris. She's seeing Mrs Gnanalingam.'

One of the other nurses smiled at her colleague and raised her eyes suggestively.

'Good,' he said stiffly as he picked up the next file on the pile and began to read it. He wondered why the nurses were being stupid but refused to engage with them.

'Angela's looking very beautiful today, Dr Walker,' said the other nurse. 'She looks like she's dressed to impress.'

He frowned and continued to read the file but became uneasy. She was probably going out with Blinkton again after the clinic. Maybe he should drag out the clinic and not let her leave until they were both finished. Then he had a pang of guilt for being so petulant.

Feeling miserable, he went in and saw the first patient, a man who was having chemotherapy for resected bowel cancer. When he was done, he went to select a file for the next patient and Angela came to do the same. His heart sank. The nurses were right. She was depressingly beautiful with her smooth skin, dark hair pulled back and a pastel blue dress that defined her trim body, showing off her bare arms and long legs.

'Bloody Blinkton!' he cursed under his breath.

'Dr Walker,' Angela said politely, 'could you say hello to Mrs Gnanalingam? I think we can discharge her. The TB is being treated by the ID team and she's feeling better. All the tests for cancer are negative.'

Rani was glowing with pleasure when he entered the room. Her husband was there with their three children, who stood respectfully in the corner, the oldest a girl of perhaps twelve.

'Dr Walker,' said Rani, 'I'm very glad I saw you. Thank you, thank you very much for curing me. I'm feeling much better.'

Walker felt embarrassed. 'No problem at all … it was a team effort, not just me.'

'I told Mrs Gnanalingam how you diagnosed her tuberculosis, Dr Walker,' Angela contradicted. 'When everyone else thought she had cancer.'

Her husband held his palms together and made a slight bow. '*Nanri tāktar vākkar, aiyā.* Tank yu,' he said in a thick accent.

The eldest daughter stepped forward, a younger image of her mother. 'My father says thank you for saving my mother's life.' She spoke confidently with an Australian accent. 'We're all appreciative.'

Walker nodded, flustered. 'No problem. No problem. It's just my job.' He shook Rani's hand. 'All the best. The ID team will take good care of you.' He turned awkwardly and strode out of the room into the corridor.

Angela followed. 'They were showing their appreciation, Dr Walker. You should be more positive in accepting their gratitude.'

'I was,' he mumbled. 'I said thanks.'

'You minimised their thanks. You said it was just your job. That makes them feel less important, and I'm sure that was not your intention.'

'But it *is* my job,' he snapped.

'What you and I do is more than a job, Chris,' she countered. Her words were soft but her demeanour was steadfast. 'Gratitude, honestly accepted and reciprocated, can be a deeply meaningful and healing experience for our patients. Telling them that it's just a job makes them feel small and unimportant.'

Walker stared at her, feeling both annoyed and embarrassed. He wanted to tell her off for her impudence. He was the consultant, she was the trainee – she shouldn't be telling him how to act. But the truth of her words bound his mouth. He knew she was right. He turned away.

The rest of the clinic was completed with them only speaking of practical topics at hand, their conversations brief and factual. But the whole time Walker kept thinking about what she said. She was right. He didn't treat his patients with respect. As the clinic progressed, he found himself listening more to what his patients said, often thanking them for their patience and commenting on their resilience in fighting their disease, even when they were angry and tense. He noticed that, generally, they seemed to leave in a better mood. He felt his own mood brighten as well, despite the difficult and often short future that some of them faced.

The clinic was finally empty and the nurses finished their chores and left Walker and Angela alone while they completed their paperwork. Walker was expecting her to say she had to leave, that she had a date with Blinkton. But she seemed to be procrastinating.

He felt belittled by the wisdom she'd shown and was in no mood to discuss anything about patients. He kept flicking through the files, pretending to read reports, hoping she'd leave.

Finally, she stopped what she was doing and turned and faced him, her arms folded over her chest. He tried to ignore her but she stood in polite silence.

'Do you need something?' he asked when he realised she wasn't going to leave.

'I think we need to talk.'

Walker sighed. 'Okay, I agree I could do better. You're right, I'm wrong. I'm an idiot.'

'Not about that.' Then she smiled. 'But I agree you're an idiot.'

He looked at her squarely. He couldn't help smiling also. 'Oh yeah?' She was leaning against the bench with her legs crossed in front. At some stage during the clinic, she'd taken her hair down and now it cascaded over her right shoulder. 'So what do you want to talk about?'

'Us.'

'Us?'

'Yes, there's something between us. But if this is going to go anywhere we have to start being truthful with each other.'

Walker stiffened. She was going to ask about Felicity. 'What do you mean?'

'Why I had the metoprolol, for one.'

Walker relaxed. 'Oh.' He stood and walked to the door. The clinic area was empty. They were alone. The lights in the corridors had been turned down and the nurses and secretaries had gone home. He pulled the clinic door closed and turned to face her. 'So, will you tell me?'

Now she hesitated. She looked away and uncrossed her arms, rubbing her hands together. She didn't look at him when she spoke. 'I wanted to kill him.'

Walker said nothing at first. He slowly crossed to the bench, keeping an arm's length away. Then he asked softly, 'Oh?'

'He was horrible. You know what he did to my mother. He was a beast. He killed her.'

Walker was silent for some moments while he contemplated what to say next. 'Did you give him metoprolol?'

'No. I chickened out. I couldn't go through with it. I realised my life is about reducing suffering and saving lives. I couldn't take one, no matter how much I thought he deserved it.'

'Did he … did he ever do anything to you? Touch you?' The image of Angela's mother came into his mind. Angela looked so much like her.

She shook her head. 'No. If he had, I wouldn't have been able to stop myself from killing him.'

'I'm glad,' he said. 'So you threw the bag away.'

She nodded. 'After he was dead.'

Walker remained silent, examining his shoes. Was he capable of the same? He spent his life treating cancer, but deep down, he knew he could kill if he had to. He closed his eyes.

He'd done bad things. Something had happened in New Guinea, something awful. If he could only remember what it was.

'I can't sleep, you know. I have dreams of Felicity. And other things.'

Angela's voice was almost a whisper. 'Things that happened in New Guinea?'

He nodded slowly, lost in his memories. 'Dreams of her drowning. I try to save her but she pushes me away.'

'Is that what happened?'

'I don't think so. Why would someone do that? Die rather than be with me?'

'What happened?'

Walker cleared his throat. 'We were training the local health workers to do TB checks in the villages. A long way from civilisation. Very isolated. Middle of nowhere.' He raised his eyes to make sure she was following. 'Felicity was working as an aid, me a doctor. We'd just left our last village way down south in the Eastern Highlands. We were walking along a creek bed with our guide, heading for Misapi Mission. It was raining. Then a massive flood came down the river and we all got washed away. It all happened so fast, we couldn't run. Felicity and the guide drowned. I almost drowned but was saved by some local natives. An old woman looked after me in a hut in the middle of the jungle. I was delirious, almost died. Then the police found me and took me back to Mount Hagen hospital.' He shrugged. 'That's it.'

'Do you have no other memories?'

He thought for a moment. 'Dreams. Feelings. Nothing definite.'

'What like?'

'A feeling of danger. But it was there before the flood hit us. As if we were being chased by someone.' He closed his eyes, trying to remember. 'And things that happened in the hut. Fragments.'

'Like?'

He shook his head. 'I don't know. Something happened. I don't know what. All I know is, it was bad.' Tears began to stream down his cheeks. He tried to stop them but that just made it worse. He let out a strangled, tortured sob.

Then she was before him. She had his face in her hands. Her light lips were on his cheek, the corner of his mouth, his lips. She hugged him tight. He pulled her close, her body firm against his.

Slowly, his sobs settled. His head was on her shoulder. He could smell her. He dragged his lips and nose across her neck. She leaned her head to the side and he kissed her soft skin. She put her hands on his shoulders then kissed him full on the lips before pushing him away.

'That's enough,' she said quietly.

Walker wasn't sure whether she meant the lovemaking or the talk. But he agreed, it was enough. He felt exhausted, but he also felt some release. He could still feel the Black, deep in his chest ready to take over, but it was perhaps a little less strong. He realised it was the first time he'd ever spoken to anyone about Felicity's death. He looked at Angela. Would she hate him for not saving Flea, like Wendy did? Had he revealed too much?

She leaned forward and kissed him again but put her hands firmly on his shoulders to prevent their bodies coming together. 'That's enough, but it's also a start. We have a way to go. We need to trust each other. And I also worry ...' She swallowed uncomfortably.

'Worry? About what?'

Her brown eyes locked onto his, pleading. 'My mother. I'm afraid I'll be like her.'

Walker shook his head, not understanding. 'Your mother? But she seemed lovely. A good mother to you.'

'A good mother, perhaps. But not a good wife. Her lust destroyed her. I don't want to be like that. I want to be in control.'

'Lust?' Walker realised he'd raised his voice and fought to lower it. 'But it was your father who forced her.'

'I saw the photos. She wanted to be with those other men.' Angela turned her face away. 'I'm afraid I might be like that.'

He stepped towards her and raised a hand. 'But you don't know your mother was like that. And you're not like that.'

She turned away completely. 'How do you know? You don't know me. You don't know what I'm capable of.'

Walker was still for some moments. He didn't know what to do, what to say. This was something he'd not expected.

Finally, he gently placed his fingers on her bare shoulder. 'Angela, you're right, I don't really know you. But I want to. And I want to care for you. Like you were saying before, we need to trust each other.' He dropped his hand away. 'If you want to take things slowly, I'm happy to do that.'

She stayed facing the other way, silent.

'Just for the record, I don't think you're like that. But if you think you need to keep things non-physical then I'm willing.'

Finally she nodded, and when she looked back at him, her eyes were moist. But she smiled. 'I would like that. Thank you, Chris.'

CHAPTER THIRTY

THAT EVENING, DARLING and his co-travellers were greeted by Berum's brother and were shown into his house, a raised hut made from grass and cane. They had a dinner of sweet potatoes, pumpkin tips and banana, which Darling considered tasty. He had a restless sleep that night on a communal grass-mat floor with insects buzzing around, and the next morning they set off at daybreak after a breakfast of leftovers, the trees full of squawking parrots, mist rising from the mountains to the south.

The road was dry and they made good progress, reaching Okapa by mid-morning, a large settlement that sat along a ridgeline consisting of several clusters of grass huts, separated by open land used for agriculture. Kora took a turn onto a dirt track that wound through coffee plantations, following the ridge southwards away from Okapa, and soon the signs of settlement disappeared from view through the rear window of the truck. The track became intermittent and Kora needed to follow the fall of the land rather than any man-made paths, moving further and further into the New Guinea wilderness.

'What was Walker doing in these parts?' Darling asked. 'This is the middle of nowhere.'

'*Past* the edge of nowhere,' Kora corrected with a smile. 'The people around here only came into contact with white men a few decades ago. They still live off the land like their forebears – slash and burn, grow crops until the soil gives in before they move on to the next plot.'

'Nice people,' said Berum. 'As long as you don't try to steal their land or their women.'

'Or their pigs,' added Kora. 'Then they will kill you.'

'And eat you.'

'Cannibals!' said Darling. 'You're kidding. In this day and age?'

'Of course not,' said Kora, throwing a frown at his colleague. 'Don't scare the detective like that, Berum.' His frown changed to a grin as he glanced over his shoulder at Darling, who was now in the back seat. 'There haven't been cannibals in this area for years. The missionaries have finally convinced them not to eat each other.'

'Not completely,' Berum muttered, staring out the side window.

'What do you mean?' asked Darling.

'It's true they don't eat each other anymore. But if they think you're a sorcerer, look out. They'll kill you, split your skull open and eat your brains, quick smart. They need to recapture the souls of their loved ones killed by the sorcerer.' Then he added quickly, 'Or at least that's what they believe.'

It sounded as if Berum might hold the same belief as the locals.

'To answer your previous question,' said Kora, looking at Darling through the rear-view mirror, 'I understand that Walker was helping with the TB clinics down this way. Didn't you know that?'

'I guess I did,' said Walker. 'He and Felicity had come to PNG to train the local health workers doing TB checks. I just didn't know which part of the country they were in.'

'Was Felicity a doctor too?' asked Belum.

Darling let out a short laugh. 'Flea. Not on your life. She hated school. Didn't go to uni. Worked as a shop assistant.'

'Why was she here?' asked Kora.

'Helping her husband. She was working as an aid.'

'What was she like?'

Darling paused and stared out of the window before answering. 'She was beautiful. In her appearance and in her heart. She was one of those delightful souls, always full of life. Loved people. And everyone loved her.'

'Sound like you loved her,' said Kora.

Darling kept his eyes fixed on the jungle. He let out a long breath. 'I did. We all grew up together – the three of us. I dated her before Walker. I loved her. But she didn't love me. She chose Kit.'

'Must have been hard staying friends,' said Berum.

'It was. But I managed for the five years they were married. Until Walker let her die.'

After that the conversation petered out and they drove in silence.

Without warning, it began to rain, a heavy downpour that gushed down the windscreen as if they'd been thrown into a river. Kora jammed on the brakes and flipped the wipers on full, then continued down the track at a crawl.

'It's the wet season. This sort of rain is common,' said Kora.

'Isn't this the same time of year that Walker and his wife were here?' Darling could now understand how they could've been caught in a flash flood if they were on a river – it would become a raging torrent within a very short time when the saturated mountain soil refused to soak up the deluge.

They continued for some time at the same pace, and Darling silently questioned whether Kora knew where he was going. The track, if that was what they were on, was no more than a strip of clearing in thick jungle. 'Are you sure this is a road?' he asked. 'What if it's a farm you're driving through? We could drive off a cliff in this rain.'

Kora grunted. 'I don't think so.' He peered through the windscreen. 'You could be right. But I don't think so.'

The rain began to clear and soon the track took a steep downward turn and they travelled like that for some time, sloshing through mud and rocks. Eventually, they reached a collection of low, modern-looking buildings made from corrugated iron, which looked like storage sheds.

'This is almost the end of the road. On the other side of the river is the Misapi Mission,' said Kora. 'That's where Christopher Walker and his wife were headed when they were caught in the flood. The road stops soon after this, near the river, and we'll need to leave the truck.'

At the bottom of the hill, they reached a clearing and Kora pulled to a halt and turned off the engine. 'End of the line.'

'Where's the river?'

'Through the trees. We need to park up here in case it floods. Don't want to lose the truck,' he added with a smile. 'Then we'd really be up shit creek.'

They got out of the vehicle into steamy heat, with rivulets of water streaming over the muddy surface of the clearing. Darling could hear the crash of rushing water through the trees.

'Will it be safe to walk along the river after this rain?' he asked.

'No,' said Kora. 'That's why we take the canoe. It's about ten kilometres. Much easier to go by boat but we'll have to walk back. We'll need to camp overnight at the place where I found Walker.'

They spent the next hour preparing for the trip – unloading the canoe from the roof racks, packing supplies in waterproof containers, then finally carrying the canoe with its contents down a muddy track to the edge of the water.

'Doesn't look very wide,' said Darling. The waterway before them was only about fifteen metres across, with thick vegetation on both sides, right up to the water's edge. The creek was swollen and fast-moving and spilled out over the banks on either side.

'That's because it's a tributary.' Kora pointed downstream. 'The main river is about a half kilometre that way.'

They launched the canoe, Darling at the front, with Kora and Berum taking up the rear, and soon they were hurtling along the stream. They struggled around the first bend, Berum digging his oar in deep while Darling and Kora paddled frantically on the other side, just missing a tree trunk.

The next bend was gentler and they managed to keep in the centre of the stream. Darling looked ahead and was disconcerted to see a group of rocks at the junction with the river. They rushed past, the bow scraping the edge of a large rock, and Kora had to push away with a thrust of his paddle against the boulder before they were spat out into the middle of a river about twice as wide as the creek.

Up ahead was white water bucking over unseen obstructions. Darling almost lost his paddle when they hit the first hump, which thrust the bow upwards, causing him to grab the gunwales. After that, the water seemed to calm but Darling could tell they were moving at a cracking pace by the way the banks rushed past on either side. Soon the river took a tight bend to the left and Berum steered close to the inner edge. They barely made the corner, despite Berum digging in again and the other two paddling on the other side as hard as they could. The bow hit the opposite bank and for a moment it looked like they would roll, but the root that had snagged them ripped, and again they were thrust forward like a bullet out of a barrel.

The river was fairly straight after that, but they still had to paddle on one side and then the other to keep the canoe in the middle and prevent it from spinning on its axis. Darling was sweating profusely, despite the mist thrown up by the river, and the muscles of his shoulders began to ache. He wasn't sure how much longer he could continue. They negotiated a few more bends and he felt as if his arms were about to give in.

He wanted to yell out to Kora that he needed to rest but he hesitated, not knowing how they could on the fast-moving river. Both banks were thick with vegetation and there was no chance of landing the craft safely. Then on the left bank, he saw a gap in the trees. Kora pointed and they paddled towards it. As they approached, Darling could see it was another small watercourse, perhaps an overflow, and they were able to run the bow into it and step out of the canoe into shallow water. Together, they hauled the craft up onto the bank before Darling collapsed onto the ground, utterly exhausted.

After a while, he sat up and looked around. The two policemen had dragged the boat further away from the water and had already unpacked most of the containers. Darling pushed himself to his feet and helped them finish the task and together they walked up a short muddy track to the top of a grassy hill. The top had been cleared and on one side, illuminated by sun shining through a break in the clouds, was a small derelict grass hut.

Kora pointed. 'That's where I found him.'

CHAPTER THIRTY-ONE

BY THE TIME they reached the hut, the sun was setting but thick dark clouds on the edge of the mountain threatened more rain. The hut was built on a raised mound with a shallow ditch dug around the edge, and consisted of a few upright poles, woven grass walls and a thatched roof. Inside, the floor was packed dirt strewn with dried grass, a circle of rocks in the centre where a fire had been built. They managed to store their containers inside just as the downpour started. Thunder rumbled in the mountains around them and lightning flashed on the peaks. From their position, they could hear the continuous crash of the rushing waters but couldn't see the river through the thick vegetation that encircled the clearing.

'This is used for short stays when they come to tend their crops,' said Kora. 'The main village is further north on the other side of the river from where we launched the canoe.'

Darling opened one of the containers, pulled out a plastic sheet and laid it out, before throwing a sleeping bag on top. He sat down on it, careful to keep his muddy boots off the fabric. There was no door and he stared out into the dim light at the vertical torrent framed by the opening. 'What a dump. I pity the poor buggers who have to live like this.' Then he realised that might have been insensitive and gave Berum an apologetic look. 'Your village was much more comfortable than this.'

But he didn't appear to have taken offence since he too looked around the meagre dwelling with distaste. 'It probably does the job. But the locals from around here are very poor.

They wish they had the comforts we've got in Lufa. They used to come to fight us and try to steal our pigs, but not anymore.'

Kora was struggling with a lamp, filling the base with kerosene and tying a white filament on the metal pole, squinting as he tied the delicate knot in the dim light. He finally got the contraption together just as darkness came and he rapidly pumped the pressure, then lit the filament, which was now saturated with kerosene. He pushed the glass outer cover down, twisted a knob and pumped some more. Light burst forward, white and bright, obliterating the view of the clearing in the muted light of dusk.

The rain pounded on the thatching above and Darling could see streams of water flowing down the inside walls, but thankfully the roof seemed otherwise intact. He looked at the circle of rocks that had been used as a fireplace, empty except for a pile of ashes. The air temperature was still warm but he knew it would get cold during the night; he also knew they had no chance of lighting a fire. Any kindling would be soaked and it'd be impossible to find in the dark.

'So, Christopher Walker was here?'

Kora nodded and pointed to one corner. 'He was lying there, probably for weeks. An old lady was looking after him. She was the wife of the guide who drowned in the flood, along with Walker's wife.'

'Tell me again what you know. I need to piece together the events, and now that I'm here, I think I'll better understand them.'

Kora was silent for a few moments as he collected his thoughts. 'What we know is that Walker and his wife were travelling with a guide from the south to Misapi Mission. They were checking on the TB treatment teams in the villages down there to make sure their training was up to scratch. They'd just about finished their tour and were travelling upstream with the guide when the flash flood hit them. They were all washed downstream. Mrs Walker and the guide drowned. Christopher Walker was found on the banks near here, caught in the trees, still alive, but only just. The villagers brought him here and left him with the old lady. She wanted to stay to grieve for her husband. When we found him here three weeks later,' he pointed to the corner of the hut, 'he was delirious. Had a fever. Was babbling nonsense. We managed to get him upriver to the Misapi Mission and called in a helicopter to take him back to Mount Hagen. It was another few weeks before we could get any sense out of him. I don't know how he made it. Another man would have died.'

'What about the bodies of Mrs Walker and the guide? Were they found?'

'The locals said they saw the bodies and confirmed they were dead. But I'm not sure what happened to the corpses. We couldn't find them and assumed they were washed downstream.'

Darling chewed over the information for some moments before continuing. 'What about the old lady? What's happened to her? I'd like to question her.'

'She's probably gone back to the village.'

'I'd like to find her if we can.' The rain continued its muffled drum on the thatched roof. 'And I'd like to talk to people from where the Walkers set off.'

'Sure, Barry,' said Kora. 'But we don't have a lot of time. My boss was lucky to give me this many days off to show you down here.'

'I appreciate it, Martin. You've been very kind.'

He smiled broadly. 'No problem. Anything for a brother of the Jungle Patrol.'

Darling glanced at Berum, who was watching them solemnly.

'It's okay,' said Kora. 'He's one of us.'

Berum reached into his pocket and pulled out a pair of rings, one emblazoned with four overlapping swords, each appearing like the letter 'P', and the other with the raised outline of a human skull with prominent teeth.

'Nice,' said Darling. 'And I expect you get a lot of chances to use them in Mount Hagen.'

Berum nodded. 'Too often the skull. But I find I'm also using the good mark lately. Things might be looking up.'

Darling laid back on his sleeping bag, bundling up his jacket to use as a pillow, and the others did the same. In the distance was the sound of the continuous rumble of thunder echoing in the mountains and closer, the rain thudding on the soft roof. He felt warm and comfortable and, strangely, the most relaxed he'd been in a long time. 'What do you think the real Christopher Walker would have done in this situation?'

'I expect he'd have done much as you're now doing,' said Kora. 'Be relentless in searching for the truth.'

'"No man can refuse the voice of the Phantom,"' Berum recited. '"Keep asking and you will find the truth."'

'Only problem is,' said Darling, 'I'm not actually the Phantom.'

They were silent for a few moments, each lost in their own thoughts as they stared at the thatched roof.

Then Berum said, 'Perhaps we should call for him. As they say, "Go into the jungle and call. The Phantom will hear."'

'If only we could,' Kora said reflectively.

After a few more moments, Darling turned onto his side. 'Well, I'm beat. I'll see you both in the morning.' He fell asleep soon after, with the rain and the thunder singing him a lullaby, and the comforting thoughts of the Phantom stalking his prey in the jungle nearby.

CHAPTER THIRTY-TWO

EPPING PUB WAS jumping, the music was pumping, the conversations were ballistic and the grog was flowing, and to Chris Walker, it seemed that everyone was at one with the universe. It was a warm night but not too humid, a welcome relief from the relentless heat of the last few weeks. Everyone was ready to party.

Walker had met Angela at her flat and they'd walked together to the pub, the parrots squawking overhead in the subtle dusk light, the air fragrant with jasmine and jessamine, and he thought it would have to take a concerted effort to feel unhappy on this perfect Sydney summer evening. Their trip was only marred by a leather-clad bikie who screeched to a halt as they crossed the pedestrian crossing, gunning his engine impatiently. Walker had the impression the fellow was staring him down. With a shock, he realised he'd seen him before, once on Glebe Island Bridge and then later in the Captain Cook Hotel. He hurried across the road and bustled Angela towards the rear stairs of the hotel.

'What's wrong?' she cried, looking back over her shoulder.

'The bikie! He's probably a disgruntled relative of one of my patients.'

Angela stopped and turned back to look. 'Are you sure? I've never seen him.'

'Whoever he is, I don't like the look of him.' He grabbed her hand and pulled her up the stairs behind him.

They pushed their way through the crowd of revellers, girls hanging on boys' shoulders, hands already straying to buttocks, breaks in the conversation punctuated by a free exchange of kisses. Despite his extensive medical training, Walker was still not certain what pheromones were but he was certain the air was full of them.

Angela already looked flushed and aroused. After his promise to keep their relationship non-physical, maybe they'd made the wrong decision coming here. He doubted he could contain himself, especially after a few drinks.

Then he decided he'd relax and see where the evening took them, follow her lead. He really liked Angela, maybe more than liked, and he wanted nothing more than to get closer to her. He didn't care about her father's death or her handling of the drugs and all that. It was ancient history, as far as he was concerned. He *knew* she was a good person. He could sense it and his gut was rarely wrong. Why should he doubt her? She was an intelligent, beautiful woman. As far as he was concerned, she was the perfect package. She was everything he wanted. He paused. What about Felicity? He'd wanted her. He had loved her deeply. His life was nearly destroyed when he had lost her. He still hadn't got over her death. But she was almost the complete opposite of Angela – blonde and Aussie as you could get. He slapped his fist into his palm. Forget it! Live for the moment. The past is the past.

Finally, he reached the bar and ordered a Sauvignon Blanc and a schooner of Tooheys and soon returned to Angela. They pushed through the crowd to the side of the room and found a space, facing each other but pressed together all around from the throng. Everyone was accepting the contact of flesh-on-flesh in good spirit and the mass seemed to have become a single pulsating organism, each individual a composite part of the whole, everyone looking after their neighbour. Maybe, Walker speculated, this is what enlightenment was all about?

They stood together not even bothering to talk, watching each other and what was happening around them. He felt comfortable and the alcohol made him even more so. Angela's face was close to his but he could sense the tension in her body as she fought her impulses. The images of her mother came into his head – the photos her husband had taken of her with other men – the look of ecstasy on her face. Or was it fear and distaste? Maybe she'd been forced against her will. It was easy for photos to be misinterpreted. But Angela seemed convinced her mother had enjoyed it. Maybe she was right. Maybe she *was* like her mother. Maybe she was a nymphomaniac, if there was such a thing. Walker felt a flush come over his body and realised the thought made him want her even more. Was there something wrong with him? Maybe he was a male version of a nymphomaniac, whatever that might be. Maybe they were both twisted. But he had to do as she wanted. They had to minimise their physical contact. He realised he should leave before they went too far. It felt crazy but that is what she wanted.

He felt her shoulder and hip, hard against his. He turned his head and found that she'd done the same and that her lips were almost brushing his. He tried to stop himself but couldn't. He pulled her lips to his and they kissed. Their bodies enveloped each other as they became one. Their lips pulled away but they stayed together, their faces twisted as if they were both in pain. And he *was* in pain. Mental pain. Angela said she didn't want them to have a physical relationship. If he wanted her to trust him, he'd have to give her time.

'We should go.' His voice was heavy, more of a moan. 'If you want us to –'

Her mouth was on his again and he felt her tongue in his mouth, her pelvis grinding against his. Then she sounded as if she was gasping for breath and he could feel her chest move against his.

'Whoa, you two! Get a room!'

They broke away.

'Blinkers! Cassie!' Walker gasped. 'What are you doing here? Together?'

'Wendy's away,' said Blinkton. 'And you know what they say,' he smirked at Cassie, 'the mice will play.' He gave a lascivious smile and looked her up and down in an exaggerated fashion.

Angela didn't look happy and for a moment Walker felt a strong camaraderie with her. But then he wondered – was she jealous? Did she prefer Blinkton over him? He still hadn't found out how their date had ended the other night. God forbid, maybe she really liked him!

A few people left a table near them and Blinkton threw his arms around it, stopping a group of girls from taking it, then Cassie and Angela moved in.

'My shout,' said Blinkton and, after getting their orders, pushed his way through the crowd.

Walker stood beside Cassie and bent his mouth close to her ear. 'Why are you going out with him?'

She glanced at Angela before answering. 'Why not? It's just a drink. He's a bit of a dick but he asked me. What am I supposed to say?'

'How about no,' Walker said curtly.

'What about you, Angela?' said Cassie. 'Are you going to have a go at me as well?'

'Why me?' she replied, looking sideways at Walker.

'I thought maybe after your date the other night …'

Walker frowned. 'What do you mean?'

'Oh well,' said Cassie, 'we all had a good time at Tracks the other night. Angela and Craig were tearing up the dance floor. They were quite a team. Exhausting to watch, actually. When Barry and I left, they were still going hard at it.'

'We were just dancing,' Angela said.

Cassie made a face. 'You seemed to be enjoying yourselves.'

'We were,' she answered. 'I like dancing.'

'You do?' said Walker.

'Yes. I do.'

Craig Blinkton returned with the drinks and must have sensed the tension. 'Uh oh, were you talking about me? I certainly hope so.' He let out a great cackle as he placed the drinks on the table.

'We were talking about you and Angela dancing,' said Cassie.

'Oh yeah!' he crowed, raising both fists. 'Angela, you're a top dancer.' He winked at Walker. 'But as you know, so am I. We made quite a pair. What about you, Kit? Have you improved? I seem to remember you were crap on the dance floor. Too inhibited.'

Walker ignored him and took a sip of his beer. 'What about you, Cassie? Are you a dancer?'

She gave him a provocative smile. 'Oh, you know, dancing of sorts. But I like it a bit more private and mostly one on one.'

Blinkton laughed uproariously. 'Yes! Cassie, you're my kind of girl!' He pushed himself against her and brought his face close to hers, leering. She stepped back, brought her drink up between them and took a sip.

'How's Barry going in PNG?' Angela asked pointedly.

Cassandra shrugged. 'Haven't heard. But I think he's in the middle of nowhere. I don't expect him to contact me.'

'Aren't you worried about his safety? I hear it's really dangerous in the highlands.'

'He's a big boy. He can look after himself.' She looked around, as if she considered the conversation boring.

'He should be more worried about things at home,' Blinkton shouted over the crowd. 'Fancy leaving a beautiful woman like Cassandra when there're men like me around.'

'I thought he was your friend, Blinkers!' Walker sneered. 'What are you doing trying to steal his girlfriend?' Walker felt shameful. He had done the same thing.

Blinkton raised his hands. 'I completely deny that allegation. I am categorically not trying to steal Cassandra as a girlfriend.' Then he grinned. 'I'm just trying to sleep with her.' He laughed madly at his own joke.

Walker leaned forward over the table. 'You know what, Blinkers, you're a complete fuckwit.'

Blinkton became serious. 'I'd watch out, Kit. I think you're the last person to criticise the notion of going behind his best friend's back. I suggest you examine your own soul before judging others.'

Angela looked confused. 'What do you mean by that?' She looked from Walker to Cassandra. 'Is there something going on between you two?'

Walker pushed his way towards Blinkton. 'Get stuffed, you wanker.'

Before Blinkton could raise his hands, Walker punched him in the jaw. He staggered backwards but the crowd behind prevented him from falling and Walker raged before him with fists clenched.

Blinkton rubbed his jaw then smiled. 'That's what I call a guilty conscience, Kit. Don't you think?'

Angela came between the two men. 'What the hell are you doing, Chris?' She turned to Blinkton. 'Are you okay?'

He flicked his chin dismissively, where a red mark showed. 'Kit's a puff bag. It'd take more than one of his puny punches to hurt me.'

There was movement nearby and the crowd parted to let two bouncers through. Angela grabbed Blinkton's arm. 'Come on, Craig. Come home with me. I'll see whether I can do something about that.'

As she led him off, Blinkton looked back at Walker, grinned and gave him a wink.

One of the bouncers grabbed Walker's arm and he shook himself free. 'It's all right, we're leaving.' He pushed through the crowd towards the pub door. He glanced back and was relieved to see Cassandra following.

Out on the street he paced back and forth. 'Blinkton's such a dickhead. He deserved what he got.'

Cassandra stood in front of him to stop his pacing. 'For telling the truth?'

'What do you mean?' he barked.

'You and I have slept together. On more than one occasion.'

'Yes, but I'm not going behind a friend's back. Wendy isn't even my friend. He hates me. And I hate him. He won't forgive me for letting Felicity die. He blames me. That's why he's in New Guinea. He's trying to find out about her death.'

Cassandra grabbed his hands. 'Chris. This has nothing to do with Barry. Things are happening that keep throwing us together.' She shook his hands. 'We need to make a decision. About us. If we keep seeing each other like this, we'll hurt those around us. I … I like you. I like you more than Barry. And I hope you like me. More than like me. If you want, we can be together properly. I'd be willing.'

Walker was stunned. He looked over her shoulder. 'But … Angela.'

She swallowed nervously. 'Angela's had her chance. And you've had your chance with her. *She's* left with Craig. She doesn't want you. *I'm* here with you.' She brought her face before his, forcing him to look at her. 'What do you say? Shall we try?'

He finally focused on her face – smooth skin, high cheekbones, full lips. But, as if for the first time, he saw something else. Honest eyes. It was as if he could see into her mind and he could see that she was genuine. And she was right. He thought he'd had something with Angela but tonight she'd made her choice – Craig Blinkton.

Walker raised a hand to touch Cassandra's cheek. He nodded. 'Let's go home.'

CHAPTER THIRTY-THREE

WALKER WOKE THE next day with Cassandra lying beside him. They'd made love, but not like the lust-driven rutting of other occasions. Last night they were slow and nervous, as if it was their first time. At the beginning, more stilted and later, tender. It was harder than the other times.

They had a quick breakfast and Walker drove her back to her flat. As he dropped her on the street outside, he wondered whether Angela had spent the night with Blinkton. If she was right – if she was some sort of sex addict like her mother – then they could well have slept together. Blinkton would have had no qualms whatsoever. He'd say that Walker was being a stupid jerk, holding himself back from a girl who was begging for it. He looked up at their window hoping for a clue but the blinds were drawn. He promised himself to ask Cassandra later, although he'd have to be careful not to show too much interest.

Thankfully, the problem with his eyesight had settled the week before, but now he noticed his left hand was a bit clumsy when he changed gears. He had to look down to make sure his hand connected properly with the gear shift, an action that was usually automatic. It worried him. He hadn't drunk much alcohol last night, so he was sure that wasn't the trigger. He also refused to believe it was some sort of heavenly reckoning for him sleeping with Cassandra. That was just ridiculous. But it *had* happened the last time they were together.

Maybe I'm just overworked, he sighed to himself as he pulled into the hospital. But he knew it wasn't that. Deep down, he had an idea what it might be.

He decided to pay a visit to Jocelyn Banks. She was pretty cluey and he thought he could ask her a few questions without drawing suspicion. People were always asking her strange things about rare pathology. She'd travelled widely and had seen a lot of things that the average Australian medico had only read about. He found her in her office in the pathology building. She said she was happy to speak to him about his patient's symptoms and offered him a seat.

'Jocelyn, what do you know about kuru? Have you ever seen it?'

'Kuru? That only occurs in New Guinea and I've never been there. I've seen Creutzfeldt–Jakob disease, which is similar. And then there's BSE – bovine spongiform encephalopathy – you know, mad cow disease, which is all the rage in the UK right now. They're all very similar. What symptoms does your patient have?'

'Oh, all pretty vague. Muscle twitches and clumsiness of … her hand. And sometimes blurred vision. Maybe double vision. Diplopia.'

'I doubt it's kuru. She'd have to be from a particular area of New Guinea and kuru has died out, on last reports. Is she from PNG?'

'No,' said Walker. 'I mean, yes. She lived there for a while.'

'I think it was endemic to the Fore people in the Eastern Highlands, from memory.' Banks lifted a finger in realisation. 'But you were in PNG, weren't you? What area? I remember you saying you were in the eastern highlands working with the TB service. What tribes did you work with?'

'The Fore,' Walker said slowly. 'But also the Keiagana, Awa and Gimi people. And you're right, kuru died out in the sixties and seventies.'

'Is your patient from that area?'

'No,' said Walker. 'It's a dumb idea. She's probably got something completely innocuous.' He smiled blandly. 'But you know how people worry about the silliest things.'

Jocelyn raised an eyebrow. 'You or the patient?'

'The patient, of course.'

'Well, if she only lived there for a while, she wouldn't have it. You can only get it from eating the body parts of an infected person, usually the brain. Did she do that?'

'No.'

Jocelyn looked at him with concern. 'Are you okay, Christopher? You seem ... distant.'

He started. 'Oh, I'm okay! I'm just distracted about these murders. Good that they've caught the murderer.'

Jocelyn let out an exasperated noise. 'Clive Johnson? He's no murderer. I've worked with him for a decade. I've met a lot of murderers in my line and I can tell you, he ain't one. I think the cops have ballsed this one up.' She flicked a finger at Walker. 'Have a talk to your mate, Wendy. What does he think about all this?'

'Wendy ... Detective Darling is in New Guinea as we speak.'

She looked genuinely interested. 'Oh? Is it something to do with the case?'

'No.' Walker shook his head glumly. 'No, it's something else.' He stood up. 'Thanks for your help, Jocelyn.'

'Good luck with your patient.'

Walker was momentarily baffled. Then, 'Yes, thanks again. I'm sure it's something I'll be able to sort out.'

CHAPTER THIRTY-FOUR

DARLING OPENED HIS eyes and caught the smell of sizzling bacon. He gazed around the dark hut to find that the others were up and had cleared away their sleeping gear. Berum was on his haunches, pushing meat around a pan in the fireplace. Kora arrived from outside shortly after with a billy of water, which he placed on the edge of the fire. He threw some small pieces of wood onto the flames, obviously still wet from the rain, since they started to steam.

Darling sat up and looked through the doorway to the sunlit grassy clearing outside the hut. He could see bright blue sky above the rim of trees.

'Wow, what a great sleep. Haven't slept so soundly for a long time.'

Outside, a collection of their containers had been arranged like a table and three chairs, the centre container already holding a plate of steaming vegetables. Darling took a seat and Berum followed with the bacon, and they proceeded to polish off the food quickly and silently. Kora made tea in the billy and they had a large mug each. There was no milk but Darling didn't care.

'What now?' he asked when he'd finished.

'Up to you,' said Kora. 'It's your investigation.'

Darling looked around the clearing and then at the ramshackle hut, not knowing what to do. He realised he really didn't have a proper plan. He hadn't thought it through. He'd hoped that if he could see the site where Felicity had died, somehow it would all make sense. With a sinking feeling, he began to understand that he'd wasted Kora and Berum's time. He wouldn't have tolerated this sort of investigation back in Australia. Why should Kora tolerate him now?

'Where was Felicity's body found?' he asked in desperation. At least he could see that.

'Not certain,' said Kora, 'But likely to have been in the bend of the river just before we beached the canoe. I'll take you there.'

Kora headed due east through thick jungle, although there was a faint path, which helped. After about a half a kilometre they reached the river, which was still rushing as the result of the previous night's rain. Kora walked along the bank and stopped at a cluster of rocks on the edge, water rushing around and over them. 'Probably here.'

Darling spent some time looking in the scrub around and even searched the lower branches. Finally, he stepped carefully into the river, keeping his balance with one hand on the largest rock, the water coming to his knees. He leaned over and felt around the base of the rocks, getting soaked in the process, but found nothing. Finally, he stood up and shook his head. 'Nothing. I'm really sorry, guys, I'm afraid I've led you on a wild goose chase.'

Kora nodded his head solemnly. 'We understand. You wanted to see where your friend died. No harm done.' He looked up at the sky. 'At least there's no more rain. But we'll have to wait for the water level to fall before we can start heading back. We need to walk along the bank and tow the canoe behind. The water is too fast to paddle against.'

They made their way back to the hut and Darling packed his stuff away. The others were tidying up outside so he decided he'd spread the ashes to make sure the fire was out. He dug a still-moist stick into the fireplace and moved the glowing embers away from each other. He was contemplating throwing dirt onto them when his stick clicked on something hard. He dug down, expecting it to be a stone, but what he uncovered appeared to be smooth and grey-white in colour. He leaned over and squinted in the dim light, digging around it carefully. It looked like a bone.

'Martin,' he called and continued digging into the ashes. He extracted the bone and flicked it onto the dirt. It was a jaw with teeth.

Kora and Berum looked down at it.

'Human,' Kora said gravely.

Berum was shaking his head, his expression stern.

'I wish we never found this,' said Kora. The policemen both looked as if they'd just dug up their mother's grave.

'What does it mean?' asked Darling.

'It's against the law,' said Kora.

'What is?'

'The old lady,' said Berum, pointing at the jaw. 'This hut's not been used for five years. That belongs to her husband. We'll have to arrest her.'

'Arrest her for what?'

'Arrest her for eating him,' Kora said glumly.

'Eating him! After he was dead?'

'Funerary rites,' said Berum.

'Cannibalism!' Darling said with disbelief. 'I thought that had died out.'

'Mostly, yes,' said Kora. 'But some of the old people around these parts ... they've been known ...'

Darling stepped away from the fireplace. 'But where's the rest of the remains?'

The policemen began to carefully examine the floor. Berum pointed to an irregular piece of packed earth near the door.

Darling stared at the place, as if a body might arise from it. 'You mean she buried her husband in the hut? Why?'

'Only the bones,' said Berum. He moved to the spot and pulled a large hunting knife from his belt and began to dig into the packed dirt. The other two watched the gruesome scene and shortly, pieces of skeleton were unearthed: a few ribs, short bones that could have been fingers, something that looked like a leg bone, and finally a fragment of a skull with two holes where the eyes sat. The top of it was missing and the edge was irregular, as if the bone had been hewn roughly.

Then Darling had a sudden thought and began to feel faint. He stumbled from the hut and fell onto all fours, vomiting into the grass like a dog. Kora followed him out.

Darling wiped his mouth and looked up with horror. His voice was a low rasp. 'Do you think some of those bones might be Felicity Walker?'

Kora didn't answer and Darling rolled over to sit upright. He grasped his head between his arms. 'This is too much!'

CHAPTER THIRTY-FIVE

BARRY DARLING HEAVED an exhausted sigh. It was late Friday morning as he sat on the edge of his bed in his lodgings in Glebe, sunlight streamed through the windows. A light breeze blew the curtains to and fro against his bed. He should be rested but he felt terrible. He'd landed at Kingsford Smith airport the night before, after the long flight back from Port Moresby to Sydney via Brisbane and he'd gone straight to bed. But sleep had not come. And any snatches of sleep he managed to get had been disturbed by terrible dreams.

He closed his eyes and the picture of the hut in the clearing on the side of the river came into his mind, like he knew it would. He'd thought of little else over the last week. He focused on the hut, the bark walls, the brush roof, the grass clearing outside ringed by jungle – anything other than the one thing he didn't want to think about.

But there it was. He knew the memory would come, forcing itself into his mind, whether he was conscious or not. He was powerless against it.

A skull with the top hewn off.

Two sets of bones with fragments of decomposed flesh laid out on a grass mat.

He stared numbly at the ceiling. Did Walker know? He'd been in the hut. He must have known. But according to his story, he'd been in a fugue for weeks and had no memory of it. But surely, if they'd done that …?

He swayed where he sat and tried to close his mind. There was a tap on the door and, gratefully, he lurched to his feet to open it.

It was Sally.

He realised he was naked.

She glanced down and smiled. 'I'd thought you'd be more excited to see me.'

He followed the direction of her gaze, not bothering to cover himself. 'What can I say?' he said numbly. But abruptly, he felt his mind clear. It was like sunshine chasing away vile shadows. Sally being here had somehow overcome the horror, at least for a moment. For the first time in a week he thought of something else. He smirked. 'I've gone all native. It's the rage in PNG right now.'

'Really,' she drawled. 'Then perhaps I should try it.'

He stepped aside and waved her into the room. 'I think you should. You never know where it might end up.'

Her chuckle was low and raunchy. 'I've a pretty good idea.' She slipped inside and he closed the door behind them.

Sometime later, Darling woke up. He'd finally found sleep. No nightmares. Sally was awake and lay beside him, propped up on an elbow, looking at him.

'So,' she said. 'Tell me about your trip.'

'It was eventful.' He would tell her everything except what he'd really found. 'It's beautiful. But quite dangerous. People will kill you just as soon as look at you. I'm glad I'm out of there. Mount Hagen was interesting. I met a lot of fascinating expats in a place called the Pioneer Club – mostly Aussies who lived a frontier life. Some of their stories were amazing. You could write a book about it.'

'And?' she said.

'And what?'

'Did you find out anything about Felicity?'

He closed his eyes. 'A bit,' he said. 'Not much. It looks like she drowned, just like they said. Not much more than that.'

'So it's all sorted then? Does that mean I have you all to myself? No more winsome longing after a dead woman?'

'Of course.'

'And can you forgive the husband – what was his name? The doctor.'

'Chris Walker.'

'Mmm. Does that mean you can be friends again?'

'Not likely,' said Darling. 'He's changed anyway. Nothing like when we were kids growing up in The Rocks.'

'Poor thing,' said Sally. 'His wife drowned, and by the sounds if it, he almost died as well. I can see why he doesn't want to talk about it. I'd be devastated.'

'I can think of another reason,' Darling muttered.

'What do you mean?'

'Nothing.'

'Did you find something? You said you were trying to find the place where she drowned. Did you?'

He nodded slowly, his eyes still closed. 'I think … I think I found her body. Or rather, her remains, plus the guide's, who was also drowned. They were buried in a hut in the jungle. The place where they found Chris Walker.'

'Oh, that's terrible,' Sally gasped. 'Does he know she's buried there?'

'There's more.' Now he'd started he couldn't stop. 'The bones showed evidence that her body had been burned.'

She grimaced. 'Burned? Like in a funeral rite?'

'Maybe.' He looked at her. 'Or cooked.'

Sally's mouth fell open. 'Cooked. But why?'

'We don't know for sure. But it's the sort of thing they used to do in that area, although it's supposed to have been stamped out.'

'Sort of thing they do?'

Darling's face was grim. 'The scientists call it transumption.' He closed his eyes again. 'Most people call it cannibalism.'

'Are you telling me that Felicity was cooked and eaten? By who?' She groaned and Darling's eyes snapped open. Her face was pale. 'You can't mean …'

'I don't know.' Darling felt sick. 'There were no witnesses. He was apparently cared for by an old woman, the wife of the guide who also drowned. The policeman who took me there – Berum was his name – he was from around there. He thought that the woman probably ate her husband's remains as a mark of respect and to help free his spirit.'

'But Felicity? She wasn't a native. Why would she eat her body?'

Darling sat up on the edge of the bed. He was feeling sick on the stomach. 'Not the woman.' He had difficulty speaking. 'They were stuck in that hut for almost a month. No one else came. They had no food. Chris Walker survived. Somehow.'

Sally remained quiet for some time. Then she said quietly, 'Do you really think it could've happened? If it did, surely Chris would remember.'

He twisted his body towards her. 'I'm not sure. But I agree with you. If it did happen, it's hard to believe he didn't have some idea, no matter how out of it he was.'

'The poor man. Imagine how you'd feel if you knew.'

Darling scoffed. 'Poor man!' He gritted his teeth. 'He's a sick bastard. How could he have done it? He'd have to have known.'

'So what are you going to do?'

Darling ground his teeth in thought before speaking. 'I'm going to confront him.'

CHAPTER THIRTY-SIX

DARLING DROVE from Glebe to work along Parramatta Road, deep in thought.

He'd decided that he'd confront Walker today about Felicity. He'd demand to know how much he knew, how much he remembered. That would be one thing he could achieve, at least. The last few weeks had been the worst in his life. First, the murder case that had been stolen from him by the wanker Wills, who was now getting all the accolades despite all the legwork done by him and Jones. But this business about Felicity had shaken him to the core. It was one thing to have her drown needlessly because she was wandering around after a useless husband who failed to save her. But the gory images of what were probably her bones refused to leave his dreams. Burnt bones.

Could her body have been eaten? He couldn't believe it.

He'd turned the radio down, in no the mood for the wacky patter of Maynard Crabbes, the morning Triple J presenter. But then a song came on that he'd never heard before and he turned up the volume. It was a soothing, syncopated song with Indian overtones and a sultry female lead singer. There was something in the words that caught his attention.

The song went on about the futility of life and something about a woman under the water looking up to see the stars from a million miles. He imagined the dead woman in the song to be Felicity, lying on her back under the water looking up at him as he looked down on her. But she was looking over his shoulder, through the shifting tide, to another place, to the stars of the universe circling above them. The terrible sadness of the lyrics and the lilting tune suited his current mood.

The track finished and he turned the radio off. One of the lines of the song kept repeating in his head. Something about the ebb and the flow of the water.

Why was it stuck in his head? Why those words? Then his thoughts flipped unaccountably to Clive Johnson and Darling felt a rising disquiet. He still wasn't sure that Johnson was guilty. All the evidence pointed to him. But …

The ebb and the flow.

Then it came to him! Johnson had spoken about the king tide and the strong ebb of the current, which had made it difficult for them to get their boat through Lake Entrance. And Johnson had claimed he'd rescued a man and his son. But the owner of the boat said he wasn't even in the country, which had dashed Johnson's alibi and led to his arrest.

Then Darling had another thought. The man who owned the boat was out of the country and so his house would have been empty. Who was to stop someone else from taking his boat out?

'Bloody hell! Did we even check for that?' He drove the rest of the way in frenzied thought and when he reached the police station, he found Jones sitting at his desk, typing one-fingered while drinking a takeaway coffee with his other hand.

'Jones! Do you have the number of the man who owned that boat? The fellow who claimed to be in Bass Strait?'

'Should have. Why?'

'Get it and meet me in my office.'

On the fourth ring the phone was answered and Darling heard a male voice, dull and slow, as if he'd just woken. It became apparent that the speaker, James Kerridge, had just returned from another stint on a Bass Strait oil rig. Yes, he'd spoken to the police about his boat. Yes, he'd been away at the time – he'd already gone through all that with the police.

'Thanks, Mr Kerridge, I just needed to confirm.' Darling paused. 'Do you think someone else might have used your boat when you were away? Someone with a small child?'

There was silence then a tired groan. 'I suppose so,' finally came the answer. 'My brother sometimes uses it. His son is eight years old. They go fishing on Lake Macquarie. Come to think of it, the portable fuel tank was empty when I next used the boat.'

'And you didn't think to tell the police?'

'They didn't ask me.'

Darling was both relieved and irritated at the same time. 'Can you give me his number?'

Darling addressed Senior Detective Sergeant Royce Wills with as much respect as he could muster but he knew he was failing. 'The brother of James Kerridge, the boat owner, confirmed that he'd borrowed his brother's boat on the day of the murder.' Darling was glad that he was in Parramatta and Wills in the city, since he couldn't suppress the smile that was forming on his lips. He hoped Wills couldn't sense it. 'He also confirms that he ran out of fuel while fishing with his son near Lake Entrance. The outgoing tide was very strong and they were being dragged out to sea. He confirms that they were rescued by two men in a large boat, a Bertram, who towed them back to the Jensen's Point Marina.'

There was a pause then Wills asked, 'What time?' He sounded more than a little miffed.

'Seven pm. Kerridge estimated they got back to the marina after eight.'

There was another pause. 'Are you sure he's telling the truth? How do you know he's not an acquaintance of the Johnsons?'

'There's nothing to suggest it.' Darling realised he'd not added 'sir' then concluded to do so now would sound even more impudent.

'So, you're saying that Johnson couldn't have made it back to Sydney in time to commit the murders at ten pm.'

'It takes over two hours to drive from the marina to Sydney. They would have had to transfer the drugs from the boat to the car and that would have taken at least thirty minutes, probably more. There's no way they could've made it back in time.'

'Are you saying that Johnson is innocent?'

'Yes, sir.'

There was another long pause and Darling allowed another small smile to form. Then Wills spat out an obscenity and hung up.

CHAPTER THIRTY-SEVEN

'SO, AFTER ALL that, we're back at the beginning,' Jones sighed. 'Three stiffs and no new clues, all the suspects have rock hard alibis and there's no one else in our sights. And the clues we had are a dead end.' He shrugged dejectedly. 'Where to now, boss?'

'At least Senior Detective Sergeant Royce Wills is out of the picture. Now we can do some real investigating.'

Despite the total stuff-up, Darling was starting to feel a bit better and he didn't even feel guilty about it. It looked bad for that deadshit Wills, and Darling hoped he would not be caught up in any collateral damage. He realised he was procrastinating about Kit. But that was going to be a very difficult conversation and right now, he felt like celebrating his success. He would deal with Walker later but he promised himself it wouldn't be long.

'Pity about Detective Bianca,' Jones continued glumly. 'I quite liked her.'

'Jones! You old dog. I was beginning to think you were made of steel. So why don't you give her a call?'

Jones shook his head sadly. 'Didn't get her number.'

Darling clicked his tongue. 'And you want to be a detective, Jones? That's the weakest excuse I've ever heard.' He pointed to his desk. 'There's a phone. I bet you a Tosca that she's sitting at her desk at head office right now, pining away for you, while Senior Detective Sergeant Wills stomps around in a bad mood, picking on new recruits and kicking small animals. Believe me, even you'd look good at the moment.'

'What do you mean, look good *at the moment?*'

Darling let out a breath and looked the tall officer up and down. 'Well, you've got to admit, Jones, you're not what you'd call a snappy dresser. And what sort of a haircut is that? That'd scare a small child shitless.'

Jones raised his hands in protest. 'It's called a uniform, sir!' Then he pointed to his head. 'And this is a standard order cut. There's not much I can do with it.'

'You could grow a moustache. You're allowed to now.'

'A moustache? I'm not one of those Village People.'

Darling folded his arms and put on a knowing smirk. 'Are you sure, Jones? I'm really starting to have my doubts. Besides, I think you'd look good in a leather cap and chaps.'

Jones looked at the phone on the desk. 'All right then, I'll call her. But not with you standing there. I'll do it later.'

'When?'

'Later.'

'Later lunchtime or later tomorrow or later next week?'

Jones took a deep breath. 'Lunchtime.'

'Good man. All right then, what about the case?' He smiled at his underling. 'Now ...' Darling clapped his hands and rubbed them together. 'Let's get back to basics.' He twisted his mouth in concentration.

'Shall I get the corkboard, sir?' Jones pointed to the board that lay on its side up against the filing cabinet. 'I've still got all the evidence in the filing cabinet.'

'I guess so,' said Darling. His mind had gone elsewhere. There must be something they had missed ...

He watched as Jones fumbled with the key to the filing cabinet.

Darling straightened suddenly. 'Keys!' he exclaimed.

Jones looked up defensively. 'You can't be too safe, sir. There's a memo about the care of evidence.'

'Not those keys.' He picked up his coat and walked towards the door. 'Come on, Jones. I have a feeling that keys just might be the *key* to this case. We've been sidetracked by

Royce's nonsense.' He raced up the corridor and made for the stairs.

'Where are we going?' Jones called after him.

Darling yelled from the stairwell. 'We're paying Dr Banks another visit.'

Darling and Jones found Jocelyn in her office in the pathology building, with a small blue porcelain teapot on her desk, along with a floral cup and saucer. Steam floated out of the spout. Darling was surprised to see a purple tin of Twinings lapsang souchong sitting nearby.

'Like your tea smoky, Dr Banks?' he said, pointing at the tin.

'Sometimes,' she said. 'Depends on my mood. This one takes a particular taste.'

'Very particular,' he agreed. 'Don't see much of that blend around here, I imagine.'

'I lived in Asia for a few years.' She twirled the teapot to mix the brew. 'Sometimes I have it just to remind myself of my time there.' She left the pot to draw and turned to face him.

'Asia? Whereabouts?' He kept his tone light.

'Here and there.'

'Lebanon?'

Jocelyn gave a curious look. 'Yes, but lapsang souchong is from China.'

'But you've been to the Middle East.' Darling was silently pleased Jones was witnessing his cleverness.

'Yes, have you?' she asked.

Darling stopped, realising he couldn't think of another probing question. All he could say was, 'No.'

She poured tea into the cup and a sharp smoky odour pervaded the room. 'Now, how can I help you?'

Darling struggled to regain his composure. 'We're trying to account for all the keys to the morgue. According to security, there are three keys. Clive Johnson and Quentin Boon each had a copy. We checked them. I saw them myself.' He paused significantly. 'But we never checked yours, Dr Banks.'

Jocelyn frowned. 'Keys?'

Darling felt his heart catch. She was going to claim ignorance. He had her.

'Yes,' he said slowly. He had to be careful. 'I wanted to make sure you hadn't misplaced yours or perhaps lent them to someone and forgotten about it.' He'd offer her a way out. If she took it, he knew he was on the right track.

Jocelyn raised her eyebrows. 'I don't have one. Don't need it. If I ever need to do an autopsy after hours, I get the assistants to open up, then I come later.'

Darling tried to keep a poker face. That was not the answer he was expecting. 'Are you sure? 'When we first asked who had access to the morgue after hours, you stated Johnson, Boon and yourself.'

'Quite sure. I have access. But I don't have a key.'

'But security says you have one.'

'Well, they're mistaken. I did have a key but it's gone missing.'

'Missing? When?'

Jocelyn appeared to think for a moment. 'Last year.' She pointed to her top drawer. 'I used to keep it in there but last year I noticed it was gone. I told security about it.'

Darling gave a bewildered look. 'But why wouldn't they have told us?'

'I suggest you go and ask them yourself, Detective Darling.'

'Why didn't you tell us before when we asked about the keys?'

'It was over a year ago, detective. I'd told security. And to be honest, I forgot all about it. I never used the key myself, anyway.' She took a sip of her tea and held the detective's gaze. 'Is there anything else?'

'One more thing, Dr Banks,' said Jones, drawing a frown from Darling. 'I interviewed two former employees and they both gave a story that the working environment here was not quite right.'

'Oh? In what way?'

'One of them, Ahmed Mohammed, said that everything here was a bit weird.'

'Jones,' said Darling, 'I don't think we should …'

'Poor Ahmed,' interrupted Jocelyn. 'He wasn't really cut out for this sort of job. I think it was best that he left for something more suitable. But I have to agree with him. It is very weird what we do. You need to have a special sort of personality to cope. Most can't.'

Jones continued doggedly. 'The other fellow hinted at the possibility of illegal activities here.'

'Jones,' groaned Darling. 'You can't make those sort of allegations –'

'Does this other fellow have a name?' asked Jocelyn.

'Frank Naim.'

Jocelyn slowly nodded her head. 'Ah. Frank. That makes sense.'

'What do you mean?' Darling said.

'Frank Naim was asked to leave his position two years ago. We suspected him of stealing items from other staff members' lockers. But worse than that, I suspected him of dealing in drugs. I caught him a few times – talking to shady characters down in the docks. I saw parcels exchanged. Couldn't prove anything and he left of his own accord so we let it drop.'

'Frank Naim!' said Jones. 'He doesn't strike me as a drug dealer.'

'He was around here about six months ago trying to get his old job back. I met him right here in this office.'

'And what happened?' asked Darling.

Jocelyn shrugged. 'Nothing. It was all a bit strange. He asked for a job, I said no, he seemed to accept it and he just left without a fight. Didn't try very hard to convince me.'

Darling glanced at the top drawer of Jocelyn's desk. 'And was it around then that you noticed the key was missing?'

Jocelyn gave a surprised look. 'Yes, it was! It was around that time.' For the first time, she looked contrite. 'That I should have remembered. I apologise. I really should have drawn the connection. But back then, who would have thought anyone would want to break into a morgue?'

Darling turned to his offsider. 'Jones, I think we should pay Mr Naim another visit.'

CHAPTER THIRTY-EIGHT

FRANK NAIM WAS sitting in the lounge room of a two-bedroom house in Auburn watching drag-racing clips on video when the police arrived.

Franks real first name was Fadel. He was a first-generation Aussie of Lebanese Sunni extraction, whereas his recent partner in crime, Ali Harb, was a Shiite, although that distinction held no relevance for him, like it would have for his father and grandfather.

He answered the knock on the door to find the tall, young uniformed copper who had questioned him in his workshop a few weeks ago. A man in plain clothes stood beside him and behind were at last three more uniforms.

'Frank Naim?' said the large copper. 'I'm sure you remember me. I'm Senior Constable Jones and this is Detective Sergeant Darling. We've a warrant to search your premises,' he recited. 'Would you please step outside? We would like to question you in regard to a group of murders that took place at Western Meadows Hospital a few weeks ago.'

Frank said nothing as he walked out onto the small front lawn of his house, freshly mowed with neat borders, virtually devoid of plants but decorated with a large number of garden gnomes. The gnomes seemed to be grinning at him. Cop cars were parked all over the street.

'We want to ask you a few more questions.'

Naim nodded but kept his lips firmly shut.

'Can you tell us your whereabouts on the evening of the sixteenth of February?'

Naim examined Jones carefully before speaking. 'I told you before. I was at the speedway.'

The one in plain clothes – Darling – spoke for the first time. 'On the night of the Mardi Gras.'

Naim examined him briefly. He reckoned he was probably Italian or maybe Spanish. Not Lebanese. 'What are you suggesting? That I'm a poof? I was nowhere near the parade, if that's what you're saying.'

'So, you weren't at the parade?' said Darling. 'And we also know you weren't at the speedway.'

Naim shut his mouth. He refused to be tricked.

'The people who you named vouched for you,' said Jones. 'But we've just come from the speedway again. The manager of the speedway said he saw you leaving at eight pm. He wasn't on your list of buddies who would stick up for you. Eight pm. That gave you plenty of time to get to the Meadows which is only a ten-minute drive.'

Naim remained silent.

'Can I prompt your memory, perhaps,' said Jones. 'You were at Western Meadows Hospital.'

'You were unloading heroin into a locker and a nurse stumbled upon you and you killed her,' Darling stated, as if it was a known fact. 'What we really want to know is who you were with.'

Frank's eyes flashed to Darling's once then away again. There was no way he would say anything about his accomplices. His life would be worth nothing.

'No?' said Darling. 'Let's see what we find in your house then.'

Naim's mouth tightened for a moment before he dropped his head defiantly. Better to say nothing. There was no death sentence. All he'd get would be a few years in jail.

Soon after, one of the officers came from the house carrying a rifle in gloved hands.

'Oh ho!' Darling crowed. 'What have we here? An SKS assault rifle, if I'm not mistaken? And what do you use that for?'

Naim opened his mouth to speak but shut it again when Darling added, 'And don't tell me it's for shooting pigs!'

Shortly after, a policewoman brought out a plastic package full of white powder, which she showed to Darling before placing it in a large paper specimen envelope. As she was labelling the outside of the bag, a third policeman came out carrying a black Adidas sports bag. He opened it to reveal it was full of cash, mostly one hundred-dollar bills in neat stacks. Sitting on top was a curved wooden scabbard of Arabic design.

Darling smiled. 'Well, I think that's enough, don't you? Mr Naim, I think you had better come down to the station with us while the team here finishes their search.'

CHAPTER THIRTY-NINE

WALKER TOOK THE long way back from a clinical meeting in the pathology building, breathing in the fresh air and admiring the blue sky as he strolled along, contemplating what he might have for lunch. He glanced down the slope to the other side of the oval where a helicopter was warming its engine in preparation for take-off. Closer to him, a figure dressed in flying gear and carrying a blue helmet was walking away down some stairs to the oval. He recognised the swagger – Craig Blinkton. Then he was surprised to see Angela dressed in her running gear, walking up the stairs in the opposite direction. It was obvious that she'd pass Blinkton and, with rising jealously, he stopped at the edge of the building to observe. He would be able to hear them from where he stood.

Angela and he had not spoken properly since the night at Epping pub, when she'd left with Blinkton. The more Walker though about it, the more he was convinced that they'd have slept together. He remembered kissing her in the pub. If there was ever a girl ready for sex it was Angela that night. They had agreed not to have a physical relationship while she worked through her issues about her mother. Maybe there was something in what she said about not being able to control her urges. But deep down he didn't think there was anything wrong with her. She seemed normal. Surely the way she felt was just grief about her mother. But maybe she *had* slept with the stupid jerk. *Why would she sleep with him and not me?* He waited to see whether they gave themselves away.

He imagined Blinkton would not be able to pass her without making some obvious comment about her appearance. Would she stop and smile at him? Caress his cheek? Kiss him? Walker swore under his breath. How could she be interested in such an oaf?

'Ha!' came a high-pitched voice over his shoulder and he spun around to see who had caught him spying.

He relaxed when he saw it was only the demented lady. She was wearing her dressing-gown and cat slippers and was accompanied by a young man, probably a relative taking her for a walk.

'Told you,' she continued, pointing at Angela and Blinkton, who had stopped at the top of the steps. They both looked towards the lady, obviously having heard her. 'Aliens! I told you so! Aliens. And look, he's got another Chinese. He'll take her, mark my words. He'll chuck her out of a window like the other one.'

The young man spoke to her in a calming voice. 'Now, Mum, I've told you before, there are no aliens. That man is a helicopter doctor. They're going to save someone.'

'Look at the thing he's carrying. He was wearing it on his head when they chased the man along this very road. Him and another one dressed in green. Aliens, if you ask me. But I don't care what you call them, boy,' she scoffed. 'Aliens, helicopter pilots. Either way, they throw Chinese out of windows.'

Walker's attention snapped to the woman. Could it be? He looked back at Blinkton. If he was wearing a helmet and dressed in his flying suit, chasing the cleaner through the hospital grounds, it would be easy for the demented lady to jump to the conclusion that Blinkton was an alien. Whatever she thought, she was specific about someone being thrown out of a window.

Blinkton was now staring at the lady. It was obvious he'd heard her. He was holding Angela's arm. Walker stepped away from building corner into full view.

Angela looked up at Walker with a puzzled expression. Her eyes also flicked to the old woman and then she turned to Blinkton.

Walker took a step towards them. 'Angela!'

Blinkton pulled Angela against his chest.

'Craig,' called Walker. 'What have you done?'

Blinkton's back became rigid and he glared at the demented woman. 'Why believe her rubbish? She's a crazy old fool.'

Angela tried to pull away but Blinkton grasped her more tightly across her chest.

'Leave her alone, Blinkers,' Walker yelled. 'She's done nothing.'

Blinkton's free hand pulled a blade from a leg pocket. 'Fuck off, Chris. If you try anything, I'll slit her throat.'

Walker froze.

Angela's face was slack with terror.

Blinkton said something to her which Walker couldn't hear. He spun her in his arms and pushed her down the slope. She tried to run away but he easily caught up to her, then dragged her down the hill towards the waiting helicopter. Angela dug her heels in and screamed but Blinkton was too strong and easily pulled her along.

'Angela!' Walker cried again, running towards her.

They had reached the helicopter when Walker was only halfway across the oval. The pilot, wearing a green suit and helmet, jumped from the chopper and helped Blinkton bundled Angela into the cabin. Blinkton jumped in behind her and shut the door while the pilot ran around the other side, tumbled into the cockpit and gunned the engine. Walker was about twenty metres away when the motor roared, causing a downdraft that almost flattened him. But he struggled on and when the craft was a few metres off the ground, he made a desperate lunge for the landing gear. His hand hit metal but failed to grasp it and he fell hard onto the ground as the helicopter lifted, pushing him flat to the grass. It hovered there for a moment and Walker could see

Blinkton staring down at him, with Angela's horrified face in front. Then they were gone, climbing rapidly and heading east.

'Angela,' Walker screamed uselessly, his voice lost in the ear-splitting roar.

The police helicopter took off from the hospital oval twenty minutes later in hot pursuit, carrying Darling and Walker. After Blinkton's escape, Walker had run to the hospital and called Darling, who put a call through to Aviation Support at Bankstown airport. The crew landed their Bell JetRanger helicopter on the oval ten minutes later, beating Darling who had driven at top speed from Parramatta, sirens wailing. After an initial argument, the pilot-in-command gave in and allowed Walker along after Darling reasoned that they might need medical assistance.

They climbed rapidly and headed east, following the direction given to them by radar control, who was tracking the escaping craft.

'Will we be able to catch them?' asked Walker, speaking through his helmet mike.

The pilot's voice came through the headset. 'Not in a straight chase. CareFlight uses Dauphins, which are faster and have a longer range.'

'What can we do then?' asked Walker.

'Follow them. See where they go. We can get them when they touch down.'

'We can call ground support if we need,' Darling added reassuringly.

'Not if they're making for the open sea,' said Walker. 'Even if they're not, there are a lot of out-of-the-way places within easy reach of Sydney. They could land on some deserted beach or in an uninhabited valley somewhere.'

'Calm down, Kit,' said Darling. 'We can track them.'

The helicopter followed the path of the Parramatta River and soon they crossed the Ryde and then Gladesville bridges, already groaning with peak-hour traffic. They flew over Goat Island where, up ahead, the soaring arch of the Sydney Harbour Bridge could be seen and just behind it, the white sails of the Opera House.

'Can we get them on the radio?' asked Darling.

'We've been trying,' said the pilot as they passed over the Opera House. 'They're not answering.'

They approached Bradleys Head, an expanse of trees that cut into the waterway, obscuring the mouth of the harbour and the open sea beyond.

'There it is,' called Darling through the mike. A white helicopter rose up on the other side of the peninsula and sped away towards the open sea, 'CareFlight' clearly visible on the hull.

'What was it doing?' asked Darling.

'Engine trouble maybe?' suggested the pilot.

'We'll be able to catch them then,' said Darling.

The police pilot picked up speed. On the other side of the peninsula, a cruise ship was entering the heads. A yellow and green ferry steamed towards Manly and just below them was a rusty container ship.

The escaping chopper flew over Watsons Bay with the police chopper in its wake and soon they were over The Gap, a sheer sandstone cliff face on the ocean side of the peninsular, a spot notorious for suicides. Walker looked ahead and was alarmed to see the CareFlight helicopter starting to pull away. Soon they were over the ocean. A large swell rolled in from the east and sleek sailing boats raced below them between yellow buoys anchored off the coast.

'Where are they going?' Walker asked desperately. 'They can't get anywhere from here.'

There was silence as the pilot spoke to his navigator on a different channel. Then his voice crackled through the headset. 'On this course, they're heading directly towards Lord Howe Island.'

'Lord Howe!' said Darling. 'Can they make it?'

'*They* can,' the pilot said grimly. 'We can't. We don't have the range.'

'Is there anywhere else they could be headed?' asked Darling.

'Not on this course. We'll keep following in case they change direction.'

They continued for another ten minutes and Walker watched helplessly as the CareFlight chopper slowly pulled away. Now they were over the vast Pacific Ocean, the coastline a low shadow behind them.

'We've dispatched two fixed wings now,' reported the pilot. 'One will shadow it and the other will head for Lord Howe. We've been ordered to return to base.'

'So that's it then?' said Walker. 'We just let them get away?'

'We have a police station on Lord Howe,' said the pilot. 'It's part of New South Wales. We'll radio ahead and he'll pick them up when they land.'

'He? There's only one copper on the island?'

'It's a small island. Besides, the fixed wing will get there first.' The pilot turned the craft and began to retrace the flight path.

Walker looked down at the water, boats and landmarks flashing under him as he thought about Angela. She'd be frightened. She wouldn't even know where she was going. For all she knew, they might be intending to throw her out of the helicopter into the sea to drown.

With a start, he realised they might just do that. He squeezed his jaw tight. There was nothing he could do. He ran the argument through his mind. Why would they kill her? She hadn't witnessed anything. They would gain nothing from it. But why not?

Walker tugged Darling's sleeve. 'I think Blinkton was involved with the murders at the hospital.'

Darling nodded. 'The pilot too, by the looks of it. Probably working with Naim. Smuggling heroin.'

'If they killed three other people, why not one more?'

'What?'

'Angela. They must be insane to have killed those three. They can't get away. Maybe they know that and are going on one last murder spree. They might even crash their chopper into the sea, taking Angela with them.' He dropped his head and closed his eyes tight.

He opened them just as they passed over the container ship they had flown over on the way out, which was now approaching the heads. There was something about it, something familiar: the stained hull, the bridge tower towards the stern ...

Suddenly he shouted into his mike. 'Turn around! That ship. The rust bucket we just passed. It's the *Sintak-5*!'

The chopper banked steeply and spun around, then hovered about thirty metres above the ship crashing through the swell approaching the heads. At first, there was nothing to see except stacked containers and two cranes on the port side, lashed tightly to prevent them from moving in the swell. The pilot hovered near the main window of the bridge but it appeared empty.

'There!' Walker shouted, pointing towards the triangle of deck at the bow of the ship. They could see movement – two people. The pilot drifted the chopper towards them and hovered just in front of the bow, hovered backwards as the ship steamed forward. Blinkton held Angela before him, clasping her tight with one muscled arm across her chest. Against her head he pointed a pistol. The wind was whipping her hair like a crazed banshee, her body stiff. She looked petrified.

The co-pilot flipped on the loudspeaker on an order from Darling, who picked up the microphone.

'Craig,' called Darling. From inside the cabin, his voice was a distorted distant groan. 'Give it up, Blinkers. You can't get away.'

In a flash, Blinkton pointed the pistol at the chopper and began firing. There was a metallic thump from behind and the craft began to wobble.

'The tail rotor!' shouted the pilot. 'Hang on.'

The chopper wobbled perilously. The pilot gunned the engine slowly and lifted the wounded craft over the bow towards the containers as it began to slowly spin.

'We're going to crash,' the pilot announced, his voice eerily calm.

Just as they reached the first container the chopper began to spin more quickly. 'I'm bringing her down.' The pilot shoved the stick forward and the craft thumped down heavily onto the container and instantly rolled onto its side. The rotor blades disintegrated instantly in a violent scream of wrenching metal but the chopper continued to slowly spin on the container top. Finally, it screeched to a halt when the destroyed tail caught an obstruction.

CHAPTER FORTY

WALKER'S BRAIN WAS buzzing. His helmeted head must have smashed against the side of the craft when they crashed but he was still conscious and, as far as he could tell, uninjured. He couldn't see properly but then he began coughing and realised the cabin was full of smoke. The thick air stunk of aviation fuel. He struggled with his seatbelt and managed to free himself, tumbling onto Darling. He heard a grunt in his ear. 'Get off me, you dickhead.'

Walker groaned. 'Sorry, Wendy. Are you okay?'

'Just get out of here before it goes up in flames.'

Walker stood and managed to push the side door open, which was now above them. He pulled himself out onto the side of the chopper, then jumped down onto the edge of the container beside the landing gear. The boat heaved in the swell and the wind whipped around, quickly clearing the smoke. He turned and helped the co-pilot, who was groaning and holding his arm. The pilot came next, apparently unharmed except for a bleeding lip.

The chopper's nose was hanging out over the edge of the container and the whole craft shifted with the next roll of the ship. The three looked at each other, dazed, then realised Darling was still inside.

'Wendy,' yelled Walker. 'You've to get out. The chopper's going to go.'

'Can't,' came the muffled reply. 'Seatbelt's stuck. Hang on, I think –'

A large gust of wind twisted the lame chopper again, then it began to slip over the edge, scraping metal-on-metal in slow motion. Walker and the pilot vainly grabbed the landing struts but the chopper was too heavy. With a final squeal, it slipped over the edge.

'Barry!' Walker screamed.

The chopper hit the edge of the ship then fell into the water, where it floated for a moment before slipping under the choppy surface. He stared at the spot where it had disappeared but Darling was nowhere to be seen. A few bubbles popped to the surface then were washed away with the next wave.

'Wendy!' he screamed again.

'Why don't you bloody well help me up then,' came a voice at his feet.

Walker looked down to see the curled fingers of two hands dug into the edge of the container. With a cry, he threw himself onto his belly and grabbed Darling's arms then, with the pilot's help, dragged him to the top.

'Are you hurt?' When Darling shook his head, Walker hugged him.

'Get off me, Kit. We're not bloody engaged, you know.' Darling pushed him away and strode to the front of the container, with Walker close behind him. Together they looked down onto the forecastle where Blinkton had been. It was empty.

They scampered down onto the metal deck and began to look for the exit. There was only one hatch and they heaved it open and together peered down into darkness.

'Leave them,' the pilot called from above. 'The Water Police will be sending boats from Balmain. They'll handle it.'

Walker and Darling looked at each other, then into the dark cavern. 'I'm going down,' said Walker. 'Blinker's a lunatic. He can't be trusted.'

'How many times have I said *that* to you,' Darling huffed. 'I always knew Blinkers had a screw loose.'

Walker started down the metal ladder and looked up. 'You coming?'

Darling moaned. 'Guess I'll have to. At least I've got a gun.'

Together they made their way to the bottom and there they stood, close together, trying to breathe quietly, straining their senses for any sound or movement in the dim hold. Somewhere water was dripping and, further away, bangs and scrapes could be heard from an unknown source. Light came from overhead through the open hatch but everywhere else was blackness. They crept forward, Darling with his Smith & Wesson drawn, until they reached a bulkhead. From there they moved towards the left, feeling along the metal wall until they reached a door. Darling pulled the handle, which screeched as the door opened and he went through, pistol first. A dim light revealed a long, narrow corridor that seemed to run the length of the ship, and together they moved along it, Walker close behind Darling. Every twenty metres or so were doors that probably led into the hold but all were closed. Finally, they reached a metal ladder going up and took it, Darling in the lead.

When they were halfway up, the ship's engines shuddered to a halt. Darling stopped climbing and peered up into the daylight. The vessel continued to roll in the swell and Walker swayed on the narrow metal ladder, his palms moist and slippery.

Darling looked down, his face in shadow against the light above. 'Water Police must have arrived,' he said. Shortly after, he was on the move again. Darling reached the top where he stopped and slowly raised his head above the deck, one hand on the ladder and the other pointing his gun.

Walker followed. The deck was empty and he realised they'd climbed up onto the bridge tower. He looked out over the side of the swaying ship. They'd stopped between North and South Heads and the vessel had rotated sideways into the growing swell, causing the ship to rock precipitously from side to side. Just off to port was a white-hulled police boat with two officers on the deck, training semi-automatic rifles at the ship.

Swaying with the rolling deck, Walker moved wide-legged towards the closed metal door of the bridge. He peered through the thick window. 'Looks empty,' he yelled.

There was a call from the stern and Walker looked back to see their chopper pilot gesticulating frantically, pointing to the other side of the vessel.

'Quick,' Darling yelled as he yanked open the door to the bridge and ran through the empty area to the other side. Walker followed, and rushed to the edge of the ship, looking down. An orange inflatable was pulling away, its engine screaming, heading towards the southern shore. In it, were Blinkton and Angela. Darling raised his pistol, then swore. Angela was seated at the rear of the boat, blocking the shot. Walker could see her terrified face clearly.

'Do something!' he yelled. 'They're getting away.'

Darling swore again, then raced through the bridge to the other side with Walker in his wake and hailed the police boat.

What seemed to Walker like a frustratingly long time later, they motored towards the shore in search of the orange inflatable. They powered past Lady Jane Beach but the boat was nowhere to be seen, just nudists enjoying an evening paddle. They went past Camp Cove, another harbourside beach, still finding nothing, then around a small headland to Watsons Bay.

'There it is,' cried Walker, pointing to the narrow swath of sand next to the wharf outside Doyles Restaurant, a swanky seafood place. The orange boat was pulled up onto the sand but Blinkton and Angela were gone. The police vessel touched the wharf to let Darling and Walker off before immediately heading back to the *Sintak-5* to alert passing boats of the danger of the free-floating vessel. The water police had said a tug was on its way but it would take at least twenty minutes, and the rusty ship hitting a Manly ferry was a bigger potential disaster than trying to save one abducted woman.

A fisherman was throwing out a line as the boat pulled away and Darling yelled at him. 'Which way did they go? The people who got out of that orange boat?'

The fellow pointed to the park behind the wharf and Darling and Walker sprinted in that direction. They jogged up the hill in the heat and finally reached the road, panting and sweating. Walker stopped and looked up and down the road. 'Where've they gone?'

On the opposite side of the road, stairs led up to a walkway, which followed the top of the cliff.

Darling pointed, grim-faced. 'I think I know where Blinkers has taken her.'

Walker followed his finger. 'For God's sake! The Gap. He wouldn't!'

They sprinted up the stairs, taking them two at a time, and paused at the top. The track went north and south, hugging the clifftop, with a sheer drop to rocks below. They could feel the boom as the waves crashed into the cliff and saltwater spray filled their nostrils. 'Which way?'

'You go north, I'll go south,' yelled Darling.

They raced off in opposite directions.

CHAPTER FORTY-ONE

WALKER JOGGED ALONG the track that traced the edge of the precipitous fall, vainly searching for any sign of Angela. On his right side, a flimsy timber and wire fence separated the track from the edge of the cliff, which was made up of irregular natural sandstone platforms set at different levels. In some places, narrow ledges of sandstone hung out over the drop.

At the points where the cliff edge came close to the fence, he paused and peered over in an effort to see the base, a stiff breeze blowing into his face. What if Blinkton had thrown her over? But he couldn't see the spot where the rock ledge met the base of the cliff, the place where a thrown body would come to rest. All he could see was the heaving swell of each wave just before it crashed onto the rocks, and hear the boom of the collision. The air was moist with spray, and seagulls floated overhead, riding the upcurrent off the cliff, their strident cries sounding a warning.

He desperately looked along the track, wondering whether he should jump the fence and scuttle along the very edge. That way he could see down as well as the track ahead, although it would be perilous. He decided to climb over but as he threw his leg over the top rail, he was halted by a piercing scream from the direction of the promontory. Then up ahead he saw them – two figures on the edge above a sheer drop, camouflaged by low bushes. They were struggling.

Walker ran as fast as he could but as he got closer, the pair became obscured again by the scrub. He stopped at the point closest to where he estimated them to be, jumped over and scrambled out towards the clifftop, crouching as he went.

He heard them before he could see them.

'Craig, please don't do this,' Angela pleaded, the swirling wind distorting her words. 'You don't have to kill me.'

'Have to?' came the calm reply. 'No. But maybe I just want to. Have you thought of that?'

'Want to? But why do you want to kill me? I've done nothing to you.'

'Maybe not you. But what about your boyfriend?'

'My boyfriend? I don't have a boyfriend.'

Blinkton laughed. 'Don't play with me. Chris Walker. Kit. The fuckin' Ghost Who Walks. I can see how much he likes you. He wants you. That's why I asked you out. To teach him a lesson. He was always such a prick at uni, always so half-hearted about everything, as if anything I was interested in was below him. He pretends to be your friend but he never commits. He's nobody's friend. Even Felicity, his poor wife. He let her die. And look at Barry Darling. Pretends to be his friend but then screws his girlfriend.'

'Cassie?' Angela sounded more disgusted than shocked.

'Ha! Didn't you know? You poor sap. What do you see in him?'

'But what has all that to do with me?'

'Not a lot I suppose. But back at the hospital today. I could see Walker had worked it out. Saw he knew I was the killer. The old lady had seen us chasing the cleaner. Gave him a clue. He's too bloody clever for his own good. And now, given that I'm almost certainly fucked, I thought I'd give him a final message. It would hurt him. Teach him a lesson that he should take better care of the people he's close to. Look after them properly. Value them.'

'So, by killing me, you think you're doing Chris a favour?'

Blinkton gave another short laugh. 'I guess you could see it that way. But mostly I just want to hurt him.'

There was a pause in the conversation. Walker could hear a scrape of a boot on rock and the whine of the wind as it came over the lip of the cliff. He crept forward, until only a scraggly bush was between them. He could see Angela's torso with her back hard up against Blinkton's chest, the wind whistling against their bodies. He lowered himself further and could see that Blinkton held a gun to her neck but he couldn't see their faces. He was about to launch himself forward when Angela spoke again.

'But why kill me? Why not wait until Chris gets here? Kill him instead.'

Walker hesitated.

There was another short pause before Blinkton spoke. 'You're a heartless bitch, aren't you? You two deserve each other. But maybe you're right. Let's wait until Walker gets here. *If* he gets here. You never know, he might have decided to let you go. But if he comes, maybe I should kill you both. You're as bad as each other.'

They went quiet, and Walker could see that Blinkton was facing back along the track from where any pursuit would come, holding Angela before him as a shield. Walker looked back that way. The track was empty. In the distance, he could hear the wail of a police siren. Soon, Darling would come when he realised they were not in the other direction. Blinkton would see him and he might shoot Angela or push her over the edge.

Walker crouched low, uncertain of what to do. If he revealed himself, Blinkton would probably just shoot him. He was only about two metres away so he couldn't miss. But if he did nothing …

He heard Blinkton's voice again. 'Well, it seems your lover's not coming. Just as I suspected, he's left you to fend for yourself. It's a pity that too late, you've found out what he's really like.'

'He's not my lover –'

'Shut up! I'm over this. Let's do it.'

'Please, please no!' Angela's voice was terrified.

It was now or never. Walker couldn't let Angela die without trying something. Her final sob spurred him on.

With a yell, he launched himself forward. In a split second, he saw that Blinkton had pushed Angela to the very edge of the cliff but she'd dug her heels in and her arms were splayed out, as if she was trying to grab an unseen purchase. The pistol was up against the back of her head. Blinkton began to turn with Walker's cry, but with the adrenalin surging through his veins, Walker jumped the two metres in one pounce, slamming into Blinkton and knocking the pistol away. There was a shot but the bullet flew uselessly out to sea.

Blinkton stumbled to the edge of the cliff and tottered there for a moment, trying to get his balance. Then he sneered and reach out to grab Angela's hair to take her with him.

With a rasping cry, Walker leapt forward and lashed out at the same time as Angela flung a hand towards her attacker.

Blinkton disappeared over the edge without a sound.

CHAPTER FORTY-TWO

ANGELA TOTTERED ON the edge, her arms flailing uselessly as the momentum drove her to follow Blinkton's path. She let out a terrified cry as she fell. But Walker lunged again and grabbed her waist as she went over, jerking her backwards just as the fragile soil gave way under her feet. He held her tight from behind, her chest heaving with terror. Then she twisted in his arms and hugged him, her face against his neck and they stood for some minutes, holding each other close, not speaking. Finally, she pushed away. 'Thank you,' was all she said.

Walker stood on the lip of the cliff and peered over the sheer drop. There was a rock shelf at the bottom where waves were crashing, the whitewater surging right up to the cliff face, throwing spray high into the air. He could feel and hear the boom as water and rock connected. Blinkton was nowhere to be seen.

There was a noise behind and Walker turned to see Darling striding towards them.

'What happened?' he asked when he reached them. 'Did he jump?'

Walker didn't answer immediately. He looked at Angela and then out to sea as he contemplated what to say. Then, 'No, he fell. Slipped. He was going to take Angela with him.'

Darling peered over the precipice. 'Where is he? Is he alive?'

'Can't see him,' said Walker. 'Maybe he's already washed out to sea.'

Darling set off back down the path at a trot.

'Where're you going?' Walker called after him.

'Police Rescue,' he shouted over the whine of the wind.

Angela and Walker followed in Darling's footsteps and walked side by side along the clifftop.

'Is it true?' she finally asked.

'What?' he said, although he knew what she meant.

'You and Cassie?'

Walker was silent as he thought for a suitable answer. 'We just fell in together, I guess,' he said finally.

Angela looked out over the surging ocean. He couldn't see her face. 'You were with Blinkton,' he added.

Her head snapped back. 'I was not *with* him. We simply went out on a date.'

'You took him home from the pub the other night.'

'I didn't take him home. I saw him to a taxi then I went home by myself.' She shook her head. 'But really, Chris, Cassie is going out with Barry.'

'Is she?' he said. 'I haven't seen him around lately and I'm sure he's not going out for drinks by himself.'

'What do you mean?'

'I mean he's probably seeing someone else.'

'You don't know that.'

'Anyway, it doesn't matter,' he said roughly. 'That's the way it's turned out. You can't help who you love.'

'Love!' she spat. 'So, you love her now? And here I was thinking it was just a dirty little affair.'

'No,' he answered quickly. 'Well, maybe … I don't know.'

They reached the park where they found Darling leaning through the window of a police car. He turned when they arrived. 'Police Rescue is on its way. The Water Police too. And they've secured the *Sintak-5*.' He looked from face to face. 'What's going on?'

'Ask Chris,' said Angela, her voiced tinged with anger. 'Ask about Cassie and him.'

'Cassie?' Darling glared at Walker. 'What are you doing now, you cheating bastard?'

He raised his hands. 'It's not what you think.'

'Have you been sleeping with her?' Darling was furious. 'What's wrong with you? Why do you have to destroy every woman I have feelings for.'

Walker squirmed and tried to sound reasonable. 'I haven't destroyed Cassie –'

'Shut up!' Darling shouted. 'I went to New Guinea. I know what you did. I saw it with my own eyes.'

'What do you mean? Saw what?'

'I saw Felicity's remains. Her bones. Her skull had a flamin' hole cut out if it. Her bones were burnt and crushed.'

'And you think I did that?' Walker shouted. 'That's just plain ridiculous.'

'As good as. You let her die in that shithole of a country. Maybe you didn't kill her, I can see that now. Maybe she drowned by accident. But you still should've cared for her. Even when she was dead. You let them desecrate her body.' Darling's face was wild, maniacal, his body shaking with fury. 'They cooked her. They consumed her remains.' He looked ready to explode. 'You ate your own wife!'

Walker stumbled back as if he'd been hit. He felt faint and sick in his guts. Without saying a word, he turned and limped away along the track back towards The Gap.

No one followed.

EPILOGUE

SYDNEY MORNING HERALD
8 March 1991
Helicopter Crash on Sydney Harbour

Sydney Harbour was the scene of a dramatic helicopter crash yesterday afternoon when a police helicopter slammed into a container ship as it was steaming out of the heads. The *Sintak-5* was en route from Sydney to Thailand when the accident occurred at approximately 3.30 pm.

Eyewitnesses from a passing Manly ferry reported that the Bell JetRanger helicopter was seen to be hovering before the bow of the ship at a low level when it began to spin and connected with one of the containers on the ship. The copter rolled onto its side and witnesses saw several people climbing from the wreckage before the aircraft sunk in the harbour.

'It just slid off the side of the ship and disappeared under the water,' said one distraught witness. 'If there was anyone in the chopper, they would have had no chance.'

Police claim there were no lives lost and the occupants suffered only minor injuries. Two men were taken to St Vincent's Hospital but were released later that evening.

The cause of the crash remains unknown and is the subject of a joint investigation by the police, the Bureau of Air Safety Investigation (BASI), and the Marine Incident Investigation Unit.

Mr Allan Smee from BASI stated that the investigation is expected to take some months. 'At this stage, there's no obvious cause for the collision between the aircraft and the ship. This is certainly an unprecedented event and we will need to interview the occupants of the helicopter and work closely with the police before we can make a statement.'

The depth of the harbour at the site of the crash is over 60 metres, and it is uncertain when the craft's black box will be secured, if ever. There's no decision at this stage whether the helicopter wreck will be salvaged.

There are unsubstantiated reports of gunshots heard just before the crash from several ferry passengers. A police spokesperson said he was aware of the reports and they were the subject of a separate investigation by the Special Weapons and Operations Section and at this time no comment could be made.

The *Sintak-5* was secured at the scene by Water Police and was able to return to dock at White Bay under its own steam. The captain – identified as Almar Shareef, a Pakistani national – along with the crew of six are helping the police with their investigation.

The *Sintak-5* was recently the subject of a police search in connection with a murder that occurred in Balmain on the night of 20 February. The ship was allowed to leave Sydney Harbour when no evidence was elicited that connected the ship with the crime. On the day of the collision, the ship was leaving Sydney Harbour after making a routine stop from Melbourne on the way to Thailand.

Police have refused to confirm or deny whether the helicopter crash was connected to the apparent suicide of a man at The Gap that took place around the same time. Dr Craig Blinkton, 34, was a medical officer with CareFlight. CareFlight management has refused to comment about any possible connection between the two events.

Page 4
CareFlight doctor dies at Gap

Police have reported this morning that the body of a man was found by their Search and Rescue unit at the bottom of The Gap at Watsons Bay yesterday afternoon.

He has been identified as Dr Craig Blinkton, 34, a CareFlight doctor. CareFlight has issued a statement saying the death was not related to any official activity. 'CareFlight was not undertaking any rescue activities in the vicinity at the time,' said a spokesman.

Police estimate that Blinkton died at approximately 4 pm. 'It is clear that Dr Blinkton fell from the cliff at The Gap around that time,' said a police spokesperson, 'but at this stage we cannot say whether he fell by accident or if it was suicide.'

When asked whether the victim had a history of depression, the spokesperson said that was not certain at this stage but would be one of the focuses of the investigation. There are reports that the doctor spent some time as an inpatient in a northern Sydney mental illness facility in 1985.

The death occurred around the time of the spectacular helicopter crash in Sydney Harbour where a police helicopter ploughed into a container ship that was steaming through the heads. Police are currently making no comment on any possible link between the two events.

A local resident, who wanted to remain nameless, stated that he saw a man accompanied by a woman walk along the clifftop in the direction where the death later occurred. He also stated that another man jogged after them a few minutes later.

'After that, the police turned up and all hell broke loose,' he said. The unnamed witness claims that a few people came back along the clifftop before the police arrived but he was unable to identify them.

A man who was possibly a witness to the death is wanted for questioning by police. He has been identified as Dr Christopher Walker, a cancer specialist from Western Meadows Hospital. Police claim that Dr Walker was in the vicinity of The Gap when the death occurred. He was questioned briefly by police soon after the incident but has not been seen since and police request that he present himself to a local station as soon as possible. Dr Angela Chee, also a doctor from Western Meadows Hospital, is helping the police with their investigation.

Police refused to comment on whether the doctor's death is linked to another event involving a CareFlight pilot. The pilot was reported to have been taken into police custody after landing on Lord Howe Island yesterday evening. A spokesperson for CareFlight would make no comment at this stage and are awaiting further details about the matter.

Homicide detectives are investigating the death of Dr Blinkton.

END OF BOOK 2

The story continues in
Murder at The Rocks

Author's note

THE MAIN CHARACTERS in this novel are completely fictional. If you think you recognise yourself or someone you have worked with then you're wrong!

This might disappoint some who think this series is some sort of exposé of a Sydney teaching hospital. Of course, like any story, all characters and situations are necessarily based on memories of real people and events. But I can assure you that all main characters are the product of my imagination.

There are many historical names that are obviously real. I have never met any of these people and any mention of them in the book is a construction of events from public records.

Many of the historical details are accurate, such as contemporary news items, names of songs and television shows, and the names and position of restaurants and pubs in Sydney in 1991. Some details are inaccurate and I intentionally departed from the facts for the purposes of this fictional story.

The medical cases are descriptions of events I or my colleagues have been involved with over the years, although the patient names are fictional.

Discover other titles by Howard Gurney

Path to Chaos series (fantasy)
Twin
The Thread Frays
Chaos

Dr Christopher Walker Murder Mystery series
Murder on the Ward
Death in a Chapel
Murder at The Rocks

Thank you for reading my book. If you enjoyed it, please take
a moment to leave a review at your favourite retailer.

Howard Gurney

www.howardgurney.com

@HowardGurney